Reckless

Jennifer Loren

Books by Jennifer Loren

The Laws of Kings Series

THE LAWS OF KINGS

DETHRONING THE KING

The Devil's Eyes Series

THE DEVIL'S EYES

THE DEVIL'S REVENGE

THE DEVIL'S SON

THE DEVIL'S MASQUERADE: THE POISON

THE DEVIL'S MASQUERADE: THE REMEDY

THE NEW DEVIL IN CHARGE

The Finding Ava Series

FINDING AVA

RECKLESS

THE LONG ROAD

Short Story

THE HAND THAT HOLDS MINE

Prologue

Sean

The decision seemed so innocent in the beginning, exciting even. How could I have ever known what was going to happen? How could I have ever known that someone could be so evil, so determined to destroy lives. I chose to ignore the advice of my brother and instead trusted - believed in friendship, believed in a woman I once loved. Now I am paying the consequences and living in hell and I have brought my family right along with me.

It all started when the rat entered our lives, and as should be expected, the snake followed.

Chapter 1

Ava

Our wedding is a few months after Sean's proposal in a secret place that only we know about - the island that brought us together again. We have our closest friends, family, and all of our island family with us when we say our vows to each other. I in a dream dress my husband made sure was available to me, because as he said, he *did not want to outdo me in his custom suit.* Standing by a small waterfall with flowers draping every place imaginable, petals under our feet and our daughter, Lillah, watching from the arms of her uncle. Lillah is dressed in a sweet ivory dress and new shoes that she makes sure everyone sees, especially her Daddy. After sealing our vows with a kiss, we are off to our reception where there is lots of food and dancing and even more laughter and smiles. The only sadness is at the end when we have to leave Lillah but it is after all - our honeymoon.

Sean planned our honeymoon all by himself, a two-week trip on a yacht that will take us wherever we want to go. I had no clue until he walked me down to the dock. Smiling his enticing smile, Sean picks me up and carries me across the ramp while I hold onto a bottle of champagne from our reception. Setting me down gently at the rail of the boat, I feel the breeze begin to blow through my hair, the stars begin to shine and the rushing sounds of water roar around us as our boat carries us away from our island. "I love you and I hope you enjoy this trip as much I dreamed you would." he said, kissing me once again.

"Well then, my perfect husband, if you dreamed of something so perfect then what do you have planned for us now?" I smile, tugging at his suit jacket and biting my bottom lip.

"Aren't you hungry? You didn't get a chance to eat at all at the reception and I hear the chef has made us something special. All I have to do is call them to bring it up for us." He twirls me into his arms as if I am being absurd to even consider sex at this moment.

"Well if the food is supposed to be that good, let's by all means eat first." I sigh. "My mistake, I thought that sex might be better. It has been two weeks since we have seen each other."

He laughs, leaning in close, "I promise you the food is spectacular but not nearly as spectacular as I am going to make you feel when I get this dress off you." His sensuous words rush through my body, weakening me all over. Smiling knowingly, Sean holds me tighter and keeps me from collapsing. "Do you want me to show you now?" he whispers against the edge of my earlobe.

Giving him my new, confident look, "I just hope you can live up to your words, Mr. Grant."

"Well then, let me show you the way beautiful." Taking my hand, he leads me to a door and opens it to a room that immediately wraps you in posh comfort. With his heated lips on my neck, his warm body nestled in behind me, and his fingers trailing up and down my bare back I suddenly have an old feeling come over me, that feeling of our first time together. "I did tell you I planned every detail myself. I took extra time with this room." I am not sure if I am nervous or anxious, which is not much different from the first time. "Take your dress off."

I turn, and seeing his superior smile I take a deliberate step back from him, "You first." I demand.

"But I want to see what you're wearing under this incredible dress."

"Give me a reason to show you, Mr. Grant. And make sure you entertain me while you do it." I grab a glass of the already poured champagne, and detour his hand away from his own glass. "Come on actor boy, show me what you got, and … *make it good.*" Pushing on his chest and sending him out into my sight, I watch him shamelessly. Staring at me briefly, he begins nodding in acceptance. Working slowly, he slides off his jacket and shows his muscles which are highlighted by his fitted shirt.

Sean loosens his tie, pulls it off over his head, and throws it to me. "Here you go sweetheart, a souvenir - try to control yourself."

Laughing, I put his tie around my neck loosely, causing an anxious sigh from his lips. "Keep going," I encourage, watching him undo every button on his sleeves, his shirt, and all the while trying to ignore his eyes on me. I breathe in deeply as he slides his flawlessly tailored shirt off behind him. I take another drink as he undoes his belt, and twirls his tongue within his mouth. Sipping the liquid euphoria once again, I watch him undo his pants, his hard excitement even more revealed as he pushes his shoes and socks off with his feet before dropping his pants to the floor. While standing in his tight boxer briefs that are hugging his body with perfection, I eye his hipbones sticking out above them, begging me to suck them.

"Good enough?" he asks.

"No, keep going, I want to see what I am going to be working with for the rest of my life." I say motioning for him to drop the remaining garment. His hand hovers against his stomach, and with a grunting sigh, he pushes his boxers down to the floor. I gulp, gazing over his sumptuous body, and giggle at the slight redness to his cheeks. He recovers quickly from his shyness with an assured smile, brushing his hands over his head and turning proudly for me. Then the cocky son of a bitch winks at me and I have to take another drink to keep from laughing.

"Happy?"

"Very." I smile with an anxious sigh.

Coming in close, he takes my drink away and hovers his lips in front of mine, teasing me. "Take your clothes off Mrs. Grant and make sure you entertain me while you're doing it," he said guiding me to where he previously stood.

"I don't know if I can get this off by myself?" Sean steps to me quickly and releases the hooks of my dress. I turn back to him with a shy smile, "I don't know if I can put on much of a show, with what I have." I said trying to encourage him to undress me himself.

"Try." He said with his tongue lingering inside his open mouth, making me crave him even more. Working up my courage, I stick my chin out defiantly and with a heavy *whish*, I release my dress to the floor. Eyeing the clothing that remains on my body, he stands silently waiting while I release my breasts and slide my panties to the floor for him. Sean's eyes widen in excitement as he gazes over my nude body, decked out in only my jeweled, high-heeled shoes and his tie. "Don't forget the hair combs, sweetheart," he says never bothering to look their way while I eye what is now mine.

With a soft sigh, I release my hair from the combs, fit his tie close to my neck, and let it dangle down and long between my breasts before proceeding to do my best runway walk towards him. I grasp the back of his head and jerk him to me with one hand, looking deep into his lust filled eyes, "Now make me feel spec... fucking...tacular, Mr. Grant."

He smiles boldly at me, "No problem." Sean takes hold of me with one arm and lays me on the bed. "Relax and I will take care of the rest," he said in a heated voice. I lean back onto the pillows as he climbs on the bed at my feet, grasping each of my legs one at a time and slides off each of my shoes. His warm hands caress my legs from my ankles to my thighs before kissing his way up and in between, rebelliously forcing his tongue into my softest of places. Clinching the pillow under my head I pant in rhythm with his movements. I let my respect for him show as my body tightens and begins to sway deeper into him. I glance down at him gripping my thighs and his eyes smiling back at me, the sensations pour through my veins. The scene is more than I can handle. Panting excitedly, I grip the back of his head and try to pull him up to me before I come, but he ignores my meager attempts and controls me until I feel the release rushing down to his mouth. Gripping his head between my legs and moaning praises to him, my body relaxes deep into the plush bed. Sean makes his way up my body little by little. Reaching my breasts, he toys with his tie before squeezing my breasts against his face and his lips. I wrap my arms around his neck while he maneuvers himself into place and smiles adoringly. My eyes close as I feel his hardened erection fit tight inside of me. His supple, full lips meet my mouth tenderly as I vow to get even. Groaning he spins us over, placing me on top and smacks my ass for encouragement. *He is so mine.* With a wicked determination, I eye him, knowing what he wants. I fondle my heaving breasts in front of him and his eyes cloud with lust once again. Moaning, I sit up high on him and slide down low feeling his grumbling groans vibrate to my core. Working up and down his shaft I arch my back, backwards and forwards, losing my fingers into my hair and moaning his name while he grips my hips tighter. Rising up, Sean loses himself in my breasts, breathing his desires and pleasures as I move along the pulsating edges of his erection. Suddenly, the sensation steals my breath away and once again, I come and collapse into his waiting arms. Sean holds me close, stroking my back and running his fingers through my hair while he catches his breath. He mouths his love for me before he rolls us over. My hands hold his head as our lips meet and his hips move deep into mine and with a soft exhale I let him take control, complete control and I enjoy every second during our two weeks together on a yacht arranged just for us.

Chapter 2

Sean

With our honeymoon barely behind us, Ava and I are off to LA for a meeting about a new film I am anxious to work on, Reckless. The script was written about an old friend of mine's Uncle, a daredevil of sorts who lived life to its fullest to the point of being destructive to himself and everyone who tried to get close to him. It is the first meeting about Reckless and I am hoping to give Ava all the details, before I give her … *all* the details. Ava and I have been living in such bliss these days, I don't want to ruin it by telling her I am considering doing a movie with my former best-friend, Joel. *He* is now married to my ex-girlfriend, whom I had planned to marry myself before she broke my heart. I assumed I would bring Ava to dinner with me to introduce her to Joel, fill her in on the details of the movie project first, and then tell her the rest. Little did I know *she* - my ex-girlfriend - had other plans. I haven't seen Rebecca since I caught her in our bed with Joel five years ago. The moment she lays eyes on me she runs up to me and secures her arms around me like we are the best of friends, holding on a little too long for everyone's comfort.

"Sean, you look wonderful." She said as I pull her off me and guide her back towards Joel. *Ava is too smart to let that display slide by unnoticed.*

"Ava, this is Joel and Rebecca Castor, old friends of mine." I said, hoping to get things moving towards the film we are suppose to discuss doing together and less on my past, failed relationships. Ava greets them each sweetly, as she always does, before we sit across from them. I purposely make sure to be across from Joel so I will not have to look at Rebecca. *She wants to make up and this is not the time.*

The discussions seem to go fine until both Joel and Ava leave to take calls, leaving me alone with Rebecca. I ignore her presumptuous smile, "I have missed you Sean."

I nod, continuing to avoid looking at her, "Good for you."

"Are you going to be mad at me forever?"

"No, it really doesn't matter to me anymore. Actually, it all worked out better for me anyway." I say sending a joyful smile in her direction.

"Good, then maybe we can rebuild our friendship."She says leaning towards me with a smile of her own.

"Can't wait." I grumble. Ava comes back rubbing her hand across my leg as she sits down. I quickly find her ear, "I missed you."

"So that call was to let me know we have a new director for Reckless. The great Daniel Kane," Joel said with illuminating excitement.

"That's wonderful Joel. I think that calls for a toast." I wave our waiter over and order the best bottle of wine available.

"To our new film – Reckless!" Joel exclaimed as we all clank our glasses together.

I look at Ava, still on my honeymoon high, and forget to keep our so far, well-kept-secret, "To my wife, I love you." I said, kissing her gently as we toast privately.

"You are not married yet." Rebecca snarled.

"Yes we are, as of a few weeks ago." I responded, annoyed by her response.

"Oh wow, that's great! Honey isn't that wonderful?" Joel said, quickly putting his arm around Rebecca's shoulders and meeting her wide eyes with a strained smile.

Rebecca eases back in her chair, "Yes, it's … wonderful." She said, looking at Ava seemingly sincerely. "So enough about this movie for now, Ava, tell us how you and Sean met. I mean after all, now that the fairy tale is complete you must tell us how it all started." Rebecca said, leaning forward and concentrating on hearing every word.

"Well, it's kind of a crazy story actually. I'm not sure I have time to tell it so that it makes sense," Ava said, looking at me for some direction.

"Oh try. Were you an extra on one of his movies or something?" Rebecca pried further.

Ava laughs as I begin to explain for her, "Ava isn't an actress Rebecca. She's an architect, and a very talented one." I say, smiling at Ava. "She actually designed my father's Cancer Center," I said proudly.

"Wow Ava that must be exciting?" Joel asked.

"I enjoy it, most of the time," she said smiling.

Our food arrives and I notice Rebecca continuing to stare at Ava. *She has more questions and that makes me nervous.*

"So Ava, you must be super smart, huh?" Joel asked before meeting Rebecca's glare. "It figures Sean would end up with a smart woman, I just didn't realize he could find one so beautiful too."

I promptly answer for Ava, "She is that and I went through a lot to find her."

"So when did you live in New York, Ava?" Joel asked as I take a drink, tensing with every awkward question.

"Oh actually about the same time as Sean, we just didn't know it until years later." Ava answered innocently.

"Yes, that was interesting to learn, but really we met because of my mother and next thing you know I was head over heels. Pretty normal story from that point on," I said, earning a bewildered glance from Ava.

"How funny that you guys lived in the same city all that time and never even knew each other existed," Rebecca pried further.

"Actually," Ava said as I search for a way to dive into my food and hide. "Sean and I did meet once in New York."

I glance up long enough to see Rebecca look over at me, "Really?" she asked suspiciously.

"Yes, we ran into each other at this little Italian restaurant. He was going there with his brother and I was standing outside waiting for my friend when Ethan's fan club came running out of nowhere and were about to trample me. That's when Sean pulled me out of the way." Ava looks over at me sweetly and I return her smile while ignoring Rebecca's glare. "He was so incredible even then. He just held onto me for the longest time. If Kyle hadn't of interrupted us …" Ava laid her hand on mine. I instantly sweep it up into my palm, caressing it with my thumb.

"Interrupted you, what were you doing?" Rebecca said harshly.

"Oh no, we weren't doing anything. It was simply a moment that we both seemed to have shared. When I ran into him a couple of years ago, I knew he wouldn't remember me since when we first met I was covered head to toe because of the cold weather. All he could see were my eyes. Eventually I told him and I assumed the meeting didn't mean anything to him, at least not like it did to me at the time. But when he showed me the locket I lost that night, I knew he did remember and he had felt the same way." I concentrate on my food, holding Ava's hand under the table like a life raft. *Silence.* I search the room for the quickest exit.

"So you *did* cheat on Rebecca, your supposed fiancé at the time, with your future wife? Damn Sean and I thought you were the innocent one in that whole mess," Joel said sarcastically.

"He didn't cheat on me, they didn't do anything," Rebecca snapped at him as he laughs.

"Whatever. I remember you finding that locket wrapped up in the back of his drawer and then asking *me* about it, like it was my fault. You thought for sure he was cheating on you because he barely paid attention to you after that night. You complained about it nonstop, thinking his brother or I had something to do with it. Well now you know ... it was because of her." He exclaimed pointing at Ava.

I instantly stop retreating and glare at him until he removes his accusing finger from my wife. Ava drops her gaze to her plate and pulls her hand away from me. "It wasn't Ava. Rebecca and I weren't really getting along then, if you recall. We would have still broken up despite Ava and me meeting," I said, trying to ease the situation. "Probably why you two ended up together as well."

"So you two met *again* years later, fell in love, married and even have a kid already - wow. You are a totally different Sean than the one I used to know." Joel said, eating his food without concern.

"A much happier Sean, thank you very much," I said, gaining a promising glance from Ava.

"Well enough about the love stuff, let's talk about the film. Ava, did Sean tell you we are filming near Atlanta so he will be able to be home while we shoot?" Joel asked.

She smiles at him. "He did, I was very happy to hear that," she said, still avoiding eye contact with me.

"So I guess we will start as soon as you're finished with your film in New York?" Joel asked.

Ava whips her head in my direction, "I thought you were going to take breaks in between films, so you could spend time with Lillah?"

"Well I thought since I will be able to stay home, then I would still be able to spend time with her," I said, reaching for her hand again to try to calm her down. Ava allows me to hold her fisted hand but I know an argument will begin as soon as we are alone.

Joel and I tried to lighten the mood since both women are now scowling and silent. I make a mistake of asking Joel whom else they have lined up for the film and Rebecca perks right up. "Well Sean, that's kind of the other reason we wanted to talk to you." Joel said sitting up straight. "Rebecca wants to play, Lacey." He said fidgeting as he looks up from his up-turned glass and Rebecca dances in her seat.

"That's probably more up to your father isn't it Joel?" I said eyeing the coward.

"Yes, but if you recommend her then he will surely allow it," he said, looking away from all of us.

"Joel, that's the primary female role. This is your movie. Do you really want to risk it?" I ask.

"Sean, you know I am good enough!" Rebecca yelled as I sit back in my chair and ignore her.

"Rebecca when was the last time you worked? And what was the last thing you did? You haven't ever had a lead role!" I yelled back at her as she sits back in her chair sulking. "No, I won't help you and in fact I will insist that it won't be her." I point back at Rebecca who shoots me an evil glare. "You can be mad at me all you want Rebecca. You should understand that this movie is too important, especially to your husband, to risk you in that role. Take a lesser role, maybe, but not that one." I relax back in my chair and put my arm around the back of Ava's chair, kissing her cheek tenderly.

"You know it has nothing to do with me, it's all about your wife getting upset, isn't it Sean?" Rebecca yelled at me.

"Rebecca calm down?" Joel says, putting his arm around her.

"No! He is so afraid that she is going to get upset with him doing those sex scenes with me and kissing me. Heaven forbid that he might find me more attractive than her." Rebecca steamed while Ava's eyes widen immensely.

"This has nothing to do with Ava. It has everything to do with you not being ready for that significant of a role. Now calm down and back off." I stare her down as tears form in her eyes and she sprints towards the restroom. I look back at Joel as he rolls his eyes. "What was that about?" I asked him.

"I know you are right Sean, and I tried to talk her out of it. I told her she could be in one of the smaller roles but she has been pushing and pushing - driving me insane about it. She even forced me to ask my father in front of her and he laughed - which didn't help matters any. I didn't know what else to do, she won't let it go." He said, looking completely beat down over it.

"When was the last time she worked?" I asked.

He waves his hands in the air, "She's been doing some local commercials and some plays here and there, but nothing of any importance. They barely get reviews. I don't know why she is so hell bent on doing this role, but she seems to think it's going to get her career going again."

"Not if she screws it up," I said. He responds with a nod and an exasperated sigh.

"Should I go check on her?" Ava asked.

"No!" Joel and I responded simultaneously.

"When she's upset Ava, it's usually best to leave her alone and stay out of the way," Joel expressed to her.

"Sweetheart, Rebecca is not one for consoling. Attention only makes it worse," I said as Joel nods in agreement.

"Well it looks like dinner is over. Thanks for meeting us and we will see you in Atlanta next, I guess." Joel said, tossing his napkin on his plate.

"Are you sure you don't want us to wait with you?" I asked him. He nodded and waved me off. I pay for everyone's dinner as Ava hugs Joel and kisses him on the cheek, making him smile bigger than I have ever seen. Ava and I leave the restaurant in silence. "Are you okay?" I finally have to ask.

"Why wouldn't I be?" She says with *that tone* in her voice.

"Because, Ava, you haven't said two words to me since we left the restaurant."

"Well maybe that's because I am still trying to figure out why you wouldn't tell me we were having dinner with your ex-girlfriend…I mean your ex-fiancé."

"I didn't know she was going to be there Ava."

"She's his wife, why wouldn't she be there? And I know there is something else that you're not telling me, so you better just do it now since the night is already ruined." I glance over at her determined expression and sigh.

"Fine, you want to know everything? Joel and I were best friends at the time I was seeing Rebecca. They hated each other, but I asked him to watch over her while I was away doing another film. I can't believe I am telling you this." I shake my head as she crosses her arms waiting for me to make it worse. "I ended up coming back early and finding the two of them in our bed together."

"You lived with her?" *shit*

"Ummm, yes."

"So you were practically married?"

"We talked about it but ..."

"But what, Sean?" She snarled at me.

I sit up and lean over to her, "I was going to say ... but then I met this beautiful redhead with gorgeous blue eyes, who made me realize that I wasn't really in love with Rebecca." She shuts her mouth.

"I thought you said I didn't have anything to do with why you broke up?"

"Well her cheating on me with my best friend had a lot to do with the break up, but you were the one that caused me to be so distant from her. That is probably why she did run to him. I thought I loved her but when I ran into you my whole world changed."

"Why?"

"Because I realized what love really is when I met you. Besides, I only wanted to marry Rebecca because I thought it would make my mother happy. Have a family and all that to distract her from my father's death. As it turned out though, she hated Rebecca and I realized I wasn't ready for marriage - not with her anyway. You know mothers' are always right." I said with a smile to match her emerging one.

Chapter 3

Sean

It is my birthday today and I am stuck in New York trying to finish-up filming. This movie is fun, lots of action and plenty of stunts for me to get excited about, but I miss my family. It didn't help me any, getting the sweet birthday video from my daughter singing happy birthday Daddy, way off key. On the way back to my trailer, I stop by the crowd of fans waiting to give me birthday cards and presents. I try to greet them all respectively but some are determined to get a hold of me and never let go. Randy, my best friend and overworked bodyguard, is always handy in these situations. He graciously pulls them off me and puts them back behind the line. However, one manages to get by him somehow.

"Oh Mr. Grant, can I please come home with you. I love you!" she exclaims.

Pulling the girl off my back, I look down at my wife and smile wide. "Baby, what are you doing here?"

"I couldn't let you spend your birthday alone." Ava jumps into my arms and I wave goodbye to the numerous disappointed women who watch me carry my wife off to my trailer. Kissing Ava is only fun for so long before I want to take it further. I can barely get started before I am called back to the set. Reluctantly, I send her to my hotel to wait for me and hope that my day ends early enough that I can spend some time appreciating my wife before the day is over. However, the day drags and the stunts become more complicated, which take longer to setup and prepare. Usually I enjoy these stunts more than anything, but all I can think about is Ava's new, frilly underwear I got a quick glimpse of before she left. By the time I arrive back at the hotel, the fire is going and the music sounds seductive, but my beautiful wife is passed-out, curled up in a blanket. At least she tried. Sighing, I pick her up and put her to bed before crawling in myself.

I barely get my eyes closed before I can feel her crawling towards me, "I love you Sean."

I glare at her approaching smile. "Prove it." I said, lying on my back watching her kiss up my chest, my neck and to my mouth.

"I said, I love you," she said, hovering over me.

"I heard you," I said as her frustration becomes obvious.

"Forget it." She huffs retreating to other side of the bed.

"Where are you going?" I reach for her quickly.

"If you don't love me, then I'm leaving."

"No you're not." I wrap my arms around her and pull her back to my chest.

"Why is that?" She asked smiling wide.

"Because I want to make love to you."

"That would imply that you love me."

"Is that right?"

"Yes, that's how it works," she said smugly.

"Oh. Well then I guess that means …" taking her lips within mine "I love you."

CER

My eyes open to the sun barely drifting in, before suddenly meeting her focused eyes. "What's this about Sean?" I sit back unsure if I am in trouble as she rattles my phone in my face. "Why is she texting you?"

"Who?" I questioned.

"Rebecca." She pronounced emphatically.

"Oh." I shy away from her judging eyes. "I am supposed to have dinner with them tonight."

"Why?"

"It is my birthday Ava and they wanted to do something nice."

"You're not going are you?"

"I already said I would."

"Can't you call and cancel?"

"No, but you can come with me. Then we will come back here and have our own birthday celebration." I reach for her, but she scoots away from me, crossing her arms.

"You're going to have dinner without me, for your birthday?"

"Baby you can come, I swear it's nothing. It is simply meant to be something nice for my birthday since I am away from my family." I mock her until she relaxes her tense frown. "Come with me, please."

"I guess, but don't leave me with her. She's scary."

"It is just dinner, Ava."

"Just dinner huh? Is it going to go better than the last time?"

"Yes, I promise." I said, cringing as the thoughts of our last dinner with them run through my mind. *It surely can't go any worse than that?*

CR&O

Ava sits silently, twisting and curling the ends of her scarf between her fingers. I have a feeling she is going to shred it by the end of the night. Grabbing the end of her scarf from her hand, I sigh as I tuck it under her coat. "It's going to be fine Ava. You don't need to be nervous"

"I'm fine."

"Yeah, you look it," I said, taking notice of her annoyed expression.

"This was planned before you got here. They remembered my birthday and … And I have said this all a million times already."

"I understand but I don't know that I should be going."

"It is fine. It's only take out. Besides, it will be a good chance for you and Rebecca to get to know each other." Ava immediately looks at me as if I am the stupidest man on earth. "I know, but I am really excited about hanging out with Joel again. He was my best friend once and I can't help that he married my ex. Please, just try to get along with her … for me? Please, Ava."

"For you I will try, but I have a feeling she isn't going to make it too easy for me."

"You might be surprised. Joel said Rebecca is so excited about getting a part in the movie that she has been a completely different woman and actually enjoyable to be around. She even commented on how sweet and beautiful she thinks you are."

"Oh, I'm so sure she did."

"Ava," I said sternly.

"I will try … for you, baby," she said kissing me.

We pull up to their apartment building and Ava is seemingly as shocked as I am by the repugnant building. I look cautiously around before I help her out of the cab. Ava swallows hard after we are buzzed in and I immediately hover around her when we enter. We walk up three flights due to the ancient elevator being out of order - since the last World War. Ava leans in close to me as a suspicious-looking man peers out of his door at us. I let go of Ava's hand and wrap my arm around her, making sure to check behind us as we walk down the corridor to their apartment. Ava knocks while I keep an eye out behind us.

"Ava. I'm so glad you were able to make it, too." Joel said with excitement as he hugs Ava and grabs my hand. We walk into the small, sparsely furnished apartment with an awkward air around us.

"Let me get your coats," Joel says as he helps Ava remove hers.

Rebecca enters the room from the closet sized kitchen, smiling. *Maybe this will be a better night than Ava feared, and for that matter, me as well.*

"Come in and sit down. We already have food laid out on the dining table. I hope you guys are hungry. Joel over-ordered as usual." she said, shaking her head and still smiling.

"Sean, we thought since it's your birthday we would get your favorite," Rebecca said as she lifted the towel covering the food.

"Uncle Wong's! Damn, I can't believe that place is still in business." I laugh, remembering how much I use to eat at that place.

"Ava, this guy ate at Uncle Wong's, I think, every day," Joel mocked me

"It wasn't every day, but probably close to it. That man was really nice to me, he gave me extra everything and I was a growing boy back then. I could eat a semi full of food in one sitting. And it was good too. But really there was just something about the place that was calming to me. I don't know, maybe it was the table waterfalls." Everyone laughs, remembering the awful décor. I glance at Ava, seeing her smile at me makes me feel much better about the night going well. "Ava, let me make your plate. I know exactly what you will like," I say, anticipating her pleasure.

"This Uncle Wong's, is it next to that bar … umm what was it … Crazy Horse?" Ava asked, getting excited about remembering the bar.

"I think that was the name of it, it's a Starbucks now, but yeah I think that's the place," Joel said before putting a fork full into his mouth.

"Did you go there too, Ava?" Rebecca asked.

"Yes, I never ate there but I was there quite often," she smiles.

"How is it that you remember it then? Did you stand outside smelling the front door?" I grin in her direction, receiving a mocking expression in return.

"Actually smart ass, Kyle and I lived in the apartment above it." My mouth drops as she laughs nervously. "Yeah, we smelled the food so much that we could never bring ourselves to actually eat there too, but … he was a very nice man."

"That's just … I don't what that is." Joel exclaimed.

I glance over at him, catching Rebecca's stern stare on Ava. "Are you sure, sweetheart?" I asked her.

"Yes, he was our landlord. We called him Bing because he liked it for some reason," she said.

I laugh, nearly choking on my food. "He liked it because I told him he looked like Bing Crosby one day and from that point on, I always called him Bing." Ava laughs with me, taking my hand. We don't even care that we are the only ones seeing the humor in it. "I can't believe that you were right above me. We must have just missed each other hundred times, at least."

"At least," she said.

"Well, until I left for LA. When I got back, for some reason, it wasn't the comforting place I use to love. I chalked it up to all the jade symbols hanging everywhere. So, I guess you moved pre-symbol days?" I smile, assuming her absence was the reason for my discomfort.

Her smile diminishes, "No, he hung those for me. It was right after Spencer … and he …"

I reach for her, "Baby, I'm so sorry. I should have never brought it up."

"It's alright, you didn't know," she said, caressing my face with a smile. "But, if you will excuse me for a second?" We all nod as Ava walks to the bathroom.

"Is she okay?" Joel asked.

I look back at Joel and Rebecca's questioning eyes. "Ava was kidnapped and attacked viciously. He hung the symbols to help protect her spirit. I remember Bing telling me about a sick girl, I just didn't realize who, until now."

"That's horrible," Joel said.

"Yeah, well if you would, please don't mention that I told you."

"Sure, no problem." Joel nodded.

Once Ava returns, the conversation moves to the dumb things we use to do and people we use to know, drinking up the wine without thinking.

"We seem to be out of wine," Rebecca said, standing up and shaking an empty bottle.

"We could go out, maybe the bar down the street?" Joel asked.

"That's probably not a good idea, maybe somewhere more..." I hesitated trying to come up with a solution.

"I know the perfect place, your Mom told me about it, Sean. And since I haven't gotten you anything for your birthday yet, then the rest of the night is on me, for everybody. Besides, I am your wife so I should pay for your birthday party, right?" Ava sits at the edge of her seat, seemingly excited by the whole idea. I grab her hand and squeeze it, feeling very lucky to be married to her.

"If you want to do that Ava, I guess we shouldn't ruin Sean's birthday by saying 'no'," Joel said shyly.

"Of course not, it will be fun and I haven't been out in forever. Oh, I need to change if we are going out though!" Rebecca excitedly runs out of the room. I try to stop her, but she is gone before I can get a word out. Joel simply sighs in the direction she left in.

When Rebecca is finally ready to go, we all leave for the cozy upscale restaurant where we are seated immediately when we arrive.

"Do you guys remember when we snuck into that upscale party for the food?" I asked.

"Oh, I can't believe you brought that up. That was crazy. Ava, your husband pretended to be some hot shot attorney and we followed him like fools, only because he was craving shrimp."

"Me? You wanted it just as bad. I seem to remember you saying, 'Oh Sean, they even have steak.' Your mouth was watering the whole time," I laugh with them.

"Well at least I was the innocent one." Joel and I laugh at Rebecca's comment. "I was. My only fault was following you two idiots."

"You may have followed, but you were the one eating your weight in chocolate covered strawberries." I laugh even harder after she smiles away from everyone. "You thought I forgot that," I said, winking at her.

"Those were some of the best strawberries I have ever had." Rebecca said as she sips her wine.

We laugh some more until I hear a few of the staff singing Happy Birthday and bringing a flaming cake towards me. I glance at Ava, who is biting her bottom lip to keep from laughing. Exasperated, I lean over to whisper into her ear, "I didn't see you leave the table but I know you had something to do with this and I will get you back." I smile, watching her laugh and sing along.

"That was great. But how did they know it was your birthday?" Rebecca asked

"I believe someone here told them," I glance at Ava, who takes a drink to hide her smile.

"You did this Ava? How? You never left the table?" Joel asked, curious.

"Yes baby, please tell us how you did it?" I asked glaring at her with an impish smile.

"I don't know what you're talking about. How would I have been able to do it?" *She looked right into my eyes and lied.* "I never left the table, so it's impossible that it was me." She wiggles a little in her chair, and in that instant I know damn well she is lying. I fork a mouthful of cake that the waiter cut for us, eyeing her disbelievingly and smiling as I plan to make her confess to me later.

"Ava?" someone calls out from another table.

"Oh no," Ava mumbles.

The man approaches our table, with a superior attitude, "Ava it is you." He said reaching out for her as she slowly stands and hugs him.

"Jasper, I should have known I would run into you here." Ava said with tenseness in her voice.

"We had a meeting across the street and decided to have dinner and a few drinks." He laughed, stopping only to stare Ava up and down while I struggle to place the name that sounds so familiar. "I think you are more beautiful now than when we worked together and that's saying something."

"Thank you Jasper. You look nice as well," she responded, still sounding tense.

"I have seen some of your recent work, Ava. I knew you were special."

"You have?" Ava asks wide-eyed.

"Yes. Are you surprised that I would keep up with my rising protégé? I do have to keep an eye out for possible competition."

"That's nice of you to say, Jasper, but I don't think I am quite to your level."

"You will be, especially if you have someone giving you the right direction." *His drooling over her is starting to annoy me.*

Ava sighs, "Jasper let me introduce you to my friends, Joel and Rebecca Castor."

"Nice to meet the both of you," Jasper said while he shakes Joel's hand and kisses Rebecca's causing her to blush.

Ava looks at me nervously. "Jasper this is Sean, my ... husband." Glancing at her, I stand up and shake his hand.

"Very nice to meet you, Sean. I thought I heard something about Ava getting married." He quickly turns back towards Ava, drooling all over himself again. *That shit is getting on my damn nerves.* "You are a very lucky man. I tried to get her to marry me." He said, as I tense and she stops breathing. "But no, she was too wild then to be contained I guess." He smiles back at me.

"Or maybe you just aren't her type." I smile forcefully in his direction. He laughs as if my comment is ridiculous. "So how did you and Ava meet?" I said though my teeth, taking Ava's hand to pull her away from him and closer to myself.

"Ava was right out of school, my sweet little protégé."

"Ohhhh." Rebecca giggled, but one look out of the corner of my eyes and she shuts up immediately.

"So she worked for you?" I said as calmly as I could. *JASPER! Son of a bitch, now I remember.*

"Yes, years ago but I still hold out hope that she will return," he said. *Over my fucking dead body asshole.* "Oh my love, you must come meet someone. I think it may be interesting for you," he said, taking her other hand. "You don't mind do you Sean?" I grip Ava's hand tighter.

"I will be right back, okay sweetheart?" Ava said, looking up at me with pleading eyes, only I'm not sure what she is pleading for. "I promise I will be right back." I nod at her and then proceed to have to watch her walk away with *him* to a table full of other men.

This is a first for me. I have never met anyone she was with before me. Now I meet him, who not only fucked my wife but proposed to her. *I want to carry Ava out of here right now. Breathe Sean before you do something stupid.*

"Sean, are you alright?" Joel asked.

"Yes. Why?" I said.

Joel kicks me under the table, jarring me to his attention. "Because you look like you are ready to kill someone."

"I'm fine," I said, taking another drink while eyeing Ava. *She is laughing with all those men, while they just stare at her.*

"Wow, you have really changed. I have never seen you jealous over anyone. So, he had sex with your wife." I instantly glare at him.

"Oohh kayyy. Just calm the fuck down Sean, it's not like he's going to do anything here." Joel backs off making eye contact with Rebecca.

"Who is he?" Rebecca asked.

"Some architect that apparently is some great talent or some shit," I said, twirling my glass on its edge.

"He's handsome, distinguished looking." She smiles devilishly at my sinister glare. "He is, Sean. I can see why she would be interested in him."

"Rebecca," Joel nudges her.

"What? He is." Rebecca said. *I feel sick.*

"Sorry about that. Jasper had a project that he thought I might be interested in." Ava said smiling at me timidly.

"I'm sure he did." I said too sarcastically, and receive a glare in return. Ava begins a conversation with Joel while Rebecca fights a smile, seemingly to keep from laughing at me. *I don't know why she finds this so humorous.*

We leave the restaurant soon after, apparently because everyone found my attitude distracting. Ava and I don't speak the entire ride back to the hotel or in the elevator, and when we get in the room I go straight to the bar.

"Do you want to talk about this or are you going to be in this mood for the rest of the night?" I glance her way but simply roll my eyes. "I did tell you about him."

"*No.* You didn't tell me everything." I shake my head and sit across from her. She follows with her head in her hands again. "Why didn't you tell me, Ava?"

"My relationship with Jasper was nothing, Sean, and when I started to realize I wanted more than just sex, I told him it was over. He thought it was because I wanted to get married, so he proposed. It was not even about that, I wanted more than sex. I wanted to feel something and I didn't for him. I didn't tell you about it because I had practically forgotten about it. It was out of desperation, he knew I was going to quit and he didn't want that. It wasn't a proposal of marriage it was more like a business deal. I don't hold onto things that don't mean anything or have any importance in my life. You are what I hold onto, and Lillah, those few years of childhood I had with my mother …" She stands up shaking her head. "But if you prefer to sit here and steam over nothing and ruin our night together, then that is your problem - not mine."

I rub my face and head. "I'm sorry Ava." I said, growling my frustration. "I was caught off guard. I guess I had convinced myself that you had never been with anyone else but me, which has been easy with you. But knowing your past with him and then seeing him touch you and obviously still desiring you. Uuuggghhhh! And the way he acted, like he was sure he could easily get you back into bed with him."

"That is his personality Sean, and you helped feed his ego with all your jealousy. He was my mentor and I worked for him because of who he is. I idolized him."

"Do you still?"

"A little bit, but I'm older now and I know the difference." She moves into my lap, facing me. "I know the difference between appreciating someone's work and not needing the admiration returned to feel good about myself. You're the only man I need, Sean."

"I'm really sorry for tonight. I love you, Ava."

Chapter 4

Ava

Sean has agreed to do some promos for the Cancer Society and they want to meet with him to go over some ideas, especially since Sean is sponsoring a majority of the efforts. Unfortunately, Sean got called back to the set early this morning to redo a stunt before they have to reopen the street. So that leaves me to entertain until he returns.

When they arrive, I open the door to four men. There are two older gentlemen with two younger men standing eagerly behind them. "Hello gentleman, please come in and make yourself comfortable. My husband is running a bit late, but he asked me to make sure you are taken care of until he arrives."

"Thank you, Mrs. Grant." One of the older gentlemen said as he reached for my hand. "My name is Donald Williams and this is my co-worker Henry Parker. We are with the Cancer Society. These gentlemen behind us are with the advertising agency."

"Ava, please." I smiled as I greet each of the older, somber men.

I have to hold back my laughter as I watch one of the younger men fidget rapidly with his bag, phone and jacket in order to produce a free hand for me, "Mrs. Grant, I mean Sean - Ava. Mrs. Ava, I mean, I am Sean … Shane … Grant, No." He winced, forcing a breath. "I mean Shane Putnam. That's me. I am Shane Putnam." Shane shamefully hangs his head as he shakes my hand and the other younger man snickers behind him.

"Nice to meet you, Shane, and don't worry. I have days like that too."

The last remaining man smiles eagerly at me, "Ava, Dillon Conrad." I put my hand out warily to him. "Oh, I'm sorry. I'm a southern boy. We don't shake hands. We hug, if you don't mind." Before I have a chance to protest, his arms are wrapped around me securely. I hug him simply, but his sniffing of my hair sends a slight uneasiness through my body.

I make sure to sit away from Dillon but despite my attempts to talk with everyone else, Dillon continues to work his cockiness back into my view. He earns quite a few swift kicks and nudges from Shane whenever he doesn't think I am watching. The two continue to bicker quietly until Shane makes a cross symbol across his chest, praying for some sort of relief. I take that sign as a signal that I should leave the room. "Would you gentleman like anything to drink?"Each of them asking for mild drinks, Dillon being a little more difficult, waits until last. I look over at him with an uneasy sigh, "And you Dillon?"

"What are you having?" He asked with a sincere smile.

"Water," I said.

"Then that's what I will have too." His contagious smile inflicts its will on me and I can't help but smile back at him.

Once in the kitchen, I grab some glasses and nearly drop them as I see that contagious smile coming towards me. "Did you need something Mr. Conrad?" I asked suspiciously.

"Dillon, please," he said sweetly.

"Dillon," I nodded.

"Yes, Ava," he said, continuing closer towards me.

"Did you need something?" I asked giving him a warning look.

"I thought you might need some help."

"Well thank you, but I think I have it handled."

"Well, I am here if you need me." He stops his approach and leans against the wall with a manly pose. "Am I making you nervous?" He asked.

"A little." I said.

"I'm sorry, I don't mean too. You are just so beautiful. I don't think I have ever seen a woman so beautiful in my life. You make it hard for me to …"

"Mr. Conrad, are you flirting with me?" I asked sternly, trying not to smile.

"It's Dillon. And why? Do you want me too?" He opens his mouth just enough so I can see his tongue trail the inside of his perfect teeth.

"Dillon, I am sure you do well with that charming smile of yours with most women, but I guarantee you that it won't work with me."

"Really?" He asked with a puzzled expression.

"No. And if I were you, I would back off before my husband gets home. You're coming on a little too strong."

"You want me to come on to you a little less?" He said, seemingly confused by the idea.

"No, I prefer you not to come on to me at all."

"But that's no fun."

"Are you always like this?" I ask, standing back from him to look him over fully.

"Like what?" He asks leaning in closer to me but I push him back and sigh. "Alright, but you're missing out. I can be a lot of fun and I am extremely good looking…but I am sure you noticed."

I laugh before I can stop myself, "I wouldn't doubt that." Dillon instantly gets excited by my response. "But I am married. *Very* happily married," I said having to push him away - again.

"He doesn't have to know. Come out and have a few drinks with me tonight. Nothing has to happen." His cockiness takes hold of him as he leans in. "Unless you …"

"No! And you better hope Sean doesn't find out you said that to me - he will tear you apart." I try to warn him but the cocky little bastard seems undeterred from his mission.

"Jealous, is he?"

"Dillon."

"Yes, Ava?" Dillon asked still hopeful.

"Yes Ava, what?" I bite my lip as Sean walks in with an intimidating approach, glaring at Dillon and his leaning posture.

"Mr. Grant. Wow, it's so nice to meet you." Dillon stupidly holds his hand out to Sean. You can see the tension in Sean's arm as he grips Dillon's hand with force and a clear understanding. I sigh as Sean let's go and Dillon shakes his hand out, behind himself.

I move between them and face Sean as persuasively as I can. "Honey, Dillon here was just telling me his ideas for the commercials. He is being sweet and helping me take these drinks out to everyone else." Sean stares at me as he contemplates whether he is going to hurt Dillon any further.

"Is that all you were talking about?" Sean asks, caressing my arm to verify that I am okay. I give him a stern look against his reluctant stance.

"Yes sweetheart, what else would we talk about?" I said, kissing him gently before whispering in his ear, "Please let it go, he's harmless, I promise." Sean huffs before loosening up his tense arms and pulling me closer to him.

"We're going to talk about this later," he whispered back to me. "Get the drinks." Sean motioned towards Dillon with a fierce look. I hand Dillon the tray of drinks, helping him position them correctly.

"Thanks," Dillon said, flexing his hand to grip the tray.

"You're welcome." I said smiling, which he returns enthusiastically. Rolling my eyes at him, I take hold of Sean's arm and walk away before the boy gets himself hurt.

The meeting proceeds without bloodshed. I did not participate, but used a nearby desk to check on some work issues, getting up to make calls in another room when necessary. Dillon follows most of my movements and Sean follows his. I try to ignore the both of them, but decide it best to leave the room, returning only once I hear them leaving. I walk in on Dillon trapped inside the threshold by Sean. Sean doesn't seem to be snarling, so I hold my place. Sean glances over at me and then back at Dillon, who is about to turn around in my direction. "Don't you dare turn around." Sean said to him. I start to get angry, but when Dillon's eyes twist as far to one side as possible to catch a glimpse of me, I grab my mouth to keep from laughing out loud. Sean glances at me in shock. "What is wrong with you?" He yelled at him.

"Nothing. Why?" Dillon shrugs.

"You know what, you're lucky I like you." Sean says holding back a smile, so I sit down and relax realizing Dillon isn't going to die … today anyway.

"You do?" He said excited and mistakenly relaxing. "You know, I knew you did and you know what? I like you too, Sean. I think we have a lot in common. We both are extremely good looking, we're both smart, and we both have great taste in women." Sean looks back at me as if to ask if I can believe what he is hearing.

"Seriously, did your mother drop you on your head or something?" Sean asked him.

"Are you kidding? There would be no way I could get my hair to look this good with a dent in my head. Like I was saying, you know I get to Atlanta quite often, maybe I can stop by. What's your address?"

"I'm not giving you my address!"

"Why not?" Sean goes speechless, staring at him in disbelief. "If you want to be my friend Sean, you should at least add me to your Christmas list. It's what friends do. And make sure you don't just sign your name, I hate that. Let me know how you're doing, what's going on in Sean's world. Don't be afraid to open up, I'm here for you buddy."

"What?" Sean snaps back.

"Hey do you ever go to Vegas? Ahhh damn, I bet you could get us into some great places. We have got to do that."

"No, we don't," Sean says, shaking his head and cautiously stepping away from Dillon.

"You know, Atlanta could be fun too. I was planning to go to Vegas next week, but sure. Why not? I will come to Atlanta and stay with you instead."

"The hell you are!" Sean yells.

"Hey, I bet you have a pool too. Does Ava swim?" Dillon asked receiving a sharp glare. "Okay, so maybe just us guys then."

"Will you shut the fuck up?" Dillon looks at Sean, taken aback by his raised voice. "I said I like you, which means I like your ideas. Not that I want to become your pen pal." Dillon opens his mouth and Sean begins to shake. "No ... be quiet. I have a film to do in Atlanta after I finish the one here. My schedule is going to be tight, so call Ethan, my brother. He handles everything for me. *Please* make sure you call Ethan. Don't call me ... *call Ethan*. Got it? Do not *ever* call me ... *always* call Ethan."

"What if ..."

"No. Never call me, always Ethan." Dillon is barely able to complete a full shrug before Sean pulls him in close by the neck and whispers something to him I can't hear, and it doesn't seem pleasant. I can't see Dillon's face completely, but he stiffens enough to tell me Sean is not wishing him well. I stomp off to the bedroom so I do not have to hear anything else. I do not want to know what Sean says to make people turn that pale. I lay across the bed, picking up one of my magazines to read when I hear Sean enter the doorway. I raise my magazine up higher in front of my face and Sean laughs. He lays down next to me, waiting for me to notice him. "Ava?" I look at the page opposite him. "Alright, why are you mad?"

"You were not very nice to Dillon."

"I was nicer than I needed to be." Sean said sternly

"He's harmless, Sean."

"Harmless? Stupid would be a better adjective for that kid." I return to my magazine in a huff. "Ava," he said, touching me softly and tugging on my clothes with the tips of his fingers.

"No. Not until you tell me what you said to him?"

He instantly rolls away from me. "I am not doing that."

"Why?"

"Because you don't need to know some things. Just know he won't be bothering you ever again."

"Sean! I handled it fine without being so harsh."

"Oh, I heard you handling it. Seemed like you only encouraged him more."

"I did not, or at least I wasn't meaning too." He glances over at me as I crawl to him. "I couldn't help but laugh at him, Sean. He is ..."

"He's an idiot and he's going to get his ass kicked badly one day if he's not careful. If you hadn't stepped in, I was seriously considering doing it myself."

"I know you were. You really need to work on your temper by the way."

"I thought I handled it pretty well, after what I heard. He was real lucky I was as calm as I was." I instantly scan his expression, worried about what he did hear. "Oh Ava! I don't think I have ever seen a woman so beautiful in my life!" He over dramatizes in a ridiculous voice as he jumps on top of me, grabs me and breathes heavily in my ear. I laugh hysterically, which seems to give him the green light to pursue whatever he wants.

I grab his hands "What are you doing?"

"Taking your clothes off."

"Sean, I have to go soon."

"No, you don't. Take a later flight," he kisses me while undressing himself.

"You know, Dillon had no idea who he was up against." I move onto his lap, pulling off my shirt and smiling into his waiting eyes. "As easy as it is for me to resist him, you are simply too irresistible for me."

"Damn right I am." Sean said, finding my lips with his.

Chapter 5

Rebecca

It's been months since I have seen him, and my body tingles all over thinking of being in his bed again. I never knew how big my mistake was until he was gone. I thought for sure Joel would be the one to make it big, but how was I to know Joel loves partying more than working? Joel's father, Butch Castor, is the richest bastard I know and even he has no tolerance for his son's lack of motivation. I am able to get money out of Butch when he is horny, which is clear when he flies me out for a weekend at his beech house. He never gives me much, but at least I get a vacation out of it. However, ever since that new blond bimbo started working at his office, I can't even get him on the phone anymore. I thought for sure I was going to be stuck with Joel and be poor for the rest of my life, until surprisingly Joel activated his one still-working brain cell and managed to come up with a decent screenplay. What's even better, is he thought enough to ask Sean to play the lead. I am on such a high over it all that it doesn't even bother me that he married that trashy redhead. Besides, after our last dinner together it is clear their marriage is on shaky ground already. If she is hiding anything from him, I am going to make sure to find out what that is, even if I have to extend some nauseating friendliness towards her. Living in their guesthouse for a few months will give me ample access to Sean whenever I please, and plenty of opportunities to make him mine again. It only takes one weak moment to destroy a relationship.

I am startled out of my daydream when Joel slows the car. "I think this is it." Joel said softly. I gaze over his home with excitement, nearly exploding from all the mental plans and changes I plan to make to the place once it's mine. I assume, after his divorce though, we will move back to LA where we belong, so really, this house is insignificant.

Before we even step near the massive double doors, Ava bounces out to greet us with her obvious, fake charm. *She needs to lighten up with that obnoxious sweetness. No one is buying it.* "Hi! I am so glad you guys were able to make it in okay," Ava said, seemingly overjoyed to see us for no reason at all.

Joel hugs her as I sigh impatiently, "Ava it's so great to see you. You look wonderful."

Pulling down my shades, I peak over the edge to review her pathetic outfit. "Ava, you look … healthy." Surprisingly, she doesn't try and hug me too before I walk past her to find a decent spot inside.

"Thanks Rebecca, so … do … you."

"I know. I can't tell you how many people bother me to say how young I look." I smiled at her. "And Ava, you don't look a day over thirty-nine yourself, you sure are handling your age well."

"That's good, because I'm thirty-two, and I believe that's three years younger than you … or was it four?" I snarl at her snide comment, only to have to watch her become amused by my reaction.

"Sorry Sean isn't here to greet you, but he went to meet with his brother about a business deal they are working on," Ava said while directing Joel to sit.

"Will his brother be coming tonight?" Joel asked her.

"No. He and his wife are staying home with the kids. Lillah is staying with them tonight, so she won't be disturbed by the party." Ava continues making small talk with Joel while I explore.

Looking around the room, I find their wedding picture and pick it up to gaze over it. Sean, cradling her in his arms, stares at her as if she is the most beautiful thing he has ever seen. I place the picture on a nearby table with no interest in putting it back where it was.

"Ava, please don't feel like you have to entertain us. We have plenty to do before the party tonight." Joel said, eyeing her closely while she bends over to pick up a nearby toy. Ava kindly hands us a key to the guesthouse allowing Joel to move our car around to the back entrance.

The guesthouse is immaculate. It has a loft bedroom and a small kitchen with a bar, and behind the stairs is what appears to be a studio of sorts. An easel, some work tables and some railings displaying some recent work. One particular piece catches my attention and I move in for a closer look when I feel Joel come up behind me.

"Ava's, I imagine. She's good."

I shrug, walking away, "I've seen better."

Joel suddenly grabs my arm and spins me around to face him. "Rebecca, don't screw this up for me."

"What the hell is wrong with you?" I yell at him as I jerk my arm away from his fierce grip.

"I am already sick of your attitude. Look, *Darling*, we both want something here and if everything goes well, we both can get what we want. So let's try and get through this without killing each other … okay?" He smiles mockingly in my direction.

I return a similar smile. "Sure dear, whatever you want."

ᑕ֍Ꮻ

Getting ready for the cast party tonight, takes me four hours, but Joel doesn't seem the least bit impressed with my efforts. "Is that what you're wearing?" Joel asked, wrinkling his face at me.

"Yes. Why?"

"It is supposed to be casual Rebecca. We're not going to the club."

"I know that, but I want to make a good impression," I said to his instant laughter. Ignoring him, I stretch out my long legs admiring them along with my new shoes. "Sean will love these." I whisper to myself.

"Are you ready to go?" Joel asked.

"Yes. Is it time? I don't want to be too early?"

"I'd say it's close enough," he said, shaking his head at me.

The house is all lit up. Servers are already greeting guests with food and drinks. I float down the path towards the main house, preparing to be greeted. Joel introduces me to each person as we approach him or her, but I really do not pay much attention to any of them. My heart begins to race when I see a broad figure on the other side of the draperies. *It has to be him.* Sure enough, he comes out the door greeting people immediately. He is so handsome, with his dark hair and green eyes. He is wearing dark jeans and a fitted long sleeve shirt, his sleeves pushed up just enough. He hasn't change a bit. I watch him smile and laugh with a drink in hand, trying not to spill it while he animates his conversation. I nudge Joel, bringing his attention towards Sean and he escorts me to him without hesitation. I reach out to him and press my body to his, taking in his heavenly scent with a kiss below his ear. Sean instantly throws his arm around my shoulders and I nuzzle into place perfectly. "Hey guys. Ava said you made it in okay."

"Yes, everything went fine. Thanks, by the way, for putting us up. Once we start getting in some money, we will be out of your way quickly. " Joel expressed his appreciation again as he gives Sean a quick guy hug, causing him to pull away from me. Joel winks at me knowingly.

"Oh don't worry about it. It will be nice to hang out together again while we finish this movie up." Sean said, lifting his drink to his lips, seemingly already a few drinks ahead of us.

"So where is Ava?" Joel asked. *He couldn't wait ten seconds to ask about her?*

"She will be out as soon as she finishes going over some things with the caterer. It shouldn't take her much longer." As if she heard her name, she suddenly appears, wrapping her arm around his waist. Sean smiles, kissing her as he adjusts to put his arm around her and let her nuzzle in where I once was. She dressed casually in her modest dress and boots. *It is chilly but they do have heaters out here, does she really need the boots? She must not think too much of her legs.* Joel, apparently trying to annoy me tonight, discreetly looks her over with a nodding smile in my direction.

We make exhausting small talk until the director comes over, introducing himself as Daniel Kane. An older man and a little strange, but he is one of the best in the industry I have been told, so I make sure to talk to him. "Sean, I had a great idea for an addition to one of the scenes," Daniel said.

Sean cocks his eyebrows at him. "Which is?"

"I think we should have Ava play one of your girls," Daniel smiles. *Is he kidding? Her?*

"That's a great idea!" Joel chimed in quickly.

"That would be up to her, of course I would love it," Sean said, looking down at Ava who is smiling up at him.

"Ava, this could be really great for the film. Everyone has such a strong curiosity about your relationship, and to get to see you two together on screen would really be something. Besides, you are so beautiful, innocent and absolutely perfect for the part. All you have to do is simply kiss your husband," Daniel pushed.

"Tell her everything Daniel, don't scam my wife now."

"No. Really. There isn't much to it other than that, I mean, except for the scene we would like to do with you two in bed together, but that would be nothing more than a simple make out scene."

"Make out with him in bed? You mean pretend were having sex?" Ava, wide-eyed, leans in to Sean more.

"Yes, but it will be easy and I am sure your husband will guide you through it." Daniel continued to push as I huff silently.

"What if we take the sex scene out and only imply it? Then all you have to do is kiss him" Joel asked.

Ava hesitates but with Sean whispering something in her ear a smile slowly emerges, "Okay, but only if my husband keeps the promise he just made to me."

"This will be great, Ava, and I assure you - you will be wonderful." Daniel shakes his fists in front of him as if he just won the best pig contest at the state fair. *I need a drink.* I search for an available bar and grab a bottle on my own, pouring a triple while ignoring the loser in his rented outfit who is trying to take the bottle from me. Returning to the Ava fan club, I become a little hopeful when I realize the conversation seems to have turned tense.

"Sean, how dangerous is it?" Ava asked.

"It's not that bad, there are plenty of safety precautions and stunt people to do the worst part." Sean explained to her calmly.

"Actually, Sean, we were hoping that you would do the stunt and do it with little gear to make it more realistic. The precautions would obviously be there, but the best shot for this is with you clearly in it. If you want it, we can do a stunt double, but we prefer you," Daniel persuaded.

Sean looks down at Ava, "What do you think?"

"I don't know, if it's something that you feel you need to do then I will support you." She cowers in his arms giving him a weak smile before kissing his cheek. "Excuse me I need to check on a few things with the caterer." She walks back into the house with Sean's eyes following her.

"Daniel, I am going to have to say 'no'. I'm not going to risk upsetting Ava over it. It's not worth it."

"Sean, are you sure?" Joel asked.

Sean nods. "Yes, it's not going to break the film."

"But it could certainly make it." Joel huffed.

"Maybe, but I am sure there is another way to make it better, isn't there?" Sean asked.

"Possibly," Daniel conceded with a sigh.

"Well, I need to go check on my wife so please go and enjoy yourselves. There is plenty of food and drink and even music if you desire to dance." Sean nudges Joel's arm, startling him out of his daydream.

"Oh yes, Rebecca would you like to dance?" Joel takes my hand without waiting for my answer. I watch Sean, over Joel's shoulder, walk into the house and find Ava inside fumbling around with something. He pulls her away from it and makes her look at him. There is some shaking of heads, some nods but eventually her highness's happiness appears once again and she is whisked to the dance floor in *my* man's arms.

"Joel, maybe we should switch partners?" I suggested.

"They just got out here Rebecca, I'm not going to interrupt them."

"Then I will." Joel tries to stop me, but I approach the sickening embrace next to us before he can get out a full sigh.

"Ava, do you mind if we trade partners?" I asked with the sweetest smile I could muster.

"Rebecca, I haven't seen my wife all day, so if you don't mind I would like to dance with her a little longer?" Sean said, pulling Ava back to his chest.

"That's fine, but save me a dance for later Sean, okay?" I said earning a sideways glance from Ava.

"Sure," Sean said moving away from us.

I spend the rest of the night trying to get Sean's attention, but no matter how hard I try I always seem to be too late or interrupted by someone else. By the time the last guest leaves and the caterer has cleaned up for the night, Sean is nowhere in sight. I force Joel to help me search for him. When we finally find them, they are cuddling together under a blanket in an oversized chair. They sit within a sectioned off area in front of French doors leading into a bedroom, which I assume is theirs. An obvious sanctuary, even though you can still see the pool, the focus seems to be the pond and trees in the back. The pergola that surrounds is strewn with vines, billowing light fabrics and an outdoor fireplace, which is already burning out. They are talking and laughing quietly to each other, so I drag Joel over to them, making sure he brings chairs with him.

"So, what's so funny?" I asked as they both turn to me.

"Nothing important," Sean said while helping Joel pull over his chair. "So did you guys have fun?"

"Yes, it was great, thank you," Joel expressed. "You guys?" He yawned.

"Yes, we did. It was our first real party since we moved in here." Sean says with his hands obviously wandering under the blanket draped around them. The discussion becomes annoying, but not any more so than Joel agreeing with everything Ava says. *Idiot.*

"The music is still playing. Should we have once last dance before calling it a night?" I asked, anticipating my long awaited dance.

"Good idea, Rebecca," Sean said getting up with Ava in tow.

I jump up dragging Joel along, but before I can reach Sean, he is already lip-locked with her. I watch them closely, waiting for a good moment to interrupt them. I have to endure watching him grab her ass and pull her closer to him. He whispers something to her, causing her to smile as he lifts her up and sticks his tongue in her mouth. "Oh, I didn't need to see that." I said, hiding my face in Joel's shoulder.

"Umm, guys, maybe we should see you tomorrow," Joel called out to them.

"Oh shit, sorry, I forgot we weren't alone. Yes, we will see you tomorrow." Sean waves us off, not wasting any time before returning to *her.*

Joel stumbles to the bar. "Did you drink that much?" I asked, shocked by his demeanor.

"What? I don't know. Just let me make one more then I will get to you in a minute."

His wretched behavior is certainly not turning me on. "I think I am going to sit outside for a little while. It's a nice night, and I need some down time before bed. Okay?" He looks up at me with all smiles as he scans me over.

"Okay, don't be too long." he said, adjusting himself.

"I won't." I smiled, exiting the guesthouse quickly with a blanket and my cell phone.

I walk back towards the main house, finding a comfortable spot near the pool to sit and gaze over the place. Holding my phone up, I take pictures of my surroundings. *I wonder how much I could get for an inside video of Sean Grant's house?* I set it to video and wander the area, taking in everything halfheartedly until I come up on their room. I can hear them laughing and talking. Curious, I kneel down to look through an opening within the drapery and watch them. *Watch him.* She sits on the edge of the bed with him standing in between her legs, caressing her legs as he kisses her deeply. I wait, anticipating, as his hand moves up her dress and without hesitation pulls her panties right off of her. My curiosity rises as I watch him hesitate and concentrate on her face again. He says something to her before kissing her again and she lifts her arms so he can pull her dress off her slowly. He meticulously removes each item she wears before laying her back in the bed gently, finding every part of her body with his mouth. I can't stop watching him. He handles her so gently. Oh, how she moans with every touch of his lips on her skin. He arouses me when he sits up to take his shirt off, showing off his masculine chest and arms. I pretend I am her, kissing his chest and grabbing his belt, undoing his pants for him and pushing them off his hips. He crawls over her kissing her tenderly, pulling her legs up around him as he enters her. My body weakens seeing all of him, I begin to moan watching him fuck her deep and slow. I can almost feel him inside of me, feel his tongue caress mine; hear his groans deepen with every thrust into my hips. I continue to watch them caressing and kissing, moaning loudly enough for me to hear now. Feeling my body begin to tighten in anticipation, I grip my phone tighter. *This is good, too good.* I smile brightly as I realize - the recording that I am getting. Happily, I am surprised to see her on top of him now, and showing quite a lot of herself from this angle. I briefly worry about him catching me, when he sits up to start kissing her body again, grabbing her ass and pulling her hard to him. The moans get louder and I lick my lips with excitement, but suddenly Sean pauses and looks out the door. I jump quickly out of sight, darting across the grounds to a safer range to view my video. With relief, I find my lounge chair and admire my new money-making video.

"Rebecca?" Startled, I nearly fall out of my chair.

"Damn Joel, you scared me half to death!"

"Sorry, I was wondering when you were coming back?" I start to yell at him for being so nosy when I notice the bottle he is carrying.

"Can I have some of that?" He nods, handing it to me. I take several drinks, "Do you want to stay out here with me?" He wastes no time crawling in next to me and fondling me. I take another few drinks while he pulls my dress off revealing my breasts to him. I take his shirt off, jerk his pants off and rub him, lick him and suck on him until he is erect in my hands. "Fuck me hard, baby!" I yell, rubbing his cock until he starts to moan uncontrollably. Finally, he takes hold of me and bends me over, my legs spread wide for him. "Fuck me!" I screamed. The more I said it, the harder he pounds into me. *I want to be loud, I want to outdo them.* I am thrilled when I catch a glimpse of Sean walking outside of their room, taking notice of us. I pose for him, twisting so the moonlight highlights my naked body. *Come on Sean watch what he is doing to me, crave it, want it and it will be yours.* I look back towards Sean to see his expression but he has already walked back inside. Anger shoots through my veins as I moan louder and louder, eager to disturb them. I come fiercely. My anger encourages my determination, so I drop to my knees baring my naked body to the moonlight proudly as I suck Joel and praise him the louder he comes. I feel superior in my attempt to outdo them, to outdo her. *I am positive Sean will be dreaming of me tonight.*

Chapter 6

Sean

Ava spent months planning this area behind our room specifically. Our place away from it all to remember our moments when we first met and it couldn't be more perfect. Ava sits in my lap, touching me and encouraging me as the alcohol within her brings out her dirtier side. I enjoy feeling her hands touch my body under my clothes and down my pants. "You're being naughty," I said, watching her lean back on my chest innocently and pulling her hand out of my pants. "I didn't say I didn't like it."

"Too bad, I'm not in the mood anymore." she said, raising her chin in a cute defiance.

"Is that right?" She nods, giggling, giving her true desires away. "I like your boots, maybe you can wear those when I fuck you later." I laugh as she acts shocked by my statement, yet she still allows me to adjust her on top of me and push her ass down onto my erection. "Feel that?"

"Yes," she moaned.

"I want to feel you, baby." She moves her arms behind her, to the back of my head, giving me full access of her. I reach down under our blanket and pull her dress up to her thighs. Kissing, nuzzling her ear and whispering dirty things as I reach down in between her legs and ... Rebecca and Joel find us and make themselves at home, *pissing me off.* I was well on my way to taking advantage of Ava's and my intoxication when they interrupted. Luckily, I am able to get right back on track after Rebecca suggested dancing. Cradling Ava in my arms, sliding my hands over her soft dress and feeling every curve of her body. "I love this dress on you," I whispered in her ear. She blushes away from me. *Damn, I get so excited when she does that.* "It's so soft, I can't stop touching you," I said, as she grips me tighter.

"Good," she whispers.

I smile, and the devil within me is starting to come out. Kissing her, I lean down to her ear, barely touching her skin with my lips. "Baby, I want to pull this dress off of you and fuck you with those sexy as hell boots still on you." I squeeze her ass, pushing her into my hard-on that is only getting bigger the more I touch her. She looks up into my eyes and I lick my lips slowly. Instantly, she pulls my head down, grabbing my lips with hers while grazing my hard-on with her hand … twice. I lose it, and let her know what I want to do to her.

Her soft moans would have caused me to strip her right there if we had not of been interrupted by Joel. I had forgotten they were there. Thank goodness, they leave quickly. I kiss Ava's giggling lips as I watch Joel and Rebecca walk off towards the guesthouse. I continue to press Ava up on me until after they go inside. Grabbing the edges of her dress, "Okay baby, we're alone now."

"Sean, no. Not out here, not with them here."

"But…. Daaammnn."

"Don't pout, and I will let you do everything you're wanting to do inside. With my boots still on." Ava winks at me and walks seductively in the house unzipping her dress slowly as she walks. *I love her so much.*

I follow her with ideas racing through my mind, ready to be dirty as hell with her until something in the back of my head resurfaces and I can't. No matter how much alcohol I have in me I cannot forget that day.

It was but only a week ago and the day was fairly ordinary, I had just finished some paper work and decided to go see what Ava and Lillah were up too. As I approached Lillah's room I could hear both of them giggling and laughing, I turned the corner and saw them playing. Ava in a big fluffy white play hat, Lillah trying to put on bracelets and oversized sunglasses on her. Ava makes faces at her every time she adds something more, causing Lillah to laugh even harder. They are both so beautiful, but never more so than when they are together - especially when they are laughing. When Ava catches me staring, she motions for me to come in.

"What are we playing?" I asked, laughing at Ava's ridiculous accessories.

"We are playing tea party. Do you want to play?" Ava smiled at me.

"I would love to. Can I, Lillah?" I ask my daughter, who nods excitedly and immediately searches for something. She finally appears with a big fluffy pink hat and puts it on my head.

"Here Daddy." she said.

"Do I need this?" She nods, clapping, and proceeds to get more.

"You cannot attend the tea party not properly dressed," Ava snickers at me. I nod back at her, feeling completely ridiculous, but when Lillah brings out a matching pink boa I know it is about to get worse. I suck it up and embrace the ridiculousness. Swinging the boa around my neck, I take my pair of sunglasses and work the outfit for her, causing Lillah and Ava to both laugh hysterically. Ava and I make fools of ourselves over doing the actions of sipping tea and discussing with our daughter, made up adventures. The whole thing … is the most fun I have ever had, and the best part is that my daughter loves every minute of it. After I put Lillah to bed, I find Ava waiting for me. "Hey, Mr. Pinky Bear."

"Ha ha, don't you call me that in front of anyone else. I do have a reputation to uphold you know. Besides, Randy and Ethan will never let me hear the end of it."

"So, I shouldn't have the pictures framed?" She laughs as I hug her with the largest smile.

"I had the best time with you both," I said.

"That's good. So did I, and I am sure Lillah did too."

"I want more days like this Ava." She looks at me with a curious expression. "I mean, I want more of this." She shakes her head at me. "Ava, come on, you know what I mean. And I know you want the same. You have had that look in your eye, ever since you held William in your arms a few months ago. I knew soon as Abbey announced she was pregnant with him you wanted to follow right after her."

"Well, it's just that Lillah is almost three now and …" her head drops but I lift it back up to look at me.

"You're not listening to me. You know I want more kids and I am ready to do that now." Her eyes sparkle and I feel a twinge of excitement shoot through my body. "I can't wait to get you pregnant, Ava."

And at that moment my world changed. Every time we have sex, it is isn't just about sex anymore it is about getting my wife pregnant. I want it to be real and wonderful for the both of us. Conceiving Lillah will certainly always be memorable and I want it to be the same with this child.

So right now, staring at her with her drunken sweet smile, I hold back briefly deciding to take my time with her. She has been off birth control for more than enough time now, and the thoughts that are running through my mind make her even more beautiful to me. I can't hold her close enough to me. I can't kiss her enough or even make her feel good enough. Everything is about her right now, and I am going to make sure she feels it. Our motions are so in sync and feel so good, until something catches my eye outside. I blink my eyes to refocus on the odd glimmer, but it disappears. A little paranoid, I hold tight to Ava and switch the lights off while laying her down under me. She is concerned, but with some simple words of encouragement on my part, I am able to put her at ease. Within seconds, I forget about my paranoia and make love to my wife as she deserves. While Ava is cleaning up for bed, I walk outside to verify what it was I saw… only I become distracted by the loud moans coming from the other side of our pool. Instantly, I regret looking up. I close my eyes tight and rush back inside, making sure to overlap the draperies so Ava doesn't see them. I jump into bed, concealing my expression before Ava walks out of the bathroom, only she starts to leave our bedroom. "Where are you going, baby?"

"I'm going to get some water … is that okay?" She smiles uneasily.

"I'll get it for you …"

"That's okay, I will get it. You stay in bed." She said, exiting before I have a chance to stop her. I wait for her, knowing what is surely to come. Hearing her approach slowly, I look up, laughing at her wide eyes and open mouth. "Sean, did you know?"

"Yes, I'm sorry. I walked outside for a second and saw them. I tried to prevent you from seeing it."

"Oh my… Sean that's …"

"Disgusting?" She nods and I laugh again. "I know. I feel like I should take another shower." I said, cringing as I hear Rebecca moan louder.

"Oh Sean, is that weird for you? She is your ex …"

"No, not weird. It's long been over between us. I can barely stand her now, and seeing her like that …" I make a face as I feel my stomach churn. "It makes me nauseous, actually. I will never know what I saw in her."

"She is very pretty." Ava said with a questioning look in my direction. "Despite her horrible personality." she mumbled.

"Trust me sweetheart, she isn't the least bit appealing to me." I said caressing her cheek with a smile.

"Sean, it's one thing for them to do that with only us here, but when Lillah …"

"Don't worry about it, I will talk to them tomorrow. I will make the rules perfectly clear to them." I said, pulling her into my arms and breathing her scent in before drifting off.

&#x0cso;

The next day, I kiss Ava goodbye before she leaves for work. I work out with my trainer, then plug in my headphones, tuning out everything and enjoy the view of our home while I do some cardio. At least, until I catch a glimpse of Rebecca and Joel in the guesthouse, reminding me of the conversation I need to have with them. I decide to get the dreaded conversation out the way before I have to leave to pick up Lillah. I hesitate at the guesthouse door, not used to having to knock on the door to my own home.

After some harsh movements inside, the door opens. "Morning." Joel said still wearing his boxers and his hair a mess.

"Good morning. I need to talk to you about something before I leave to go pick up Lillah and the boys." I look at Joel as sincerely as I can. He instantly steps aside and motions for me to come in and I am immediately met with arms wrapping around my waist.

"Good morning, Sean," Rebecca giggled. Grimacing, I undo her hands from my waist and she happily skips to Joel's side, staring up at me eagerly, and waiting for me to speak.

"Like I was saying, I really need to talk to you both about last night." I watch both of their clueless faces stare at me. "Anyway, Lillah will be back here and she is only two. We would like you guys to keep your …" *How the hell to say this?* "Your escapades hidden behind closed doors, if you would?" I tried to explain.

Joel seems to understand perfectly, "Oh, Sean, I am so sorry. We were both so drunk and not thinking at all. I am really sorry."

"Not a big deal, but I wanted to make sure you are more careful when Lillah is around."

"Absolutely. This is your house and we should have never disrespected you or Ava like that. Is she angry?" Joel asked.

"No, she's not. We both actually thought it was kind of funny."

"Funny?" Rebecca exclaimed loudly.

"No. I mean, we were surprised and drunk ourselves …" I tried to explain before Joel puts his hand up.

"We understand Sean, don't worry about it. And rest assured, it won't happen again. We promise." He looks over at Rebecca and then back at me, emphasizing his point.

I nod, feeling a lot better, "Great, then we will see you for dinner tonight?"

"Sure, looking forward to it." Joel smiled.

I walk back out the door as fast as I can and almost make it to the car before Rebecca stops me, striking her usual come-hither pose. "What?" I ask her with a sigh.

"Where are you going?" She asks, touching my arm and twirling her tongue.

"I told you I'm going to get Lillah and the dogs."

"Can I go with you?"

"Rebecca, I'm not going anywhere exciting and I have to meet with Ethan. Trust me, you won't have any fun or interest in coming with me."

"But it's boring with nobody here." She pouts, and I huff at her while motioning towards the guesthouse. "Joel is working, so I will be sitting here all day by myself. I would much rather go out with you than sit around here by myself." She pouts profusely, sticking her bottom lip out and putting her hands in her back pockets of her skintight pants.

Rubbing my face, I swear silently, "Fine, get in. But no complaining." I emphasize until she nods. She jumps for joy and runs to the other side of the car. *I know I am going to regret this, I just know it.*

"Why can't we take that car?" Rebecca asks pointing to Ava's car.

"Because that is a wedding present I got for Ava. It is a special occasion car for her only."

"So, does that mean you can't drive it?"

"No, but it's a little difficult to get a car seat and two full grown dogs into an Aston Martin, Rebecca."

"So why did you get her that car? Is that her favorite or something?"

"Kind of."

"Kind of? What's that mean?"

I sigh loudly. "Because I have the same car, so it reminds her of me. We enjoy riding together."

"Oh. So how is your brother?"

"Good. He and Abbey just had their second child a few months ago." I said, trying to make a long conversation as short as possible.

"Abbey? His wife?"

I look over at her, forgetting that she probably wouldn't know that. She has not seen Ethan since we were dating, and only briefly then. I am not even sure Ethan would remember her. "Yes, Abbey is his wife. They were married a couple of years after ..." I glance over at her.

"After we broke up?" She said with a disgruntled tone.

"Yes."

"Well that's nice, I'm happy for him."

"Wonderful," I said, exasperated.

"And I'm happy for you too, Sean."

"Great."

"So are you excited about the role you will be playing?"

"Sure."

"It will be great working with you again." She smiles, patting my hand.

"Uh-huh."

"So do you like Atlanta?"

"Uh huh."

"Even better than LA?"

"Uh huh."

"Sean!" Rebecca screamed.

I jump, staring daggers at her, "Don't fucking do that!" I yelled.

"Well you're not listening to me," she pouted.

"You know I don't like fucking chit-chatting Rebecca," I said, watching her cross her arms and proceed into full pout mode.

Damn! I should have said no and drove off as quickly as possible, my own damn fault she is here. "Fine, what do you want to talk about?" I smiled sarcastically at her. She ignored the sarcasm and goes right back into her questions. *I can't drive fast enough.* I pull into Ethan's, grateful for the interruption... at least until I see my mother's car. "Rebecca, my mother's here. You might want to sit in the car and wait. I promise, I won't be too long."

"Why do I have to sit in the car?"

"Seriously?" I ask her, shocked that she would ask such a stupid question. "If you recall, you and my mother don't get a long too well."

"Oh. That was a long time ago, I am sure we both have matured since then," she said, jumping out of the car and waiting impatiently for me to lead her in.

Please Dear God, let me get through this. I enter Ethan's house as if it is my own and find Lillah in the floor playing with Collin. I sneak up behind her, putting one foot on either side of her and staying silent until she notices me. She looks down at my shoes, grabbing one and instantly throwing her hands up to reach for me.

"Daddy!" Picking her up, I kiss her energetically on her neck until she is laughing uncontrollably. After I sit her back down I find Collin, giggling already, as he scoots away from me and holding his chin as close to his chest as he can.

"And where do you think you're going?" I grab him and throw him over my shoulder, turning him upside down and kissing his belly until he can't take any more. I sit him back down to pick up Lillah who is determined to be the only one getting my attention. Abbey and my mother sit watching the giggle fest with great enthusiasm.

"Hello Sean," Abbey said, smiling as she folds some clothes.

"Abbey, you look beautiful as always," I said kissing her on the cheek. "You too mother," I said, kissing her cheek with a cocky smile.

"You better not forget me," my mother stressed with a smile.

"And what about me?" I look up to the second floor, spotting Ethan blowing kisses at me.

"Oh, I'm coming for you next sweetness."

"Make sure to use tongue, you know how I like it," he laughed.

"Ethan!" Abbey yells at him with a dirty look.

"Don't worry Abbey, I'll take care of your husband," I give Ethan a wicked grin.

"Sean Grant, don't make me call your wife," Abbey said, glancing at me out of the corner of her eyes.

"Abbey, I thought you liked me?" I whined.

"I do like you, but I have enough little boys to take care of around here." Abbey said as I look up at Ethan and smile.

"I heard that," Ethan yelled as he walks down to us.

I turn to him quickly to fend off any possible attack coming my way only to see his mouth drop open. "Rebecca?" Ethan said quietly.

"Hello Ethan," Rebecca said with a perfect smile taking over her face.

My mother instantly glares at me. "Rebecca you remember my mother, Mary?" I said pleading for peaceful actions.

"Yes, how are you?" Rebecca said unafraid.

"Very well, thank you. And you?" My mother said, nodding stiffly towards her.

"Great, thank you." Rebecca said happily.

"And this is Abbey, Ethan's wife," I said, moving away from my mother's reach.

"Nice to meet you" Abbey said, holding out her hand to greet Rebecca, unaware of the history.

"Nice to meet you as well," Rebecca replied as she shakes her hand.

"Please, have a seat." Abbey motions for her to sit across from them. Rebecca sits down, seemingly unaware of the uncomfortable air in the room.

"Okay I'm going to be only a few minutes, then we can go." I said, waiting for Rebecca's half nod. I try to avoid my mother but she has a way of drawing me in, but her glare nearly ignites me before I am able to look away from her. I follow Ethan up to his office and try not to think about the conversation that might be going on downstairs, only to realize Ethan is staring at me silently. "What?"

"What!" I move back in my chair shocked by his anger. "Sean, how could you bring … *that* woman into my house?"

"Whoa, calm down. I didn't realize it would be that big of a deal Ethan."

"Well, it is."

"Okay, so now I know. Do you mind telling me why it is?" I ask, sitting back slowly in my seat.

"I don't like her and I never did. Why are you with her?"

"She and Joel are staying in our guesthouse," I said calmly

"You aren't serious?" Ethan said, slamming his fists on his desk.

"Ethan they don't have enough money to pay for a second place here. You should have seen where they are living in New York."

"I don't care. You shouldn't bring her into your home. I can't believe Ava is okay with this."

"She wasn't real happy about it, but she saw how they lived and agreed for during the shooting of the film they could stay with us. Then they can go back to New York with a little more money in their pockets and hopefully a lot better off."

Ethan sits shaking his head at me and sighing, "This is going to end badly Sean, real bad if you're not careful."

"I will be careful Ethan, don't worry. The next few months will fly by."

"I hope so."

We sit in silence for a few minutes until he finally moves on to more important issues. When we are done, I walk back downstairs alone and to an uncomfortable silence. *Damn this day.* My mother meets my eyes and moves quickly to head me off. "Oh shit." I said under my breath.

"Sean, can I speak to you for a minute?" My mother asked as she walks into the other room, waiting for me.

"I guess," I mumbled as I follow after her.

"Well?" She said with her arms crossed and her foot tapping in front of me. *I have not seen this stance in a long while.*

I rub my face. "She and Joel are only staying with us until shooting is over and then they are going right back to New York. She wanted to get out of the house for a little while today, so she begged to come with me and I didn't think it would be that big of a deal… but I am really regretting that decision." I rambled.

"I hope you are regretting it. You keep your distance from that … "She tensed, shaking her head before looking at me again. "Sean, be careful." I nod, defeated. Once she seems somewhat satisfied, I sprint away and quickly gather my daughter before ushering Rebecca out the door. *I could swear I am forgetting something.*

"Daddy where the boys?"Lillah shrugs at me as if I am an idiot.

I kiss Lillah on the head, "Thanks sweetie." I run back into grab the boys and load them into the back of the SUV before speeding off towards home, relief washing over me instantly.

"Oh Sean, could you stop at that store real quick?" Rebecca asked, pointing to the convenient mart on the corner.

"Why?"

"Because I need to get a few things." Irritated I pull over and motion for her to go. "Thank you," she said happily.

"No problem," I sighed.

I look at my watch, then toward the doors of the store willing Rebecca to hurry the *hell* up. When I hear a rumbling vibration, I take out my phone but quickly realize it isn't mine. *Surely Ava didn't leave hers in the car.* I reach down under the passenger seat and pull out a phone, but it isn't Ava's. I start to put it back when I take notice of the incoming text and recognize the name immediately. A slimy reporter that loves to capitalize on celebrity mishaps and tragedies or anything he can get his hands on to exploit them. I hesitate for a second before pushing the button to read the text.

"I would be very interested in a video of Sean Grant and his wife. The clearer the more money I would be willing to pay. Call me as soon as you can and we can meet up to review the video and discuss."

My body tenses and I start to shake. "Rebecca..." I seethe, while searching her phone for videos. When I come to one labeled Sean and Ava, I shake my head, hesitating to view it. I glance back at Lillah playing quietly in her car seat and push play. As soon as I see Ava naked and riding me, I am ready to choke the hell out of somebody. *I knew I saw somebody last night. That bitch, that fucking bitch! And she was going to fucking sell it!* I clear her entire phone before taking out the memory card and sticking it in Rebecca's diet soda and then driving over her phone several times. I recover the mangled mess and lay it in the passenger seat beside me, breathing deeply as I glance at my daughter's innocent face in the rearview mirror. Rebecca skips out of the store while I hold tight to the steering wheel, denying myself the pleasure of running over her with the car. She opens the door, spotting her mangled phone right away. "You got a text while you were gone. I guess you are going to get a great offer on your video," I fist the steering wheel as she eases into the seat next to me, leaning against her door as much she can. She starts to open her mouth. "We'll talk about it after I get Lillah home." I said through my teeth.

"But..." Rebecca tries to say.

"I said, not now." She turns away from me, sitting in silence the whole way home. I park the car and let the boys out before getting Lillah out of her seat and taking her inside. Rebecca foolishly follows. I ask our housekeeper to watch Lillah for a few minutes and I kiss my daughter, reminding myself that jail will be a bad thing for her to visit me in. I leave her room, forcing my footsteps to remain calm. Grabbing Rebecca harshly by the arm, I drag her to the other end of the house and shut the door. I look at Rebecca as she rubs her arm pitifully. "Talk, Rebecca. Talk before I call the police and have you arrested!" Her eyes focus on me in shock. I cringe. "Rebecca!"

"Okay, yes. I watched you two last night and then I got the idea to record it. I don't know why at first. Curiosity I suppose, and a little drunk too." She said as tears start flowing out of her eyes.

"Why?" I asked, shaking my hands in front of her.

"Why?"

"Why would you do that?" I yell. "Why would you sell it?"

She cowers from me, "I haven't yet."

"Yet?" I yelled.

"I mean, yes, I was thinking about it, it's a lot of money Sean."

"That's why? For the money?"

She sighs, "No, not really."

"Then why?"

"Umm ... I guess I wanted to get even with you," she looks up at me sorrowfully and I roll my eyes.

"Why, Rebecca?"

"You left!"

"You cheated on me. Or don't you remember fucking my best friend in our bed?" I said sarcastically as my voice grows louder.

"I know that, and that's not when I meant. I meant when you left to go to California to do that movie. You left me in New York, all alone."

I narrow my eyes at her, "Are you fucking kidding me? You're mad at me for going to work ... years ago?"

"You rarely called me and I really needed you then."

"Rebecca this is ... I don't know what. Childish and stupid. You seriously need to grow the fuck up."

"Grow up?" She yelled back at me.

I get right back in her face. "Yes. You act like a fucking child all the time with your temper tantrums. I was sick of it then and I am not about to put up with it now."

"Maybe I wouldn't have been so upset all the time if I hadn't been pregnant with your child!" She yells in my face. "If I hadn't had to abort your child by myself!" I step away from her in shock.

"What the fuck are you talking about?" I said, starring into her lying face.

She calms some and digs into her purse, pulling out a folded up piece of paper. "This is what I am talking about," she said, handing it to me.

I read the clinics name and then Rebecca's name, stating who the patient was getting the abortion and the time and date of the abortion. Then off to one side, was marked if known, who is the father, and there it said ... Grant. I look up at her, "This was while I was in California, Rebecca."

"I know, I wanted to tell you before you left but I couldn't. I didn't want to ruin your opportunity by making you stay to help me." She starts crying, as I stand dumbfounded. "I was all alone and felt horrible all the time and so completely lost and I needed you. For you to tell me it was going to be okay." She looks up at me, crying hysterically. "The worst part …" she drops into a chair doubling over. "The worst part is the abortion was botched somehow, so now I will I never get a chance to get pregnant again." She cries even harder and I stare at her horrified.

"Rebecca…" I stumble, searching for words.

"I'm sorry Sean. I saw you two so happy and I hated you in that instance. I hated you for making me go through that on my own and I blamed you for taking something from me that I can never get back."

"You didn't say anything Rebecca, how was I supposed to know?"

"You weren't listening to me anyway, remember?"

"Probably not, but I would have listened to that, I'm sure."

"I wasn't even sure if you were coming back."

I pace the room searching, for what I am not sure.

"I am sorry Sean and if it helps any, I would have never actually gone through with selling it. I never made the copy I was asked to do and I only contacted the one guy and that was last night when I was still drunk. By this morning, I was regretting it all. Can you forgive me?"

I look at her tearful eyes and seemingly sincere, apologetic face feeling guilt like I have never felt before.

Chapter 7

Ava

The house is silent. Peaceful, when I arrive late from work. I shouldn't be surprised, but it is still unsettling. With a deep breath, I cautiously walk through the house practicing my innocent expression. I finally find Sean lying in our bed and looking suspicious himself, relieving me of my guarded composure. "You look as if something is on your mind."

"It's been a long day, is all." he said, forcing a smile.

With a soft sigh, I assume his issues. "I can understand why, considering what I have heard."

"And whom did you hear it from?" He asks, with his piercing eyes flashing.

"First, there was your mother. Then Abbey followed right after, telling me for the second time what happened today with Rebecca." He nods, leaning back further into the pillows that he positioned perfectly behind himself. When his expression turns somber, I crawl into bed and try to reassure him. "So, tell me how I can get your smile back?"

He manages a weak smile. "You already did," he said, welcoming me into his arms. "I love you."

"And I love you." I said.

Cradling me in his arms, he tightens suddenly. "I love you so much, Ava," he whimpered.

"Sean? What's wrong?"

"Nothing. Sorry, I'm overly tired and I was worried about you being out so late is all."

"If it's something your mother said, I can talk to her and ..."

"No baby, it's alright. I think today brought up some bad memories, which are making me that much more grateful for the life I have now."

"Are you sure?" I ask as he traces his fingers along the edges of my face.

Nodding, he smiles sweetly at me. "Promise me you won't ever lie to me?" He asked, holding my eyes with his.

"Sean?" I said trembling.

He immediately shakes his head as tears well up in my eyes. "I'm sorry, forget it." Kissing the side of my head, he twists my body around him as I try to fight my own tears. With all my fears coming to the surface at once, I can't hold them back. I fist his shirt, fighting the tears from falling any further. *What if he finds out? I don't know how I will ever begin to explain why I kept it from him.*

☾✦☽

I have started working from home every other day, so I can spend more time with my daughter. Today is one of those days. My once true love of architecture is slowly fading into the background behind my family. "Okay Lillah, are you ready to go outside and play?" I asked my rosy-cheeked daughter.

She nods anxiously. "Yeah."

"Okay, let's go." I said, picking her up and grabbing her arm floats on our way out the door. The pool is warm and feels incredible. I ease Lillah in as she squeals and giggles. "Watch Mommy, Lillah." I move down under the water, just enough to get my mouth under and blow bubbles. I come back up to her overly excited wiggling, "You ready to try?" She nods. "One … two … three…" I help her gently under the water and then back up again. "Good job, Lillah." I said, clapping along with her.

"If you need to learn how to swim, Ava, you can watch me." I turn to see Rebecca setting up her lounge area by the pool, sporting pieces of fabric that barely cover key parts of her.

"Thank you, but I think I got it down. I am trying to teach my daughter now."

"How sweet." Rebecca said, lying back in the chair without ever glancing my way. Ignoring the Bitch to my side, I continue with Lillah. "Ava!" Rebecca screamed.

I pop up out of the water. "What's wrong?"

"Your … dogs." she shakes her hands at them with a sour face. "They're everywhere! Do they need to be out here?"

I narrow my eyes at her as the boys try to get Rebecca to throw their ball for them. "Are they bothering you?" I asked.

"Yes, they are. They stink and are constantly bringing me that disgusting thing. Can you do something with them? Put them into a cage or something?"

I smile happily at the boys. "No, and if you so much as breathe harshly at my dogs, I will put you into a cage." Rebecca huffs at me while I go back to ignoring her.

Rebecca slams back into her chair, managing to ignore the boys after all. However, the nice silent treatment she is sending my way doesn't last long.

"I like your bikini Ava." Rebecca called out to me.

"Thank you." I respond warily.

"I didn't know they sold bikinis that - *big*. You must have found a great mommy store." Rebecca giggles to herself.

"Well, I prefer not to dress like a whore in front of my daughter."

Rebecca instantly sits up. "Are you saying I look like a whore?"

"No, I said I prefer not to dress like one."

"Sean!" I heard her yell. I look up to see Sean walking towards us after arriving home. Rebecca runs to him and jumps all over him, rather like a distressed dog. "Sean, what do you think of my swimsuit?" she said while modeling her suit in exaggerated poses.

"I guess it's fine, Rebecca." Sean said, pulling her off to one side before approaching the edge of the pool and kneeling down to wait for Lillah and me. "How's my girls?"

"We are doing well with our swimming today." I said.

"Really? Can you show me, Lillah?" He asked. Lillah nods excitedly, almost jumping out of my arms into the water. We show him everything we worked on, earning applause from Sean. Lillah claps sweetly along with him, proud of her own work.

"Are you home for lunch," I asked him.

"Yes, is that okay?"

I lift Lillah to him as he holds out her towel to wrap her in. "Very much so." I said, walking out of the pool and watching Sean's eyes light up. "You like my new tassels?" I asked him with a wink.

"You know that I do." I cradle the back of his head as he leans down with a kiss.

"Are we eating lunch or what?" Rebecca said with a huff.

CR&O

As soon as Sean gets home for dinner, Rebecca begs him to help her with a part in a commercial she managed to get. I am not even certain the part really exists, but she sweetly talks him into helping her anyway. I walk in on them and sit, pretending to read my book as I watch Rebecca consistently find reasons to touch my husband.

"I think you have your lines down, Rebecca." Sean said, pulling away from her again.

"Yes, but I want to run through them completely with you." I glance up at him catching his eyes on me briefly.

"I'm not kissing you Rebecca." Sean warned her.

"You don't have to. Only everything right up to it will be fine." She said happily. He let her take his hand and pull him in near her while Rebecca puts on her lipstick, seductively, in front of him. Her lines are few and stupid, but she overacts them anyway to a pretend camera. Obviously, she is ignorant of the absurdity. Sean pulls her in close to him as she feels her way up his chest, up his neck, to the back of his head. She pulls him down to her, pausing to stare into his eyes. He starts to move away but she grabs his lips with hers and holds on tight. Sean grabs her hands and shifts away from her quickly, both of them looking my way.

"Oh, don't worry Sean. Ava understands it is only part of the job." She says, smiling.

I want to say something, but Sean's silent expression begs me to let it go. Sean's phone rings, its peal cutting through the tense air in the room and providing him an easy exit. I don't even want to look at her. I know if I do, I might do something horrible to her.

"Ava." Rebecca whispers. Shaking my head, I continue to ignore her. "Can you believe I barely touched Sean and he became hard as rock?" My head snaps in her direction. "Not that I didn't enjoy feeling it, but if he calls my name out tonight, don't be offended. It happens a lot with me." My body is up and moving before I even realize it. I am in mid-air when Sean catches me and sets me back on the floor.

"Rebecca, I think we should all call it a night." Sean said, continuing to hold tight to me. The bitch doesn't say another word. She slowly walks out of the house, still wearing that smile I want so badly to rip off.

"You can let go of me now." I said as he releases me slowly.

"Will you please try to not let her get to you like that?"

"Will you tell *her* to shut her mouth?" I yell.

He grabs my waving hands in his face, "She is threatened by you. She will calm down if you ignore her. I'm not telling you to be best friends, but try to be patient with her."

"Sean, she kissed you right in front of me! And did you hear what she said to me?"

"I heard her Ava, but you know it's not true and the kiss was nothing. It had nothing to do with me. She was trying to upset you and it worked. Don't let her get to you and she will stop trying."

"I want them out of our house, Sean. I see nothing but problems from that girl."

"I can't do that Ava. Joel has too much going on right now to worry about trying to find another place to live. And Rebecca..." He sighs at my still-rigid stance. "She hasn't had a whole lot of great influences in her life, Ava. Her mother was a drug addict and her father was in prison most of her life. She's been on her own, practically, since she was sixteen. She's tough, but she's had to be. She craves attention because she never got any when she needed it." Sean rubs his hand over his face. "Please be patient. We are almost a month in already. It will be over before you know it." He sighed, pleading with me. "I am enjoying getting to know my best friend again, and with him, unfortunately, comes his wife. I promise I will talk to her and makes sure she understands that her behavior will not be tolerated." Sean raises my chin so he can smile into my eyes. "If you do this for me, I will take you, Lillah, and the boys to Ireland for a few months. The house renovations should be completed by then, and we can all enjoy it together." I nod. "I love you." he said, waiting for me to look him in the eyes.

"I love you too," I want to win this argument, but I am not sure how I can. Something within him is wanting to protect her and I am not sure why but I am going to trust that he knows what's best.

CZ&O

Rebecca stretches out in a lounge chair, smiling at the sun as if she owns it. Aside from Spencer, I do not think I have ever hated anybody in my whole life. However, she is working her way towards that line...if not past it. I try to ignore her abrasive smile while I sit in the grass playing with Lillah and the boys, but when Sean comes home for lunch Rebecca is up and at his side before I can even turn around.

"So how was your day Sean?" Rebecca, like a terrier at her master's feet, barks for his attention as soon as he approaches. Sean's forced smile fights through his obvious exhaustion. Rebecca clings to his side, following us inside and talking non-stop. Sean is clearly annoyed, and I begin to feel sorry for him.

As I set food down for Sean and Lillah, I force a smile at the bikini princess. "Would you like something Rebecca?" I asked as nicely as I could.

"Oh aren't you sweet. I am fine with my vitamin drink, but thank you for asking." Rebecca says with an obnoxiously sweet tone, and pats me on the hand.

I sit down next to Lillah, helping to make sure she eats, not at all paying attention to the conversation Rebecca is forcing on Sean. "Is your tea good?" I turn towards Sean as he tugs at my shirt.

"Yes, I finally remembered what I was forgetting."

He smiles at me nodding, "Good."

"What kind of tea is it?" Rebecca asked.

"Something my doctor told me about when I was pregnant with Lillah."

"It's good for you then?" She asked and I nod.

"Can I try it?" Rebecca asked. I push the pitcher over to her, and she pours herself half a glass. "Oh yuck! What is in this?" Rebecca soured.

Sean laughs, "No one seems to like it but Ava. I think she has forced herself to get use to it." He leans over to me and kisses my cheek gently, "But whatever she wants, I am willing to get it for her."

"Are you willing to watch your daughter for the rest of the day so I can go to work? Kyle got a call for some last minute changes and he needs all the help he can get." I ask him, assuming he will not be able to.

Cocking his head to one side, he allows a slow smile to emerge. "I have a short day today. I can take her with me for a few hours, but I want to see you tonight after I put her to bed. So, don't be coming home too late."

"Okay, deal." I kiss him happily.

"If you want, Sean, I can come with you and watch Lillah while you are on set." Rebecca exclaims, forcing a humorous smile at Lillah.

"That is nice of you, Rebecca, but I think Ethan and Randy can handle it. They enjoy the distractions anyway." Sean says, grasping her hand in appreciation. Thankfully, his decision makes it easier for me to leave my daughter behind.

CRBO

It has been a long day and an even more stressful one. I'm not sure how much longer I can hold onto my secrets. I want to tell Sean. I want to tell him before things get out of hand, but I fear they already have. The amount of time I am spending with Jasper these days would surely not go over well with my husband. The more time that passes without telling him makes the lie that much worse and harder to tell.

A nice, long, hot shower should help rejuvenate me. When I walk into our bedroom, it is lit up with candles while a shirtless Sean greets me with a smile and a tray full of food.

"I assumed you didn't eat dinner while you were out." Sean said.

"No, I didn't. Thank you for saving some for me."

"You're welcome." He sits next to me and plays with my hair as I eat and I slide in close to him. "Do you like it?"

I nod.

Catching sight of the lit up bathroom and the running water, I smile. "Are you getting a bath?"

"Not exactly." he says kissing the side of my head.

"Just running water for no reason?" I ask smartly.

"No…but if you're finished eating, I can show you?" He said, prompting me to push my tray of food to the side. "Come with me." Taking my hand he leads me into a whole room full of candles and my favorite - movie star rose petals. The bathtub is full of water, and floating petals. "Do you like it?"

I nod with a smile.

"Good. You know, they say it is important to relax when you want to get pregnant." Sean says, pulling me to him and running his fingers through my hair. He waits until I look up at him to kiss me deeply and begins removing my clothes for me. With soft hands, he pushes the fabric from my skin before fondling my bare breasts with the palms of his hands. With a low growl, he whispers his admiration for my body, but all I can hear is the sound of the zipper on his pants and the quiet *whoosh* of them falling to the floor. Immediately, I feel his erection pressed against me, already searching for what it wants. "Not yet baby." He smiles trying to calm me down. Picking me up he moves us both into our bath for two. Sean shocks me when he sits down casually with me straddling him. He puts his arms out to either side, and exhales softly - as if he is waiting for me to make the next move.

"What are you doing?" I asked.

He laughs. "Relax." I narrow my eyes at him and move off him trying to do as told. He kisses the side of my head, "Relax, sweetheart."

"I don't think I can." I pout. *I am way to tense and I want to have sex...now.*

He wraps one arm around me, burying his face into my hair. "Do you want me to help you? Relax, I mean," he whispered.

"How?" I mumble with growing excitement.

I can feel his smile against my cheek. "Trust me baby...I know how." He holds my head in place as he noses through my hair and begins to play with my nipples. Thumbing them and massaging my breasts, he causes a soft moan to escape from my mouth.

"Does that feel good?" Sean whispered into my ear.

"Yes." I said, as his hand slips down my stomach and between my legs. I gasp as he spreads my legs, massaging each of them as he moves them to either side. Swallowing noticeably, I feel his hand reach my center, his fingers finding their way to my spot. My eyes naturally close as he skillfully plays. My head falls back and I begin to shake, gripping his arm tightly.

"How do you feel now?" He asked, looking smug.

"Good." I breathed.

I watch him look down at his hand and his expression changes to pure pleasure as he feels inside of me. I move against his hand, gripping his arm tighter with every wave flowing through me. My moans become uncontrolled.

"Are you going to come?" He asked.

"Yes." I breathe.

He stops instantly, lifting me out of the tub to sit me on the heated edge. Moving between my legs, he changes from his fingers to his tongue and works me into a frenzy. I can feel the vibration of his groans, with my every moan of his name.

"Sean!" I yell. *I can't breathe.* I release in overwhelming pleasure and he pulls me back into his warm arms and the soothing water with a confident smile.

"Are you relaxed now?" He asked, cradling me to him. I close my eyes and nod, falling deep into his arms. He relaxes and I can't get over his gorgeous green eyes on me, so warm and loving. He gently brushes his thumb over my bottom lip and I kiss it, enjoying his smile. "You are so beautiful, Ava."

I hold his hand against my face and breathe in before catching a glimpse of him sticking proudly out of the water. I smile up at him to see if he is going to let me. He is amused, but shows no sign of preventing me from getting what I want. I pull his hand behind me and ease myself onto him, watching his eyes surrender completely to me as I rock myself down on him then feel him deep inside. His lips find mine as he takes hold of my hips. I search for his tongue, stroking it with the same movement I make on his erection. He feels so good that I move faster and kiss him harder. Sean suddenly picks me up and carries me to lie down on our cozy fireplace rug. A place we know well. Sean hovers over me, pulling my legs up. He moves deep, shallower, and deep again, faster and faster ... pushing hard inside me, causing me to cry out and exhale our orgasms together.

"Do *you*, feel relaxed now?" I asked him as he collapses around me.

He laughs, "Are you making fun of me?"

"Never, baby."

"Well then yes, I am."

I follow Sean to bed, holding his hand the whole way until I am safe and warm in his arms.

CRð€

Another last minute change on the project and everyone goes crazy. It is supposed to be my day off, but after scrambling to find a babysitter, I manage to make it into work to ease tension before chaos erupts. The only problem is - I was not able to get away from Rebecca. She insisted on coming with me because she doesn't want to sit at the house alone. Since she has no car, she is dependent on anyone who does. If she had not threatened to burn down my guesthouse after I left, I would have not thought twice about leaving her behind. I walk into the office and everyone seems to have calmed down since I agreed to come in and help.

"You made it! Thank goodness. I was afraid you were going to change your mind." Kyle says, giving me a hug as I come in.

"Hi." Rebecca says, coming in behind me. She seems anxious to meet my co-workers for the first time.

My shoulders drop and I give them each a wary smile. "Oh yes, Kyle ... Michael ... Anna - this is Rebecca."

"Nice to meet you, Rebecca." Michael says genuinely as he sticks out his hand.

"Please tell me you're not gay. I could really enjoy getting to know you." she said. Kyle interjects for *his* man by holding out his hand and firmly shaking Rebecca's.

"I like your outfit, Rebecca," Anna said.

Rebecca beams, "Thank you, it's very expensive."

"Oh, well, I would love to get something like it. Where did you get it?" Anna smiled at her with honesty.

Rebecca laughs joyfully at her. "Oh honey, I don't think your body is made for clothes like these. Not that you are fat dear, it's just that not many people can have a body like mine." Rebecca glances at each of my friends. "Besides you all have such cute little outfits. You must have dug in bins for those all day."

Rebecca pats my friends like dogs and proceeds to tour the office on her own.

Oh, please dear God … don't let me kill her today.

Kyle immediately gives me a hard look and shakes his head. "Thanks for introducing us to your friend Ava, she's a real joy." he said sarcastically. "Looks like we are going to have to break out the bitch slapper today." he mumbles back to his office.

"It's going to be a long day." I exhale deeply.

Chapter 8

Rebecca

Ava's office is small, but nice. Not that I would ever tell her that, but I assume Sean helped pay for most of the things in it. I ask her about each item trying to make that point, but she swears that she and Kyle paid for everything.

Sitting at Ava's desk, she allows me to play on the internet while she works with the others. I take the opportunity to snoop and see if I can't find something that she may not want me too. It feels like I've spent hours searching, when Ava's office phone rings. Typically, I wouldn't dare think to answer it and play Ava's receptionist, but the name on the ID makes me too curious. "Ava Kelley's office ..." I say with a sincere tone.

"Yes, Anna - this is Jasper. Tell Ava I will be back in town tonight if she needs to call me. I will try and come in some time tomorrow and meet with her on the details I discussed with the client."

"I will do that Jasper, and where can she reach you tonight?" He sighs in annoyance but tells me his number anyway. Hanging up with him, I simply smile.

०ঙ৪০

Joel wonders what I am up to, but doesn't care enough to ask when he drops me off in midtown. Dressed perfectly for my plans for the night, I make one call and beg for assistance...assistance for Ava. Jasper arrives quickly and I meet him at the door.

"Where is Ava?"

"I'm sorry, Jasper. I confess I tricked you into meeting me. When I found out you were in town, I begged Ava to give me your number. I am such a big fan and ..." I hide my bushing smile. "Well, I am in such awe of you." His ego is instantly stroked and my plan begins easily. He buys me dinner and drinks, then eagerly rushes me to his home. I am shocked to find out he owns a condo in Atlanta and has for months. I could easily seduce him. He is already obviously expecting sex at this point, but I want more than just sex. Slipping an effective drug into Jasper's drink, I not only have him hard and horny, but crazed. He grabs me forcefully, throwing me to the ground and ripping at my clothes. I encourage it silently so my cell records only what I want it too.

I encourage Jasper to spank my ass, push me down, pull my hair and say all the dirty things he has always wanted to say to a woman. He fucks me hard, "You like this? I bet you do, you little whore. I like fucking you. I knew as soon as I saw that short dress of yours that I was going to have it on my floor." He says jerking my head back by my hair. I glance at my cell with ... a tear.

Now all I have to do is edit my video properly before I show it to Ava. Lucky for me, she is home waiting up for Sean when I get back. Ava immediately sighs when she sees me coming. "Oh don't be that way. I have a surprise for you. I will let you have it, if you do me a favor?" She rolls her eyes and pretends I am not here. "I want to spend some alone time with Sean." I said, to which she begins shaking her head vehemently. "Doesn't have to be much, maybe you could suggest a threesome? Or hell, I am willing to share Joel. Maybe we could ..."

Ava instantly turns around, breathing fire, "No! I don't know why you think it is okay to even suggest such things. Don't you have any respect for your own husband?" She seethes.

"Alright, you can't blame a girl for trying. It might have been fun - you don't know. But, if not in his bed in real life, then how about on set? Convince Sean that I should have your role. Should be easy for you to do. It's not as if you wanted it in the first place."

"Rebecca, go away. I am in no mood to deal with you today." She said, shaking her head before starting to walk away.

I grab her arm forcefully, "Oh, I think you're going to do exactly what I want for as long as I want." I pull out my phone and show her my video. "He raped me, and I am going to press charges. He even stupidly recorded it. Luckily, I was able to escape with a copy to prove his guilt. I bet this would be *very* bad for anyone associated with him, or ... for any company he owns or recently bought a major share of. Wouldn't it ... Ava?" Recoiling from me with wide eyes, she begins to tremble, "How much money does he have invested in your little firm exactly? I was kind of shocked when he told me last night. That's a lot of money Ava and to know that all you wanted to do was retire and be a full time Mommy. Jasper really wants you back, and apparently will do anything to work with you again. Maybe you're not such a boring lay after all."

"Jasper tricked us. We thought we were making a deal with another architect, not him. If I had known it was him, I would have never signed that deal. I only wanted to surprise Sean. We want to have another baby and I want to stay home with them. To be home when he is home. I can't do that owning so much of the firm. I needed to let it go so they could find someone to help carry the firm after I leave. They wouldn't sign the deal unless I stayed on through this last project. I didn't see anything wrong with that. Sean gets so jealous and I didn't want him to worry. I thought I could finish the project and retire without him ever finding out. Jasper won't stay here once I am gone anyway."

"That is a sad story Ava, too bad for you I don't care … about you anyway. Either give me what I want or I will take my video and go crying to the police and ruin everything for everyone you know… including Sean."

"I will recommend you for the part. You're right, I don't care about it. But, after this is all over, I want a video confession that you made it all up. And, I want you to leave here and never come back."

I think happily about her agreement for a few seconds, "You have a deal, Ava. But you better make sure I get that part. Oh, and part of this deal is that you never tell Sean about any of this. I don't need him getting all upset over his wife breaking his heart and ruining my big break." I hug her stiff posture happily. "You know, this really is going to be a great movie, especially with me in it."

My night is satisfying and more than a little successful. Now all I have to do is wait for Ava to hold up her end of the bargain.

⋘⋙

I wait anxiously for Ava to do as she promised and I know she held up her end when Joel walks in with a scowl. "Bad day, baby?"

"What did you do?" He says, stomping his way towards me.

"I don't know what you are talking about."

"You know damn well what I am talking about! Ava has decided against doing the movie and highly recommended you take her place. She begged Sean to give you a chance since you two have become such great friends as of late." Joel stresses with clenched fists.

"Oh, I never would have thought she would go to so much trouble for me. She really is a sweetheart. I accept of course, but we should do something nice for her. A gift basket of some sort, I think." I smile happily as I prance away from my glaring husband.

"You know I needed her on this movie."

"I know you said that, but I have no idea why."

"Rebecca! I swear…" He cringes, fisting his hands above his head. "Do me a favor and hold off on your scheming and evil ways, now that you have what you want. Give me a little time…"

"Oh darling, you are so cute when you're angry. For you I will try to be good, but I can't make any promises. If you're nice to me, I might be able to talk Ava into having sex with you. I know you would like that." He glances my way.

"Shut up, Rebecca." He says more calmly, walking upstairs to go enjoy the image I put in his head.

It is a perfectly beautiful day, so I decide to take advantage and go layout by the pool. With a renewed excitement, I strut around the corner to the pool only to have Ethan jerk me out of my daydream.

"What the …? Let go of me!" I yell at him.

"I know you must have done something horrible." he accused. What are you holding over Ava? Whatever it is, I want you to let it go, now. I want you out of this house and on your way back to New York."

I shake my head, huffing as I cross my arms. "Oh Ethan, don't be ridiculous, you are still such a drama queen."

He stomps back on the balls of his feet. "Don't screw with me Rebecca. I know you, and I of all people know what you're capable of." I glance down to study my nails, exaggerating my boredom. "If I were you Rebecca, I would get the hell out of this house and leave my brother and his family alone or…"

"Or what?" I stand up to him, sending him back on his heels in shock. "What are you going to do Ethan?"

"I'm going to tell Sean everything," he said assuredly.

"I don't think you are. Even if you had proof, which you don't, I don't think you want your precious wife to find out about our little arrangement."

"That was before, Abbey."

"Was it? As I remember it you were already dating each other." I said confidently.

"I have no doubt in my mind that Abbey would believe me over you." He said as his eyes continue to keep check on our surroundings.

I smile. "I still have the pictures Ethan. All of them time stamped. You look so good, too …" I take hold of his face reaching in to kiss him but he turns away from me in a huff.

"That's history, and Abbey will forgive me."

"Maybe, but Sean won't." I lean into him, putting my arms around his neck. "Now would he?" I pout.

"Get off of me." he says, jerking away from me.

"Oh Ethan, you have so many little secrets and unfortunately for you, I know all of them." I said as he shakes his head at me in disgust.

"I'm warning you Rebecca, tread lightly or I will come after you. I don't care who hates me in the end. I won't let you destroy my brother's life again."

"What are you talking about? Sean was happy with me. He would have stayed that way if not for you and … *her.*"

"Only in your delusional world. He left early for California to do that movie and stayed long after it was over just to avoid coming home to your pathetic ass. He begged me to get his stuff for him so he wouldn't have to look at you." I smack him and he smiles widely in my face. "Watch it Rebecca, you might accidentally show some real human emotion."

"Fuck You Ethan." I snarl at him. "You better go to your wife while you still have her. Otherwise, we might have to test that theory of yours. Will she care or won't she? Do you really want to risk losing her and those two cute little boys of yours?" I smile as I step around him. "Goodbye Ethan." I wave as I continue on with my day.

Chapter 9

Sean

Screaming. SEAN! NO PLEASE! NO!

I awake abruptly to Ava screaming. "Ava!" I yell and instantly she crumbles into my arms. "What's wrong?" I ask her, but she won't stop crying. "Ava, talk to me. What's wrong?" Her tear filled face pains me as she holds my face. "What Ava?" She buries her head into my chest. "Baby, talk to me please. You're scaring the hell out of me."

"You were gone. I lost you." she said. "It felt so real, you left me … alone."

Taking her into my arms, "It was just a dream Ava, I'm right here." She holds me desperately and in total fear. I haven't seen her like this since she was worried about … *Spencer.*

CʒՑ

I am flying to New York to film some Cancer Society promos. I had not planned to take Ava and Lillah with me, but after last night, I have decided to give Ava an early birthday present. Plans are quickly changed and Randy arrives packed and ready to escort us all with his usual watchful eye.

"Are you *all* leaving?" Joel asks as I help Randy pack the car.

"Yes. I changed my mind at the last minute. Ava seems on edge lately, and I am worried about leaving her alone."

"Why is that? Did somebody threaten her?" Joel asks.

"No. She had a nightmare last night, and I haven't seen her respond like that since she was worried about Spencer. She has been working so much lately, maybe if I give her a nice vacation she will feel better."

"From what you told me about what happened to her that is probably a good idea. I can't imagine it would be something she can easily get over. I hope she is going to be okay. Let me know if you need me to do anything." Joel says with sincerity, making me feel good about our renewed friendship. "Well don't be gone too long. Otherwise, I will have to dust off my actor persona and take over your part. Hello, I am Sean Grant." He mocks me with a bright smile.

"I would say something smartass, but that was actually pretty good." I say glancing at Randy who nods in agreement.

"Yeah, well now you know not to test me." Joel laughs, waving goodbye as he leaves in his own car.

♋

Lillah clings to me as I carry her into the studio, while Ava leans in at my side holding my hand. This was a better decision than I thought. I love having them here with me. When we walk into the studio, the first thing I see is Dillon already acting the fool. I walk up on him talking to Shane about me, causing me to be more curious about his obnoxious behavior.

"Oh stop being so uptight Shane. Besides, Sean loves me." Dillon exclaimed proudly.

I roll my eyes. *The kid needs help.* "Who said that, Conrad?" I said, causing the both of them to jump. If Lillah had not have been in my arms, I might have said something more appropriate to him.

He approaches me with his insufferable smile and his hand out to me. "I'm pretty sure you did." he said confidently.

"Well, I think that depends on the day when it comes to you." I glance at the pretty girl standing next to Dillon, wondering if maybe my wish has come true. Perhaps I will be able to seek revenge on him for hitting on my wife. I shake Shane's hand as he approaches, but Dillon's approach towards Ava interrupts me.

"Ava, you look beautiful as always." He says, taking her hand and kissing it. *Really? Is he going to start this shit again?*

I pull Ava's hand away from him before he drools all over it. "Watch it Conrad, I warned you about my wife."

Dillon laughs as he turns to introduce the young, blond, Taylor. *Damn, I hope he is head over heels for this girl so I can fuck with him.* She is sweet, and touches Dillon more times than I can count in the few minutes it takes to introduce her. From the way he smiles at her, I know he is doing his best to impress her. Before I get too excited about seeking revenge on the young Mr. Conrad, he moves towards Lillah.

"And I don't know this beautiful girl." Dillon said, taking Lillah's little hand and kissing it, causing her to giggle into my shoulder.

"This is Lillah. Lillah say hello." I said to her as she smiles at Dillon. *Oh no, don't fall for it Lillah.*

"Hi." Lillah blushed. I am relieved when she covers her mouth as she says it and buries her face into my shoulder. At least she still needs her Daddy to protect her from scary men who are up to no good.

"She is adorable." Dillon said.

"Thank you, but she is a bit shy until she gets to know you. Then she won't leave you alone." I said, trying to get Lillah to stop hiding. "Alright, Daddy needs to get to work. Can you stay with Mommy for a little while?" She shakes her head at me. "Lillah, you can too." She pushes her bottom lip out as far as it will go and holds onto me tightly. She is preparing to stand her ground with me - I recognize it immediately. She gets that same look Ava does, and as cute as it is, it can at times be inconvenient. "One second. She is like her mother and has a bad stubborn streak. She doesn't handle not getting her way very well." I said, glancing at Ava who is not amused.

"Only because she isn't used to you telling her 'no'." Ava leans across me reaching for Lillah. "Come here, Lillah." Lillah surrenders to her mother with only a slight whimper. Ava's smug expression is expected.

"So maybe you're right, sweetheart," I said to her.

"Maybe?" Ava pushed.

Fine, stubborn. "Always, I meant always."

"Sure you did," she said. I laugh, kissing her and Lillah on the head before walking away with Shane and Dillon.

After we finish shooting the promo, I sit talking to the director when Dillon comes hopping over, eating an apple and nodding happily at me. "What do you want?" I ask to the annoyance.

"I only wanted to see how you're doing," he smiles.

"How *I'm* doing?" I pause, watching him try to seem interested. "I'm fine, thank you. How are you doing Dillon? In fact, how is your girlfriend doing? What is her name, Taylor?" He nods. "She's pretty. How long have you been together?"

"She's not my girlfriend, were just friends." He tried to proclaim, innocently.

"Uh huh," *I do not believe a word he says.*

"No - really."

"Whatever." I said sarcastically. "How long have you known her?"

He shrugs. "Four or five months, I guess." Either he is blind or he is lying to me.

"So, five months and you bring her here to impress her, but you don't like her?" I pressed.

"I like her, but not in that way." He said. *He is an idiot.*

I shake my head at him, ready to burst into hysterics. "If you didn't hit on my wife, Conrad, I would think you're gay because that girl is hot. Most guys would have already ..."

He instantly sits up straight. "Yeah maybe with most girls but Taylor is... she's not..." He looks me up and down, sticking out his chest and staying focused on my eyes. "Forget it. You wouldn't understand." He said as his face turns red and his muscles tense.

"Try me." He shakes his head, pulling another snack from his pocket. *I have no idea where he got that.* "Now I am curious Conrad, so tell me."

"Taylor is great, and I could see her being a wife-type person... you know." I shake my head, not understanding at all. "Well, I guess you could say that I like her too much to get involved with her and ruin what we have. The last time I got involved with my best-friend... it didn't end very well."

"What did you do?" I ask, laughing as I imagine what stupid thing he did to mess that relationship up.

"Nothing!" He jumps suddenly. "She simply disappeared and I never saw her again." Dillon says, looking too distant and dejected for me to want to push him.

"Well, I would say it never hurts to try someone new. Sometimes the perfect person for you helps you forget the one you thought was for you. She likes you, I can tell. A little innocent for you, but otherwise I approve, Conrad." Dillon rolls his eyes. "But, if you're going to act, you'd better act quickly. A girl like that may get tired of waiting and move on."

"Nah, I am too hot for her to ever look anywhere else." Now I have to roll my eyes. "No seriously, Sean. I don't know what exactly it is about me but women just can't get enough. I think it's the combination of my handsome face, great body and incredibly huge..."

"Alright... I have had enough of this conversation." I get up and walk away.

"What? Sean! I was only going to say personality! But hey, if you want to go there..." I turn around and see him smile, doing a dance only a moron would do.

I walk away shaking my head, "Dumbass."

Dillon catches up to me as I look in on the girls.

I motion towards Taylor. "If I wasn't married, I would find some time for her. I like the sweet, innocent ones." I smile at the poor fool, who is now turning several shades of pissed off. I enter and walk straight over to Taylor. "So Taylor, Ava says you're a fan of mine?"

Taylor stands, already with a wide smile, "Oh … yes! I mean, I …"

"Do you want to get a picture together before I go?" I ask and Taylor instantly rushes to her bag. I glance back at Dillon, who is annoyed, to say the least. Taylor forces her camera into Dillon's hands with bouncy excitement.

Running back to me, the once-shy girl suddenly becomes aggressive. She jumps against me, wrapping her arms around my neck with one hand and rubbing across my chest with the other. Her heart beats rapidly against me, and Dillon is ready to come out of his skin to kill me. "Dillon, do you mind?" I motioned for him to hurry up and take the picture before his girlfriend molests me any further.

"I'm getting to it, hold on." He said as he walks over to Taylor. "Don't you think that's a little inappropriate?" He said, glancing daggers my way.

"No, just take the picture." Taylor impatiently asked him again.

"Fine!" He said angrily. "There!"

"You might want to take another Dillon, to make sure you got it." I said innocently, but my smile begins to give away my true intentions.

"Yes Dillon, take another one to make sure." Taylor insisted.

As Dillon readies himself to take another picture, I kiss her on the cheek…and immediately regret it.

She goes weak and I have to hold her up. "Taylor, are you okay?" Dillon said, rushing to her. She nods with a starry-eyed expression, causing Dillon to roll his eyes.

"Ummm…." Taylor waves her hands at Dillon.

"*Dillon.* My name is Dillon."

"Oh yes, Dillon. I think I'm going to go to the restroom and splash some water on my face." Taylor said. "Thank you Mr. Grant, and so nice to meet you all …oh wow … this has been the best day!"

"What the hell was that about?" Dillon asks me.

I try to play surprised. "I don't know what you're talking about?"

"You know, with the touching and all that shit. Did you really need to get that close to her?"

"No, but it sure was fun watching you get jealous as hell."

"I'm not jealous." He said.

I laugh and turn towards Ava who is biting her lip to keep from laughing at him too. "Did you hear that sweetheart?"

"I did." Ava said.

"You are so screwed man, and you don't know how happy it makes me to know that." I say with a wide smile.

He looks so confused. "If you're referring to Taylor, I'm not jealous. I'm only looking out for her is all." I shake my head, laughing. "Whatever. I know what I am." He snaps

"Okay Conrad." I pat him on the back before I escort Ava and Lillah out the door. As soon as they are out of hearing range, I lean back inside. "Don't worry Conrad you'll be fine ... as long as you don't have sex with her." His eyes widen. "You're so screwed!" I laugh hard, knowing he can hear me as I walk away.

C3&0

We have a great room, a great view, and Lillah is sound asleep after a long day. I have decided to celebrate Ava's birthday tonight, so I wait patiently for her with candles and my best smile. When Ava finishes checking on Lillah, she walks in the room with the reaction I was hoping for.

"I hope Lillah doesn't wake up and see this." She said.

"Me too, so hurry up and get over here."

"Wait, I didn't think you would be in the mood after such a long day, but since you are I have something special for you." She smiles, stepping backwards towards the bathroom. My mood greatly improves, anticipating what she has in mind.

"So, what do you think?" She asks, entering the room wearing a single red ribbon that wraps her body in the most seductive of ways. "I like your red heels." I said, looking over her body as she bites her bottom lip and waits for me to release the bow across her breasts. Instead, I stand up and make her stand in front of me so I can walk around her and admire every available inch of her. I fumble with the edges of the ribbon with my fingers, tracing lightly underneath the plush edges, teasing her until one of us breaks. "It's not my birthday ... nor Christmas ... not Valentine's Day ... what is this gift for?" I breathed against her cheek.

"I know, but it is my birthday," she said. I press my lips to her exposed skin, enjoying her soft exhale.

"Please, Sean," she begs, as I toy with the edges of the ribbon across her breasts.

"Please what? What do you want Ava?" She moans as I move my fingers up under the ribbon to her ass and back down between her thighs.

"Stop teasing me Sean, or I'm going to go to bed and leave you standing here, hard and alone."

"You wouldn't dare." I whispered to her.

"Try me," she said jutting her chin out and crossing her arms.

"But baby, I don't want your outfit to be simply torn off and thrown to the side, forgotten and abused. I think we should show it some respect." I move behind her, running my mouth up her neck and forcing my thumbs up under the ribbon to her breasts. Her head falls back against my chest and she grabs my thigh to pull me closer to her body. We both moan as I move into her further. I am not sure the ribbon is going to hold up much longer. I am too hard and my erection is starting to break through the edges of the ribbon and forcing its way against her ass.

"Oh Sean, I want you so bad." She says, enjoyably caressing my thigh and ass.

"We're not going to make it to the bed." I said, gripping the ribbons around her thighs and jerking them up above her ass to give me ample access. Ava leans against the wall, giving me a full view of what I want and I take it. Tasting her skin along her shoulders, I pull her hips to me and instantly slide into her, feeling her wet desire surround me completely. With every slide out, I groan. With every push in, I feel the pulsating edges of her soft wetness, sending me into passionate desire. Running one hand through her hair and cradling her head to mine, I kiss her lips and earn her tongue. Holding her hips in place, I enjoy the sight of my dick sliding against her ass as it pushes between her thighs and reaches for that sensitive spot that makes her quiver and whimper for more. *And oh, does she whimper.* Watching her closely, I take hold of the end of the ribbon across her breasts and release them into my hands. She reaches up above her head and allows me to play with all of her. My hands wander to her wettest of places and encourage her orgasm to a maximum eruption. "Happy birthday, baby. I love you." I said, bringing me to the tip. I hold her closer and push deep into her, coming more inside her with every thrust. I collapse, breathless, against her. Ava spins around and winks at me happily. With a smile on my face, I lean against the wall and hover around her. "Happy Birthday." I mouth to her. She wiggles her happy dance into my arms, making me laugh. "You are such a dork."

"But you love me anyway?" She asked.

I look into her sparkling blue eyes. "Forever and always, my love." I said, carrying her to bed and crawling in after her. "So, what do you want to do for your birthday?"

"You mean besides having constant sex with you?" She smiles ridiculously.

"Dork." I whisper as she scrunches her face at me in disapproval. "Yes baby, besides my fucking you to complete exhaustion." I laugh at her.

Her expression turns almost serious, as she contemplates. "I don't know."

"I have an idea." I said calmly.

"You do?" I nod. "What?" I stare at her, trying to conceal my smile as I make her wait. She smacks me playfully. "What is it? Tell me." I laugh, reach under the pillow next to us and hand her an envelope I pull from beneath it. She looks at me surprised. "I really thought you forgot."

"Why would you ever think that? You know how much I love buying you things." She holds the envelope up, admiring it. "Open it, Ava!

She peeks inside before pulling out the tickets. "Sean!" She yells, turning to me in shock. "Really?" I nod. "The playoffs?" She whispered.

"Yes, the playoffs. Courtside."

She vibrates with excitement. "You are the only girl I have ever met who gets that excited about basketball."

"Thank you so much," she said, hugging me tight.

"You're welcome." Ava holds the tickets up, continuing to stare at them. "Give me those. Enough of these, they are for another day." Taking the tickets from her, I put them aside and enjoy her lying on my chest. She is completely content with her tickets. *She's so easy to please.* I reach under my pillow, pull out a small box, and lay it in front of her.

"What's this?" She asks.

"Open it and find out."

"Sean, you know I don't like you spending a lot of money on me. The tickets alone have to be…" I press my finger to her lips.

"This is not much, only something simple to remember who loves you." She huffs at me. "Open it, Ava." She sits up, examining the box carefully, turning it and shaking it. "Open it already."

"Okay." She pulls the decorated top off and removes the delicate charm bracelet as I relish watching her perfect smile take over her face. "Sean, it is so beautiful."

I wrap myself around her as she takes delight in all the sparkling charms. Her smile is already enough, but I still want to show her more. Taking hold of a charm, "You see this one, this one represents the little island we met and married on … and this one is Lillah … the boys … our little house in Ireland … and the one in Atlanta."

She grasps my hand. "And what about this one?" she asked, holding up the remaining charm.

I stare at the radiant emerald heart, and squeeze her tight. "My heart." I whisper to her. Whispering her love for me, she curls up under my arm. I watch her play with the bracelet that is now dangling from her wrist until she finally falls asleep.

CSEO

Rebecca walks on set as if she is the star of the movie. It doesn't really bother me, but she is irritating everyone else. Tami approaches me with a sour expression. "Sean, you know I am not one to complain, but…" I sigh, expecting what is coming. "That girl has to go. She is horrible, and so full of herself I can't take being around her and we haven't even started working together yet. I can't imagine working late nights with her. I know I should go to Kane with this, but since this girl is clearly screwing him …"

I perk up instantly, "What? She's what?"

"Oh, come on Sean. She is going into his trailer constantly and he keeps adding lines to the script for her. He even said that when she is around other women in a scene, to make them look less appealing so she stands out more. She is unbelievable!"

She sighs, obviously feeling bad about ranting to me. The set has been a joy to be on until recently, when Rebecca took Ava's part and became the queen of the set. I assure Tami I will take care of it and she hugs me with relief. I am not sure how best to handle this, but I know how to get what I want done quickly. I contact Joel's father and tell him blatantly that Rebecca has to go. I even agree to talk Ava back into to doing the part. With that, he makes a call and makes it happen. Instead of leaving it up to Kane to handle her, or force Joel to be the bad guy to his own wife, I decide it best to talk to her myself…only I find her arguing with Ethan.

"I swear Ethan, I will get even with you!"

"I don't know what you are talking about you crazy bitch!" Ethan yells back at her.

Rebecca gets back in his face. "Crazy? You haven't seen anything yet. Now you get me back into this movie or I will make sure you regret it." Ethan pushes her back off his chest and I recognize his breaking point.

Rushing to her, I pull Rebecca back and look down at her until she calms. "I got this Ethan, you can go." He hesitates, still huffing before finally walking away mumbling under his breath. "Ethan had nothing to do with you getting fired. I did." Her shoulders sink and she suddenly looks as if she has lost everything. I feel horrible for having to do it to her, but maybe I can help her in some other way. "Honey, listen. You have got to learn to be more respectful of others. You are not at the point you can demand appreciation. This part isn't that great anyway."

She backs away from me and begins to cry. "I can't believe you would do this to me. I thought you cared about me, that you were sorry for how you treated me before. And now you throw me away …*again*!"

"Rebecca, this is not that big of a deal. If you will humble yourself a bit, then I promise I will help you get another start. A better one." Rebecca's expression changes briefly to something I have never seen from her before. A sinister glare forms and I wait for her to snap, but instead she steps back and breathes easily with a soft smile.

"You had to do what you had to do, Sean. I don't blame you, and I know you will do everything you can to help me." She reaches in and kisses my cheek. "I love you. Know that I don't blame you for this. I am disappointed, but I am sure I will have a better day ahead of me." She smiles sweetly, shocking me. I expected her to be out of control and inconsolable, but instead she is acting mature and accepting. I couldn't be more proud of her.

"I am sorry about this." I say, leaning down to hug her. "I will buy you dinner sometime and we can talk about your future …okay?" I wink at her, enjoying her beautiful smile.

"Well, I better clear my things and find a way back to your house."

"I am not sure if you want to but you can wait around for me to take you. It looks like I am going to get done early tonight. I was planning on surprising Ava but ..." I said.

She perks up, seeming to consider it, but begins shaking her head instead. "No, thank you, I think I really want to get back now. Don't worry about me I have other plans tonight so you can continue with your surprise. I will be sure not to tell Ava."

C3&0

Arriving home early for once, I am excited about being able to surprise Ava. Smiling wide, I walk towards the house from the garage and notice a strange car parked in the drive. Before I have a chance to check it out, I see Jasper walking towards me. My heart speeds and I stop dead in my tracks. My silence seems to shake the ground until it reaches Jaspers spine. He looks up and instantly steps back.

"Good evening." He says with a nod. His clothes look thrown on, and not at all like the man who never has a hair out of place.

"What the fuck are you doing at my house?" I demand. He holds out his hands trying to slow my anger when Ava rushes out of the house and Rebecca comes running out of the guesthouse.

"Oh my ... Jasper, what are you doing here?" Rebecca asked, holding her hand over her heart. She looks slowly at Ava. "Oh no, no ... you did not do this to him."

"What are you talking about?" Ava yells.

Ava looks over at Rebecca with her mouth open.

"Sean, this can all be easily explained." Jasper begins with a superior attitude.

"Get the fuck off my property!" He starts to speak again, "Get away from me before I do something to you that you won't be able to recover from." My every word breathes like fire as he carefully walks around me and speeds away.

Turing to Ava, I focus on her every movement. "What is *he* doing here?" I asked her.

"I didn't even know he was here, Sean." She pleads.

Rebecca huffs. "Ava, how else would he get in here? I mean I know you are working with him again ..." I snap my head towards Rebecca, wide-eyed. "Oh Sean, I'm sorry I didn't tell you. She promised me her part in the movie if I would keep quiet about it. She said it was innocent, but if I had known ..." Rebecca rests her head against my arm. "Oh honey, if I had known she was screwing him I would have told you - I am so sorry."

I force my eyes back towards Ava. "You are working with him?" Her eyes float down to the ground before looking back up at me with tears in her eyes. "Why ... why didn't you tell me that?" I yelled as she cringes. "Why was he here? I can't imagine that he would be here without you knowing about it."

"I didn't know Sean. Rebecca is the one sleeping with him. She must have let him in." She cries.

"How dare you bring me into this ... I don't even know him." Rebecca claims.

"You lying whore!" Ava yelled with a passion I have never seen before.

"Go back to the guesthouse, Rebecca." I said, focusing on Ava.

"But Sean ..."

"Go!" She walks slowly away whispering - *if I need her*. The only thing I need are answers. I walk towards the house looking down at Ava as I pass her. "Come in here."

Once inside, Ava's posture changes significantly. My eyes widened watching her start to tremble. Her eyes search the silent room that surrounds us. All I can hear is my heart, beating louder and louder, reaching its breaking point at any second. I straighten and take a deep breath while I prepare to concentrate on every word, every sound and every breath she is about to make.

"I don't know how you couldn't tell me. How you could ..." I cringe, trying to voice my frustrations calmly. "How could you?"

"Sean, he bought my portion of the business. I didn't know it was him until it was too late. In the agreement, they demanded I stay on full time until the end of the current projects. I didn't want to upset you, and it was all supposed to be a surprise for you ... a gift."

"A surprise?" I yell at her. "You thought this would be a gift for me?"

"No, Sean, you don't understand. I am only working with Jasper so ..."

"I understand! I understand that you have been lying to me and seeing your old lover behind my back. I understand that you bribed Rebecca with your part in the movie so she would keep her mouth shut. I can't imagine why you would do that unless ..."

"No, Sean! No. I would never. I can't believe that you would think that."

"Then why, Ava? Why?"

"Because she threatened to say Jasper raped her. She had a video of them having sex and she threatened to take it to the police." She said, as if that makes anything better.

"He raped her?"

"No. She only made it look that way."

"How do you make it look like you're being raped? Ava, I don't even know who you are. You are defending him, protecting him. Why do that unless you are sleeping with him?"

"He owns part of the business now Sean. For Kyle's sake, I gave up a part I didn't even want. Not for Jasper. I don't care about Jasper. I am not cheating on you, Sean. I love you. Do you really believe I could do that to you?"

"I don't know what to believe anymore, Ava." She approaches me with pain-filled eyes and tries to take hold of me, but I push her hands away.

"There is nothing going on between me and Jasper, except work. Please believe me." She pleads, grasping for my hands again.

"Why should I?" I shake my head at her, pushing her hands away from me again.

"I wouldn't lie to you, Sean."

I start to laugh, "But you did Ava."

"No, I just ..."

"You what? Just didn't tell me, so you don't think that's a lie?"

"Yes, but I didn't think you would like me working with him and ..."

"You're damn right I wouldn't have!" I roar at her. I look down at her as she cries into her hands. "I would have helped you figure out another way, Ava. You didn't have to hide it from me." I pause, rubbing my face and head, doubling over and back up again with tears in my eyes. "You didn't need to keep it from me!" I cringe, shaking my hands in her face.

"I know, but I didn't want to upset you and I wanted to finish this last project. It is really going to be beautiful. I wanted to see it through, I wanted ..." She holds her face, crying hysterically.

"SHUT UP!" I screamed sending chills through both of us. "I don't give a damn about what you wanted." I said, gripping my face and feeling the pain eat me up.

"I'm sorry. I wanted to tell you. I did, and I should have."

"You think so?" She nods. "Now you do at least, huh?" I inhale, looking down at her furiously. "I'm going to ask you this one time and you better not lie to me." She nods slowly. Snarling, I look her up and down, causing her to cower away from me. "Did you fuck him Ava?" She instantly shakes her head. I grab her face, forcing her to look into my eyes. "Did you fuck him and then come home to me?" I look into her tear-filled eyes, heartbroken.

"NO!" she cried. "No, I would never do that." I watch her, hoping to see the truth somehow. Pushing her away once again, "Leave me alone, Ava. I don't want to talk to you anymore tonight."

"Sean. Please, if you would just listen to me …"

"I'm going to go get a shower. Please don't interrupt me." I turn away from her, feeling every step that takes me further away from her.

The steaming hot water does not ease my pain but does calm my anger. *I want to believe her. Damn, I want to believe her. I just hope it's not blinding me to what might really be going on.* Tears begin washing down my face. *I love her so fucking much. She wouldn't do this to me. Please God, tell me she isn't lying to me.* Leaning against the shower wall, I fist my hands, shaking and pleading. *I don't think I could handle it if I lost her … she's everything to me.* I manage to get control of myself once the numbness creeps in.

Chapter 10

Ava

I will never forget his face. There was so much pain in his eyes, and I was the one that caused it. I would do anything to take it away. To let him know how much I love him, to hold him or touch him. I don't know how to get back to where we were before I screwed up. Grasping my head, it takes me some time to stop shaking and stop the tears from flowing. I approach our room quietly, changing in the silent darkness before crawling into bed with him. He is lying on his back. I hope that his usual posture is a welcoming sign. Scooting over I reach out for him. I touch his chest softly, only to have him push my hand away before turning away from me. I cannot breathe. I move away from him and find my own place, by myself. He never turns, he never speaks, and I wait all night for him to.

⋐⋙

Dinner tonight is good, however, the conversation isn't. Joel and Sean talk about the set and all of their ordeals of the day, leaving Rebecca and me to exchange wicked glares and snide remarks.

"Do we have anymore wine?" Rebecca asked, holding out her wine glass as though waiting to be served.

"Yes, we do." I said, not moving.

"Well, can I have some?" She huffs. I ignore her and she slams her glass down. "I don't know where you keep the wine, Ava, so can you please get me some more? I will be forever grateful." She said, forcing a smile.

"Fine, I will be right back." I go and pull out a new bottle of wine and take it to the table. While fitting the corkscrew in, my hands begin to shake. I fist them a few times and try again, but suddenly my vision goes blurry and sideways. I try to shake it off, but in reaching for my head I end up knocking the bottle of wine to the floor where it shatters. *Damn it!* I quickly bend down to pick up the pieces. Joel, the only one to respond, is kind enough to bring me a towel and a trash can. "Thank you." I said to him as he nods with a concerned look. I have almost all the pieces when my vision goes sideways again. "Ow!" I cried out when my hand tightens around a shard of glass, slicing it.

"Are you alright?" Joel asked looking over my hand. "You should go take care of that. I'll finish this up for you. Please." He insists. I leave him and stand up, glancing at Sean who is watching me carefully. I clean my wound, but find it difficult to bandage on my own. "You need some help?" Joel asked, putting the trash up and bandaging my hand delicately. "There. Not bad if I do say so myself."

"You did perfectly." I said, matching his smile. Sean walks in, looking us both over with a scowl before leaving again.

"What the hell is up with him?" Joel asked.

"We got into a fight." I say staring down at the floor.

"It must have been some fight. He is being a total ass to you tonight."

"I deserve it, I suppose."

"You deserve better than that. I don't care what you did." I smile, kissing him on the cheek, but my innocent affection arouses him. He slides his arm around my waist and caresses my cheek as he leans into me. "You know Ava, if you were mine I would do everything I could to make you happy." Joel forces his lips to mine and I push him away.

"Joel, what are you doing?"

"I thought you wanted me to." I back away from him as he shyly looks away from me. "I'm sorry. I don't know what I was thinking." I nod, but the awkwardness between us is obvious. "You go sit down, I'll get Rebecca's wine," he said, but grabs my arm. "Ava, I didn't mean to… my marriage isn't exactly going well either." He looks down with a deep sigh. "I think I was only trying to get back at Rebecca. She throws herself at Sean every chance she gets, you know? Anyway, I really am sorry."

"It's okay. I won't tell Sean as long as we can go back to being good friends and lose the awkwardness." I said as he smiles, hugging me. I leave him to go back to the dining room, trying to eat but feeling to dizzy to care. Sean glances at me a few times, mostly eyeing my hand. I assume because of the injury but when I look down, it is shaking out of control. I pull it back to me quickly, hoping no one notices… but he already did. After dinner, Sean and Joel leave for the guesthouse to shoot some pool. I bring Lillah into the living room with me to play while I sketch, hoping it will calm my nerves as well as my shaking hand. Unfortunately, Rebecca follows me.

"Ava, I found the perfect product for you. It should help keep your skin from aging any more than it already has, but don't get your hopes up too much. I don't think it can work miracles." She holds up the product page with encouragement. "No?" She smiles, shrugging. "I will keep looking then."

I jab my pen into my pad causing the wound in my hand to tear open again. "*Augh*!" I cringe, cradling my hand while looking for something to stop the bleeding.

"Will you watch Lillah for a second?" I asked Rebecca, who instantly makes a sour face at me.

"And these nasty dogs too. I mean, really Ava, how could you let things so disgusting near your child? They should take your child away from you."

"I will put the boys outside. Just watch her for a few minutes while I clean my hand up. Please?"

"Fine." She says, waving her skinny, nasty hand at me.

I let the boys outside and rush to get my hand cleaned up. I grab a bandage and wrap it best I can before going back into the living room to find both Lillah and Rebecca missing.

"Rebecca?" I yelled.

"What?" She replied, walking out from the bathroom nonchalantly filing her nails.

"Where's Lillah?"

"I don't know, she's your daughter," she said, disgusted.

"I asked you to watch her!" I yell at her.

"I have better things to do than to do your job, Ava."

I panic, looking everywhere for her when I hear the boys barking outside wildly. I look to see what they are barking at, and that's when I see my daughter dangling her little feet into the pool, trying to get in as she cries. I stop breathing as I run to her, watching her screaming and crying. "Lillah!" I scream as Sean jumps the fence from the other side and grabs her.

He holds her to him gasping for breath himself, "It's okay, Daddy's here." He said, calming her as she cries on his shoulder. I hold my hands to my mouth as Sean looks over at me. "Where were you?" He yells with a fierce intensity in his eyes.

"I … my hand started bleeding again and I …"

"You left her?" His eyes widen at me.

"No, I asked Rebecca to watch her for me."

"Ava, you said you were taking her with you. I would have stayed in the room otherwise. And you are the one that let the dogs out before you left." Rebecca says, walking up from behind me to touch Sean sweetly. "It was an accident, Sean. I am sure she didn't mean to leave the door open."

"I didn't…" I tried to speak.

"Ava I don't care what happened, but you could have at least made sure the gate around the pool was closed today." Sean accuses me again.

"It was closed, Sean, and I didn't …" He gives me a dirty look as he walks around me back into the house with Lillah. Rebecca walks back to the guesthouse smiling back at me. I fist my hands and try my best not to run after her. Instead, I go to check on my daughter. I try to take Lillah from Sean's arms, but he avoids my reach, skeptically eyeing me. "Come here Lillah." I take her anyway, holding her as she grips me.

"Are you sure you should be carrying her?" Sean asked me crudely.

"Why?"

"You haven't exactly been … all that together today. Have you eaten at all today?"

"I'm fine." I snap, taking Lillah to her room without looking at him. Sitting down in our rocking chair, I kiss her tear stained cheek and wipe away the remaining tears from her face. "Lillah, I'm sorry I left you." I said, as she plays with the charms on my bracelet. "I promise I won't leave you again, okay? Do you forgive me?" She nods and rests her tired body against me as I rock her. "Why did you go outside, honey? Did you want to go swimming?"

"No, Becca took me. She said I stink like the boys." She begins to get upset again. "She said I need to get a bath. I told her that is not where you get baths, but she said I couldn't come back inside until I smell better …" Lillah says, crying and burying her face into my sweater.

"Oh honey, you don't stink and neither do the boys. Becca stinks and Mommy isn't going to leave you alone with her ever again." *And, I am going to do my best not to kill her when I talk to her about it.*

After I calm Lillah and put her safely to bed, I leave Sean with her and go to talk to Rebecca. Thankfully, she is the one that opens the door. Her obnoxious smile is quickly knocked off her face. I step over her fallen body and growl with pride. "Touch my daughter again, and I will make sure there is nothing left of you to bury." I start to turn away, but I know she will say something smart as soon as I turn my back. With a freeing smile, I kick her in the jaw and send her crashing back to the floor where she belongs. I walk back into the house powerfully when Sean looks up at me. "Just so you know, Rebecca put Lillah out at the pool and told her she couldn't come back in until she took a bath - in the pool."

"What? Ava you can't be serious. Why would Rebecca do that?" Sean starts to dismiss me, but I lean down into his face so he understands me clearly.

"I don't need your input on the matter. I only wanted to tell you myself, that yes, I admit it. I knocked the shit out of that bitch! And if you don't like it - tough!"

CREW

Sean never says a word about Rebecca's noticeable wounds to me. Even though he hasn't really said much of anything to me the last few days, I believe he is ready to talk though and let go of the tension between us. His late nights on the set are becoming more frequent, but I wait up for him tonight and hope that I can convince him to listen to me.

I meet Sean before he can get through the door. Holding me back with one arm, he says, "I am going to be staying at a hotel for the next few days with Joel. We are behind now, and are having to catch up with several late nights. Neither one of us should be driving afterwards."

He walks around me but I stop him. "You're running away, rather than talking to me?"

"I'm not running from you." He sighs, walking away again. He grabs a bag to pack and catches a glimpse of me in the background. "Ava, I am really tired and I don't feel like talking right now."

"Then when, Sean? When will you be ready? How long are you going to punish me for something I didn't even do? Lying to you is one thing, but you act as if I cheated on you and you know damn well that is not true."

"The evidence says otherwise."

"What evidence? You're being ridiculous. If you really believed I cheated on you, then why are you still coming home to me every night? Why not kick me out or ... ask for a divorce? You don't believe it Sean, and with good reason. You know in your heart, I love you and no one else. You know I would never do anything like that." He tries to walk around me again, but I stop him and grab hold of his face, forcing him to look at me, "Sean, I know you are hurting, but please listen to me. All I wanted to do was let go of the business, take a backseat and be able to stay home more." He suddenly focuses a little more on me. "Once we decided to have a bigger family, I wanted to surprise you and be home more for you and our family."

"You would never leave that job." He huffs.

"I would never leave it for something that doesn't mean anything to me, but I would leave it for you and Lillah and for … whoever else may come along." Pulling my hands away from his face, I hope he finally listens to me.

"I want to believe you Ava, but I am afraid to. Rebecca says Jasper has been coming over here while I'm gone. That you two spend hours inside, that she saw him kiss you …"

"That is not true Sean."

"I found a tie clip under the sofa. It had Jasper's name engraved on it." He says looking me over.

I sigh in disbelief. "It is not true. Rebecca probably put it there. I told you she was at his place." Frustrated, I grip him tighter, "Jasper has never been here. You can ask him yourself. I will call him and you can talk to him."

"I don't need to talk to *him*. Forget the tie clip, you're telling me that he bought your company and forced you to stay on long enough so he could work with you, but he didn't want anything more?"

Hesitating, I know it is better to tell him despite the reaction I expect to get. "You're right, he did it all in hopes of somehow getting me back. And yes, he did corner me one night after everyone left." Sean's eyes widen. "I stopped him. I punched him in the eye, actually, and I made sure he understood it is never going to happen. I wouldn't say he completely respects that decision, but he doesn't try anything anymore." His hands are fisting as he steams even more. "I don't know what else to do to convince you. I don't know why you would believe Rebecca anyway. She is nothing more than a lying whore and will do anything to get what she wants."

"I don't know who to believe, Ava." Before I can argue with him any further, he growls frustratingly. "I am so tired! I only want to get this film done and then, maybe, we can talk." He says. I shake my head, defeated, and go to bed. There is no use fighting with him when he is this tired.

I lay in bed for several hours before I hear the door open. Sean lies in bed next to me, and after a soft sigh I feel his hand brush the hair out of my face. Running the back of his fingers across my cheek, he expects me to be asleep but I open my eyes and look into his for the first time in days. I don't give him a chance to say anything. I push myself deep into his chest and hold onto him desperately. He doesn't hold me as tight as he has, but he doesn't push me away either.

❦

The next few days are impossible and miserable. I feel like my whole body is rejecting me. I can't sleep, eat or even manage a clear thought anymore. It's difficult, but I manage to get Lillah dressed and take her outside along with the boys to play, hoping the sunshine will help me feel better.

"How sweet." Rebecca said, walking over to us. I sigh instantly. "Oh, don't get all worked up, Ava. I am only teasing you." I grab my drink so I can move us further away from her, but she follows. "What are you drinking? I thought you always drink that nasty tea stuff?"

"I made more, but it's not cold yet so I am drinking water. Is that okay with you?" I asked her as she shrugs.

"Whatever. Are we eating soon?" she asked.

"You can eat whenever you want. There is a kitchen in the guesthouse." I said, exasperated.

"Oh Ava, don't be ridiculous. At least tell me where I can get something to drink, and I don't want water."

"Oh yes, I would hate for you to go without alcohol much longer. It is after six." I smiled at her, earning a mocking one back.

"Go to hell, Ava."

"You first." I said as she walks into the house. Since Joel has been staying with Sean at the hotel every night, it leaves me to deal with his wife alone. The only good part about that is she is not able to be around Sean either.

By the time I put Lillah to bed I feel exhausted and want nothing more than to go to bed myself. Sean is supposed to call within the hour so I try to keep myself busy so I can stay awake long enough to talk to him. I let the boys outside and clean up the patio some before concentrating on Lillah's toys in the living room.

"Ava." A voice steams in my direction. I snap my head around and lose my breath instantly. "I missed you." Shaking my head, I fall to the floor and scoot away from the approaching figure. "I told you I would never let you go. You are mine, and I will take you back."

Screaming, I run to let the boys inside but they seem more alarmed by me than anything else. Pausing, I search the room and find nothing, no one. My heart is still racing as I check on Lillah and call security to check things over for me. They find nothing and I begin to believe that my exhaustion is causing my nightmares to surface. After all, *Spencer is dead. How could he be talking to me in my living room?*

CRBO

I had trouble sleeping last night, even after I moved to the bed in Lillah's room. With the doors locked and the boys at my side, I kept watch on security lights, which stayed solid throughout the night. I decided to make an excuse to work from home today. I am able to get some sleep when Edelmira, the nanny, comes in to watch Lillah for me. My dreams are erratic until his voice slithers into my dreams. "I always liked watching you sleep, Ava." Slowly, I open my eyes, but before I can scream he covers my mouth and holds me down. "Don't scream or I will kill everyone in this house, including your precious little girl. Do you understand me?" I nod, slowly. "Good, now take your clothes off and turn over." I begin to panic and shake my head hysterically when he presses down harder on me. "Don't fight me!" Spencer yells at me.

"Mrs. Grant? Are you awake?" Edelmira calls out as she knocks on the door. I stare at Spencer wide-eyed.

"Get up and get rid of her." He says.

He lets me up and I walk slowly towards the door. As soon as I reach the knob I turn it quickly, grab Edelmira by the arm and rush to Lillah causing the boys to become alarmed and bark madly. I sound an alarm and close us all in Lillah's room to wait for help. I don't know where Spencer went or how he got away, but security swears that they can find no one. Edelmira tells me to get some sleep, but that is the last thing I can do. Sean arrives quickly and rushes in, checking me over in panic.

"What happened?" He asks. I begin to cry in relief to see him. "Calm down. You're okay now. Tell me what happened, Ava."

"I don't know exactly. The other night, I was cleaning and I saw Spencer. Then, when I was asleep, he woke me up and held me down and told me he was going to kill Lillah if I didn't do what he asked." I ramble before I think about what I am saying. Sean backs off me with a questioning expression on his face.

"Ava, that is impossible. And security says that they found no one here. Are you sure you didn't just have a bad dream?" Sean caresses my face as if I am breakable. "You look exhausted, baby."

"Sean I ... I have no idea what I saw ... if I saw." *It was real, wasn't it?*

Chapter 11

Sean

Ava looks half-crazed. Her eyes are dark and her hands are shaking. I feared those nightmares would come back. I had hoped she would find a way to deal with them, or at least recognize them as nightmares and nothing more. Security assures me they checked everything several times, and even the boys acted as if nothing was amiss. I feel bad for leaving her alone, even when I knew the nightmares were affecting her lately. I need to be home with her, but until I can, I have Randy move in to help her feel better.

It is only a day later, and in the middle of the night, when Randy calls. He would never call unless there is something horribly wrong. "Sean, I think you need to come home. Ava is hysterical. She swears she saw him again." Sighing deep into my hands, I hear him do the same. "Sean, she is injured too."

"What? What do you mean she is injured?"

"She has cuts and bruises on her arms and legs. There is no one here, Sean. There is no one anywhere on the grounds. I checked myself." Randy said.

"What are you telling me? She is hurting herself?" I ask and he sighs again. I get up and begin to pack, but before I leave, Joel walks in.

"Where are you going?" He asked with a surprised expression.

"It's Ava. She is having those nightmares again and she is hurting herself now. I need to be with her as much as I can."

"Sean, you can't be serious. We need you on set. We need you to be fresh. I know you are worried about your wife and it is understandable, but what are you going to do that Randy and security aren't? Besides, don't you think this is all a little convenient?" He cocks his head at me as I stare at him in confusion. "Come on Sean, she happens to have these nightmares right before you go out of town? Seems convenient now that you two have been fighting and you move to a hotel for a few days. She seems to be fine when you are with her."

"Ava isn't like that."

"I am sure she isn't meaning to consciously, but sometimes a woman just wants attention. Then, when she doesn't get it, she over dramatizes things to get you to notice her. She probably doesn't even realize she is doing it." I shake my head, even though it makes some since. "Listen, it is too late for you to be going home now. You will have to turn around and come right back. Call her and talk to her, then get some sleep. Get through tomorrow, and then go home to her. If she knows you are coming home, she will calm down."

"Maybe, but I have to go home and check on her myself."

"You should get more sleep, Sean. I think the lack of sleep is affecting your judgment." Joel pats me on the back before walking towards his room.

"Are you just getting in from the set?" I asked him.

"Oh, yeah, I got so involved in watching the dailies I forgot the time." He says shrugging.

"You work too much, talk about someone who needs more sleep. The movie is going to be great, you shouldn't worry so much." He laughs and I leave to go to my wife.

Chapter 12

Ava

Sean came home and slept beside me, and Randy was kind enough to stay and sleep in Lillah's room. It was a bad night and everyone is now walking on eggshells around me, as if I am about to go crazy at any moment. In a way, I feel as if I am going crazy. Even after talking to my therapist, I believe that I am dreaming it all. After getting enough sleep last night and even some this afternoon while Edelmira was here, I feel better and want to do my best to look lively before Sean gets home. When Joel comes home, I call out to him before he goes into the guesthouse.

"Hi Beautiful, are you feeling better?" He says, seeming to be on the same eggshells as everyone else.

"Yes, thank you. Is Sean going to be here soon?"

"Should be, I believe he was right behind me." He says nodding and obviously wanting to get away from me before I go crazy again. "You know, you should get some exercise. Go for a run or something. It might even convince Sean that you're not so scared of the dark after all." I smile and he leans in, "You're not, are you? I mean, if you are, then you might want to consider going to a hospital for help. I only say that out of concern for you. There is nothing wrong with it."

"I'm fine. I don't need to go into any hospital. But thank you for your concern."

"I didn't mean to upset you, but Sean is really worried about you and it is affecting him badly. I love him like he brother and I would do anything for him, so anything you can do to prove it to him that you are okay, I would be grateful." I nod and he smiles, hugging me lightly, but Rondo suddenly approaches with a light growl, causing Joel to back off.

"Rondo! What is wrong with you? I'm sorry, I am not sure why he is acting like that." I said, holding Rondo back by the collar.

"It's okay, but where is the other one? I don't want him to sneak up behind me." Joel laughs nervously.

"He is inside sleeping, so you should make it the guesthouse safely. I'm sorry, I don't know why he is acting this way. He must have woken up on the wrong side of his dog-bed." I laugh, hoping to ease his tension.

"He must have." He laughs with me. Joel steps further away from Rondo who is watching him intently. "Well better go check on Rebecca before I have to go back to the set. You should consider that run, it would really prove you are not afraid of the dark, you know?"

I didn't like my conversation with Joel, but the idea of a run isn't a bad one. When Sean arrives home, I spend some time with him before asking if he minds watching Lillah while I go for a run. He seems shocked by my request, but excited by the idea, which makes me feel better about easing his stress some.

The cool night air is nice and the run feels great, but I can't help but watch every movement around me. I still feel as if someone is watching me. I keep telling myself I am okay and it is my imagination, but the overwhelming feeling increases more and more until I decide I have to turn around and go back home. The fear becomes too much and I am in tears when Joel pulls up beside me.

"So you decided to take my advice after all." I force a smile when he notices my tears. "Are you crying? It is okay you made it halfway at least, baby steps sweetheart. Get in, I will take you home." The idea of running home alone is not something I am willing to attempt so I eagerly jump into Joel's car. "I hope you don't mind, but I have to go pick up some wine for Rebecca. She can't sleep without her favorite wine. I mean, after all, it is after ten o'clock and she isn't falling down drunk yet." He laughs.

"It is after ten already?"

"Yeah, how long have you been running?"

I can't believe it is that late already, Sean must be worried. I am having so much trouble focusing lately, and now I am completely losing track of time. Maybe I should be worried. "I didn't bring my watch but I didn't think it had been that long."

"Well I didn't bring mine either but the clock in this rental clearly says ten-fifteen," he says, tapping the clock. I nod but stop listening to him so I can focus on calming down before I see Sean. Being out this late is going to have him worried enough. While Joel is in the store I close my eyes and breathe. My heart begins to steady and I am almost asleep when he returns to the car and drives off.

"Did you get her wine?" I ask but he doesn't answer. Opening my eyes, I see Spencer turns to me, and smile. "No! You are not real!" I scream.

"Shut up!" He knocks my head into the window and the world begins to blur and goes dark. By the time I wake, I have nothing more than my underwear and shirt on. My body is thrown into the backseat and he jumps in on top of me. I instantly begin to fight him, knocking him in the face and feel something strange. As the moonlight hits his face, I see a mask pushed off to one side. "Good job, Ava. You just ruined a perfectly good disguise. My Dad's art department spent days on this for me."

Shaking my head, "Joel? Why are you doing this?"

"You mean why am I going to fuck my best friend's wife? Because I have to know what it is like to fuck you. Since he is not willing to share, I will just take it. Joel leans down and whispers in my ear. "The best part of this is, everyone thinks you are a *liar*. A crazy woman who is seeing a dead man wherever she goes. So, I can do whatever I want to you, whenever I want, and no one will ever believe you." Holding my hands tightly he kisses me hard. "Fight me if you want to Ava, it only excites me more. Besides, the drug I gave you while you were passed out should be taking effect here soon and then you will be an easy lay for me." He pushes his erection in between my legs and laughs as I cringe at the feel of him. Ripping my shirt off, he grabs my breast and tries to remove it from my bra as he kisses my neck. I fight him and struggle, kicking and screaming until I reach out and find a pen on the floorboard. Holding tight to it, I ram it into Joel's arm and send him racing backwards out of the car. "Son of a bitch!" He screams, looking at his bleeding arm. Dropping the pen, I jump out and kick him before running away.

Running fast and hard, my mind begins to spin and the world becomes hazy. I fall to the ground, trembling, as the trees surround me and the darkness makes it nearly impossible to understand where I am. Stumbling to my feet, I search for the road, struggling to focus. I concentrate on my feet and the sounds around me. I feel as if I have wandered for hours and hours. My feet are swollen and bleeding, my head is ready to roll off my shoulders, but I continue to fight to make it to the main road to search for help. When I finally hear a car, I open my eyes to the bright lights and scream as they rush towards me. The screeching tires come to an abrupt halt as the ground rushes towards me. I do not know if I should cry for help or run, but I cannot open my eyes to judge clearly as the footsteps rapidly approach.

"Oh God, Ava!" My head is lifted and my eyes open to the blurry stranger. "Ava? Ava, are you okay? Sweetheart, please be okay." I jump, screaming and trying to fight. "Ava it's me! It's Sean!" *Sean?* "Baby, are you okay?" When I feel his warm lips touch my face, I relax in his arms.

"I want to go home." I mumble, burying my face into his shoulder as Sean wraps his jacket around me, picks me up and carries me to his car.

Our house is full of people when Sean carries me in, all of which instantly surround us. I try to hide myself from them as Sean grips me away from their line of sight. "Everybody, she's fine. You can all go home now."

"Sean, we should take her to the hospital," I heard Ethan say.

"*No*, she's fine. I'm going to take care of her and get her to bed. Just go, please," Sean said, standing in place and holding me so tight I wonder if someone is trying to take me from him.

"At least let us know how she's doing?" Kyle exclaimed as he feels for my hand. "Sean?"

"*Okay*. I need to put her to bed, so please go."

"Do you want me to help you get her to bed?" Joel said.

His voice instantly sends chills to my spine. I start screaming and push away from Sean until he drops me and I cower away from everyone. "No! Get him away from me!" I screamed.

"Ava… calm down. What is wrong with you?" Sean pulls my face up to his.

"He tried to rape me. He left me out there," I cried.

Sean sits back, glancing at Joel who shrugs with concern. "When Ava? When did this happen?" Sean asked.

Thinking back, "Ten-fifteen" I said, confidently.

Sean sighs, watching me. "He was here Ava. He was right here with everyone else." I shake my head, as I look up at Joel, seemingly sincere in his concern. "Yes, it had to be someone else, or …" I look at Sean as he hesitates.

"Or what? Or I'm making it up? I'm lying to you again?"

"I don't think you're making it up. I think you're really tired and …"

"And crazy?" I cry to him as he tries to pull me to him.

"Will everyone please go," Sean said, holding me still as he waits for us to be alone. He focuses in on me, "It's just after ten now Ava." I shake my head at him. "Yes, it is. What's going on with you?"

Tears flow as I search the room for some sort of answers. *Am I losing it? Maybe it wasn't Joel, maybe none of it was real. I don't remember, I don't remember anything clearly.* "I don't know," I cried.

He reaches out slowly, laying his hand on mine. "You're shaking like a leaf. You look dazed lately and ..."

"I'm cold!" I snap at him as I realize he is accusing me of more than simply being tired.

"Ava?"

"I'm cold." I pull my hand away from him. "I don't care if you believe me." Sean looks at me with concern and I know what he is thinking. "I said I am cold. Why won't you believe anything I say?" I force myself up and take five steps before I fall against the wall, trembling uncontrollably. Sean takes hold of me and instantly lifts me back into his arms. "Sean, I don't know what's wrong with me. I don't know what's wrong." I cry, unable to control my emotions or my body.

"It's okay. I'm going to take care of you now." I look at him, confused, as he carries me to our room and helps me get a bath. Now calm, I climb into bed as Sean comes in with a tray of food and a glass of tea, setting it directly in front of me. "Eat something, and then go to sleep. I am staying with you tonight, so no reason to be scared." He said as he sits in a chair next to my bed, watching me closely.

My determination surfaces and I get angry, knowing I am right. "Sean, I know I sound crazy, but it was Joel. He has a mask that makes him look like Spencer. He tried to rape me and make me look crazy.

"Oh Ava, we have already talked about this. He was with all of us, and worried as hell about you. I had to stop him from going out himself to go find you."

"That's because he knew where he left me." Sean rolls his eyes at me, shaking his head. "He found me running and picked me up in his car. Then took me out into the woods and gave me some kind of drug. And then ..." Sean throws up his hands, huffing. "*And then ...* he put me in his back seat and tried to rape me. I fought him and ..." Suddenly the memories are becoming clearer. "*I stabbed him!*" Sean looks back at me with suspicion. "I did, I stabbed him with something and he let go of me and I ran."

"You stabbed him? With what? Because he sure looked fine to me."

Twisting into my pillows, I cry, surrendering to what must be delusions. Grasping my wrist, "Oh no, I lost my bracelet." I sit back up, apologizing emphatically to him.

Sean leans down over me, hushing me and kissing my head, "It is okay baby. I can get you another one. It's okay, just go to sleep.

Chapter 13

Rebecca

I wake up completely rested, this bed is so much more comfortable than the one we have at home. I can spread out completely in the soft sheets as the sunlight washes over my room.

Randy had to leave to help Sean at the set, giving me the day to drive Ava crazy. She is already half way there, she looks like she hasn't slept in months and after last night's drama no one's expecting for her to make it without psychiatric help much longer. I cannot believe Sean fought everyone on it, he seems to be in bigger denial than she is. Of course, all this may have something to do with the drug I have been crushing into her, *special tea*. The shit is so nasty, you cannot possibly notice any bitterness. Although, it could be Joel dressing up in that stupid mask too.

With a joyful feeling overtaking me, I get up and change into my best bikini before joyfully making my way to the main house, especially when I see that Sean is still here.

"You're not working today?" I asked.

"Yes, but I'm going in a little later. I have to run a couple of errands this morning."

"Like what?"

"I'm taking Lillah over to my mother's for a few days."

"Why, Ava can't take care of her own daughter now?" Sean looks up at me with a sharp scowl. "Sorry only commenting on the obvious."

"*Ava* is fine."

"Okay, she's fine, then why can't she watch your daughter?"

"She's sick and needs to rest. Which means I don't want you anywhere near this house until she's better."

"Sick?" *I know better than that.*

"Rebecca, mind your own business."

"Okay. I didn't realize it was such a big deal." Sean huffs looking away from me. "Well is there anything I can do at least, maybe I can take care of her, you know make her meals and drinks?"

"No thank you, I have someone else watching her for me. You're welcome to hang out by the pool but if I find out that you went anywhere near Ava I will ..."

"Got it, damn." He walks off in a horrible grump. I swear under my breath as I shuffle outside collapsing into a lounge chair. *This is unbelievable! How am I going to get to Ava now? I nearly have over the edge.* Sean comes outside with that child, and sits in a chair nearby helping her put on her shoes. I watch Sean tickle her and cradle her, being so sweet that I nearly vomit but it does give me an idea. "Sean, you know I hate for you to take the child so far away from her mother. Leave her with me and I will watch her and that way you won't upset Ava. We can play and then when Ava wakes up we can spend time with her and help her feel better." Sean pauses seeming to consider my idea. "I can't imagine how upset a mother would be if her child has been taken away."

"I'm not taken Lillah away from her just giving her some time to rest."

"Sean, do you really think Ava is going to see it that way?" I asked as he starts to nod in agreement.

"Maybe, what do you think Lillah?" he asks the child playfully. "I really appreciate the help Rebecca, thank you." He said forcing a smile at me.

"Happy to help anyway I can, of course. Besides what else do I have to do all day?" Getting up I go to them and lean down, "So ..." *What the hell was her name?* "... are you ready to spend the day playing with Aunt Rebecca?" I said with my perfect smile before glancing up to Sean's gorgeous green eyes.

Suddenly the child reaches over and smacks me in the face rudely, "No!" She screamed at me. *Oh I am so going to make her pay for that one.*

Sean grabs her hand looking at me shocked before staring back at the evil spawn, "Lillah that wasn't nice, you don't hit people." The child instantly starts crying and throwing some disgusting tantrum. "Lillah stop? Do you want a time out?"

"No Daddy," she cried.

"Then you apologize to Rebecca," Sean said trying to look at her as she buries her face deep into his shirt. "Lillah?" She pushes even deeper into his shirt. "Okay then you're going into a time out until you do," Sean picks her up and takes her to some imaginary area away from me. *Talk about a drama queen.* I look back at the child, who is calming down but still has her bottom lip out and her arms crossed. "Why did you hit Rebecca, Lillah?"

"Don't want to play with her." She whimpers.

"Why not?" He asked as she remains silent. "Lillah, why not?"

"I don't like her, Daddy."

I look at the little disgusting, nuisance appalled. "That isn't nice Lillah, why would say that?"

Fidgeting she keeps trying to get back into Sean's arms rather than explain herself. "Cause … she stinks." Sean glances back at me with a strange expression. "Come on Lillah," Sean said picking the child up and letting her bury herself back into his arms. "I think it is best I take Lillah to my mother's Rebecca, thanks for the offer. And don't forget to stay away from Ava." Sean leaves abruptly without any explanation.

CS&ED

I try unsuccessfully to sneak into the house and make sure Ava is still drinking her tea but that Edelmira acts like she is working for the secret service and Ava is her charge. I spend the rest of the day bored out of my mind, waiting for Joel to come home. I had been staring at the door for hours when he enters.

"What's wrong with you?" He asked walking past me to the bar.

"That bitch has been laid up in secure quarters all day."

"So?"

"*So?* So she's not drinking her tea I am sure of it."

"How do you know? Because the Gestapo Witch has been making her special meals and drinks to help her get better."

"You will just have to think of something else Rebecca."

"Me? Why does it always have to be me?"

"Because dear, you're the one that wants her husband."

"And what exactly is it that you want my beloved?" I said sarcastically as he sits down.

"His life as he knows it … destroyed," Joel said relaxing comfortably into a chair.

Chapter 14

Sean

The last few weeks have been excruciating. It was all I could do to concentrate on getting up in the morning, forget about trying to go on each day as if my life is perfectly fine. My wife can barely stand up straight, her eyes have been noticeably dilated at times, she barely eats at all and I'm not sure she is in touch at all with reality. I do not know who she is anymore. The strong, vibrant woman I fell in love with has become … I don't know. Then there is Jasper. After I drop off Lillah at my mother's I stop by Ava's office to let Kyle know how she is doing and to my surprise Jasper is here too.

The moment I walk in, Kyle runs up to me, "Whoa, Sean, please don't start anything here."

"I only want to talk to him, Kyle." I said concentrating on my breathing. Jasper gets up and walks over to me but remains more than arms length distance. "What is going on with you and my wife? And you better not lie to me."

"There is nothing going on between them, Sean. I can't believe you won't believe her!" Kyle yells at me.

"I am talking to him … so, Jasper, what is going on between you and Ava?"

"Nothing is going on between us. She told you that, hell she hit me when I simply tried to kiss her on the cheek." I roll my eyes. "I don't know how all this got started but believe me there has been absolutely nothing but business between us. She was so afraid you would be angry with us working together she would work from home on the days I was working here. The night at your house was the first time I have seen her in months."

"Then why were you there?" I asked him but he shakes his head. "You're not going to tell me?"

"I … I guess I was hoping to make you mad enough to leave her so she would run back to me for comfort." He said strangely. Kyle looks at him in shock.

"But that's not why." Kyle said before Jasper shakes his head at him.

I take a second to rub my face and consider the events and that my wife was telling me the truth after all. I turn to walk out but then remember something else she said and he confirmed. I turn and step to Jasper quickly, "By the way, don't ever touch my wife again." I say punching him in the jaw.

ڽۀ

I bargain with Kane to save the last scene for the next day, so I can leave early. The drive to and from home is a rare peace lately, I usually welcome it although tonight I am anxious to see Ava. I hesitate getting out of my car, breathing in and out forcefully to prepare myself for whatever might be waiting for me inside. As soon as I get out of the car I hear the dogs going nuts, and my head immediately starts pounding. *Who put them outside, they won't be happy unless they are with Ava?* They are muddy and a complete mess as they fight to get inside. I hold them back from getting inside, "Boys go play, I don't feel like cleaning you up just yet." I ease into the house hoping they will be quiet long enough for my headache to go away. Of course, they sit right outside the door whimpering as they look up at me with innocent eyes. "Ten minutes, that's all I ask," I said before making my way to our room. As soon as I reach the hall, I see Joel opening the door to our bedroom. "What the fuck are you doing?" I yelled startling him.

"I thought I would check on Ava," Joel said releasing her door.

"Why? I specifically said for no one to bother her."

Joel looks around nervously as he grips his mouth, "Honestly Sean, I had a suspicion about what the problem may be but I wasn't sure until Rebecca told me about a man showing up here earlier … to bring her these." Joel said holding up a bottle of pills. "I think you should search the house for more, there is no telling how much more she has." He said handing me the bottle of pills. "I was hoping I wouldn't find anything and then you wouldn't be hurt anymore than you have been but … you have to do something to help her Sean. You have no other choice."

I stare at him in disbelief, "How … how would Ava even know how to get these?"

"Apparently she does. I hate to ask this Sean, but how well do you really know her?"

I go into our room and Ava instantly sits up groggy but curious. "Where did you get these?" I said holding up the bottle of pills to her but she simply shakes her at me. *Sighing.* I look around the room and begin going through all her drawers.

"What are you doing?" Ava asked.

"I'm searching for more." I said but I find nothing in our room but I do in her office. My whole body sinks as I take the other bottle to show her.

"That's not mine." She says looking at me in shock. "I saw you Ava, your eyes dazed, your hands shaking and you wouldn't eat. I watched you get worse and worse, hoping, praying that you would handle it on your own. I thought you were stronger than this."

"I didn't take them, he's been sneaking them to me somehow." She said pointing at Joel. "I can't believe you don't believe me, you especially, I would think you would believe me." She said tears suddenly flowing down her face.

"I want to get you some help," I said watching her close her eyes hard. "I only want to get you some help, stop being so stubborn and let me." I sit next to her calmly. "Please, Ava. I love you. I only want to help you get better so you can come back to me. There is no reason you should have to take drugs to get over your past." I hold her face still as she cries and nods, hugging me tight as I exhale in relief. Wiping my tears away I hold her out from me and force a smile, "Ethan found a place that can help, I haven't seen it myself yet but I will go do that now and if it seems right then I will make ..." I breathe in deeply facing my own reality. "I will make arrangements for you. Okay?" She nods reluctantly and I kiss her gently before leaving her.

I ask Joel to look after her until I get back and borrow his car in hopes that no one will recognize me admitting my wife into rehab. The last thing she needs is the press rehashing her past. I can barely contain my emotions as I drive down the road, I am so emotional I nearly hit the car in front of me when it slams on its breaks to make a sudden turn. *Thank goodness, Joel's breaks work.* I pull up slowly to the stop light, hoping to get a hold of myself but instead I become intrigued by a bloody pen that has rolled towards my feet. I don't move until the horns of the cars behind me become belligerent and then I pull off to park his car. It takes me some time before I can bring myself to get out and search his car. When I do, it doesn't take me long to find what I feared finding the most. Stuck in between the cushions of the back seat is Ava's charm bracelet but even more unbelievable is the mask I find stored in a backpack deep in the trunk of his car. Shaking I pull out my cell and dial, "Randy ... I need you to meet me at my house as soon as possible … I'm going to kill Joel." I end the call and race home.

Chapter 15

Ava

As soon I hear Sean leave, I jump out of bed and pack my bags. I have to get away from here, I need some time to think. I do not know what is happening to me but I know I am not doing it to myself. I gather my things and rush through my door running right into Joel.

"Going somewhere?" Joel asked while threatening me backwards.

"Get out of my way." I said trying to look strong.

Joel laughs, "You're still weak aren't you. It's okay, Sean is going to put you somewhere that will help you."

"I'm not going, now get out of my way."

"Oh I think you are … unless you want me to help you."

"Help me? How can you help me?"

"Well I am Sean's best friend, he trusts my opinion on things. I can talk him into giving you another chance. Keep you around for awhile. You know as soon as he puts you away, he's going to forget about you." I shake my head but he laughs at me. "Oh Ava, don't fool yourself. It happened to Rebecca, out of sight, out of mind and *you* will be, very soon. But if you do some things for me then I might be willing to help you out."

"I'm not doing anything for you." Joel shakes head, looking down at his hands as he pulls out rope from his back pocket. Panicked, I shove my suitcase into his chest and run past him but he catches up with me and holds me down, while I scream. "Sean will find out and he will kill you!"

"Sean isn't going to find out anything, he doesn't believe a word you say remember? You're a drug addict whore, who sleeps around. Trust me he isn't going to give a shit about you when I am done."

I scream harder, fighting him until … *Whack! … Whack! … Boom!* Joel pauses after the loud crash startles us both but the sudden rumbling coming from the floor beneath me, causes me to smile. Rondo and Prince round the corner with their target's image mirrored in their eyes. I lay flat on the ground as they both fling themselves atop of Joel, showing no mercy to his screams. Jumping up I immediately grab my bags, call for the boys, and take them both along with me as I drive away. *I don't know where I am going, but anywhere is better than here.*

Chapter 16

Rebecca

As soon as I saw Joel leave with that rope and the needle, I knew he was asking for more than we are both willing to bargain for. He told me to follow, he told me to bring the video camera but I can't see this going the way he thinks it will. He should have just let her go, let Sean put her in that rehab place. He is so damn stubborn, I know he has been set on having her since he first laid eyes on her. He has been determined to win her over and steal her from Sean. Only Ava, is only interested in being his friend. Now he has lost his damn mind and he is going to take me down with him, if I'm not careful. While searching the guesthouse, I hear the dogs going nuts and I do not dare go outside now. They sound like they are going to kill somebody. As soon as the thought enters my head I hear the crash followed by Joel's screams. *Shit! What the hell am I going to do now?* Remembering back to how I got the last bit of money from Joel's father, I take in a deep breath and then slam the door against my arm and then my face before throwing myself down the stairs. *I hope I got blood everywhere because that hurt like hell.* I take a half a step outside wondering what to do next when I see Ava rushing down the drive with both dogs. I look back at the destruction of the now open house and stand frozen as Joel hobbles towards me.

"Have you lost your mind?" I asked him.

"What the hell happened to you?" He asked.

"I'm covering my ass, because you are obviously going to be killed."

"She's gone and is probably never coming back. I will tell Sean that she was trying to get away and I held her back but that the dogs thought I was hurting her and attacked me, helping her get away." He said as he walks into the guesthouse and cleans himself up.

"Okay boy wonder? What are you going to do when she does come back?"

"*If*... if she comes back. And if that happens, I doubt he believes her, he is getting ready to put her away. She will probably go straight to the loony bin before he hears her say anything."

"Well excuse me if I don't take part in this crazy plan."

"Fine Rebecca! Do whatever you want. Stay here and makeup your own little stories, handle it all on your own. Hell, call Ethan, he has been so helpful to you in the past."

"Shut up! I can do just fine on my own. I don't need you." He laughs at me as he walks out the door. "You however do need me, or at least you will. When Sean and I get married you're going to need my help, you just wait and see."

"Go have another drink Rebecca, you're delusional again. I am going to go wait for my best friend and console him when he finds out his wife just left him. And I might let him know that I know how he feels, because my wife is also a cheating whore. Maybe then we can bond over needing to get a divorce from our crazy wives!" He smiles ignoring my huffing as he walks back towards the main house.

Chapter 17

Sean

I pull into our drive still shaking as I picture myself, strangling the son of a bitch to death. I am out of the car before the engine completely shuts off. Rushing towards the house, I notice the destruction of our back door. The sight of it reminds me of what I should have been thinking about. Rather than killing Joel, I should have been worried about protecting her from him.

"Ava!" I stop short at the bloody mess outside our bedroom door. "Ava!" I search our entire house, becoming more hysterical by the second.

"Sean," Joel rounds the corner calmly. "Sean - she took off."

"Why? What did you do to her?"

He seems shocked by my accusation, "I didn't do anything, I tried to stop her but the dogs came after me, I guess they thought I was ..." Before he can finish his sentence my rage takes over and I grip him hard as I throw him up against the wall.

"What did you do to her?" I scream as he struggles to reach the floor with his feet. "What did you do to my wife?"

"Nothing! Sean calm down I didn't do anything."

"The hell you didn't! You drugged her didn't you? You tried to make her crazy pretending to be Spencer and then tried to rape her." I watch him shake his head in disbelief. "You son of a bitch, I know you did. Now tell me where she is!" He shakes his head trying to get away from me. "Tell me!"

"I told you! I don't know." The lying piece of shit tries to look me in the eyes and I lose it, ripping his shirt sleeve I find the puncture wound from where Ava stabbed him with the pen. I focus on his eyes as he searches for a way out. "Sean she came on to me and I admit I was willing but then she went psycho on me and I got scared."

I slam his back into the wall as I take hold of his neck. "Tell me where she is!"

"I don't know!" I relax my hand and a new calm comes over me. "Sean, I'm telling you ..." The blood that spews from his mouth as my fist hits his jaw doesn't even phase me, I cannot stop now. The pressure I feel to my fists plowing into him over and over, doesn't seem to help relieve any of the pain or guilt that I am feeling but I continue to try.

"Sean!" Ethan yells as he and Randy drag me off Joel. Still vibrating with anger, I cannot take my eyes off him. "Sean, what is going on? What happened?"

"He did it, it was him and I blamed her and the whole time it was him." I cried out.

Joel staggers back to his feet holding his bloodied body with a scowl, "You're fucking right I did! And you know what I loved every second that I rammed your wife's face into the ground as I fucked the hell out of that whore." Jerking away from my brother and Randy's grip I lunge at him only to be pulled back again. "Keep coming Sean, I already got enough to put you away and take all your money. If you're nice enough, maybe I will send you pictures of Ava and me fucking, hell I think I even got video. My resistance against my restrainers grows as he enjoys my pain. "Ohhh don't worry, I didn't hurt her too much, she enjoyed it ... trust me. Hell maybe since she isn't on birth control, I will get that son I have always wanted." Suddenly the grips on me - release, and I take my revenge out on Joel once again.

"Okay Sean, that's enough." Randy helps Ethan to pull me back again.

"Joel I wouldn't be so confident, if you raped Ava," My body tenses as my brother speaks. "She is going to testify and put you in jail, no one is going to care what Sean did to you. It is his home."

Joel continues laughing, as blood runs from his nose down into his mouth, "Oh Ethan, still trying to be so innocent are you? I know what you have been up to, maybe we can work out a little deal but as far as Sean, he's going to jail and I am taking everything he's got."

"No, you're not." Rebecca says coming up from behind us. She stuns us all with her tattered clothes and gruesome appearance, "I found these," she said releasing a bag full of pill bottles. "Plenty of evidence to prove that you have been drugging his wife in hopes that enough of them might make her want to sleep with you. I watched him go after her, I tried to stop him but he made sure I couldn't. I'm sorry Sean, I tried. I heard her screaming and there was nothing I could do."

"Where is she?" I asked her.

"I don't know, when I was finally able to get up, she had taken off." Rebecca said as she began to cry pitifully. "I tried to leave myself but Joel came back and told me if I said anything that he would kill me."

"You're a fucking bitch! Do you know what you have done?!" Joel screamed at her. He tries to move in her direction but is unable to do anything but stumble to the ground, with his swollen face and broken body.

Rebecca had called the police before she came over with her confession and they showed up a few minutes after she did. Joel was dragged off and I assured Rebecca that she could stay in the guesthouse when she gets back from the hospital. Her arm is clearly broken and I assume it's not the only thing, she looked terrible. If Joel can do that to his own wife and I can only imagine what he did to mine. I call her every few minutes, search for her everywhere I can think of, but she is gone and I am not sure when she is coming back. I can only hope that she does.

ϠϡϠ

It has been days and no word from Ava. Ethan has convinced me somehow that working will help take my mind off things but being on set everyday is not helping anything. I am not even sure if I want to do this damn film any more, but Joel's father has made sure that I realize I am under contract. The asshole even made me aware that his son has been released from jail since Ava is not here to file a complaint against him. And since I allowed him on my property, I am as guilty as he is for fighting. Castor says he will not sue me if I promise to be a good boy and finish the film and not touch his son again when he returns to the set. It takes Ethan some time before he can get me to calm down but he reassures me that despite Joel, the script is still just as good as it was when I signed on and the chances of Joel showing up anywhere near me is slim to none. It really doesn't matter because I am numb to it all right now, I only want Ava back.

It is towards the end of the fourth day and her name finally appears on my cell. "Ava? Where are you, baby? Everything is okay now, Joel is gone, and I know everything …" I pause as I hear cry.

"I need you Sean. I need you." She cried, mumbling repeatedly until I can finally get out what is truly wrong. Not that it matters, she needs me and that is really all I needed to hear. As always, I drop everything for her and go to her immediately, damn anyone who has a problem with it.

CR&O

Ava ran away to her grandparents' house, in Lexington, the place she has known since her parents died, her true home. However, the woman that raised her and has comforted her through everything, passed away quietly in her sleep sometime last night.

The funeral was somber. I stood by Ava the entire time with my hand on her back as she stood strong. She said her goodbye and her tears flowed, leaning into me a little more and more as time passed. I do not know who amazed me more, Jack or his granddaughter. I kept an eye on them both waiting for some sort of breakdown. Instead, I am dealing with Ava's relatives, most being wonderful, but some are simply obnoxious and annoying.

"Hey Sean, do you think you could beat me in an arm wrestling contest?" Cousin Doug asked me for the fifth time.

"Yes I do," I said finally not ignoring his stupid question. For some reason he seems to think his gigantic size means he can take me in almost anything and maybe he can if it is an eating contest, otherwise, he doesn't stand a chance in hell.

"Oh well lets go then son!" He said dancing around and waving for other cousins to surround us. He sets his arm down with stern focus. I casually walk around the table, take my jacket off, roll up my sleeve and sit with a humored smile. "Come on, stop trying to delay the inevitable."

"Doug please, leave Sean alone," Ava yelled at him.

I wave her off, "No baby I got it." Cousin Doug smiles with grinding teeth, ready to take me down. I take his hand and watch his eyes as he tries to predict when we will be released into battle.

"Go!" Cousin Nate yells.

I hold him in place for a time, enjoying his struggle until his heavy breaths begin to turn his face a bright magenta. "Sean please," Ava calls out from across the room. I smile and wink at Cousin Doug before taking him down.

"Sorry fella's the wife calls," I said standing up and putting my jacket back on, glancing at Jack who is hiding his chuckle behind his hand.

"One more time Sean?" Doug called out to me.

I ignore him and find Ava in the kitchen arranging numerous dishes of everything imaginable. "Do you want some help?"

She throws her hands up. "I just don't know what to do with it all. It's not going to all fit in the refrigerator, we can't possibly eat all of this, and you can't freeze most of this." I walk over to her and hold her still.

"Stop, stop trying to do everything. It doesn't matter," I said as she collapses into my arms, allowing me to console her fully for the first time.

"Everyone is leaving now," Jack said causing Ava to straighten up and clear her face quickly.

"Okay well make sure they know we have plenty of food, if anyone needs something to take home." She said.

"I'll tell them but that's just going to prolong the idiots from leaving my house." Jack said with a scowl.

I laugh and Ava smacks my arm, "Don't laugh at him, it only encourages him," she scolds me.

After everyone leaves and Ava gives up trying to rescue mountainous amounts of food the three of us finally sit down and take in the day.

"Grandad, I need to make up the extra bed for Sean, do you know where the …" Ava asked Jack.

"No. Just sleep in the one room, don't go messing up two rooms just because you don't like sleeping with your husband in a small bed. He's your husband now. Lay on top of him if the beds are too small. He'd probably prefer that anyway," Jack said pointing at me with his cane.

"Do you have to be so crude?" She said watching him narrow his eyes at her.

"You know what I forgot to turn off the lights in the barn," Jack said scooting to the edge of his chair.

"Sit back down, I'll do it," Ava said running out the door before he can stop her.

"Is she this annoying at home?" He asked me.

"She's trying to help you," I said.

"Stubborn as hell is what she is and don't you dare argue with me." *I wouldn't dare argue with that.* "So tell me what started this whole mess with you two?"

"What do you mean?" I asked him.

He laughs at me, "I might be old Sean but I'm not stupid and I know my granddaughter. You two had some fight and it's written all over both of your faces."

I shake my head looking away from him, "It's nothing."

"That bad huh?" I glance at him out of the corner of my eye. "If you don't tell me I will tell her that you told me everything and that I'm on your side."

I huff, "You are a mean, nasty old man."

"Start talking before she comes back, it won't take her long to figure out all the lights are already turned off." I laugh at him as he waves his hand at me.

I explain the details to him while he nods seeming to understand. "Now I don't know how to get her to forgive me for being stupid and not believing her over everyone else."

"You sleeping in the same bed?" He asked.

"Not much lately, I was staying in a hotel and then she was sick. Not much *sleeping* together going on."

"Well there you go." He said sitting back in his chair nodding his head.

"There you go?" I questioned his illogical response. He simply nods assured of his stance. "Okay. Well I still worry about her, I think she is having those dreams about Spencer again."He looks me over with a sudden concern.

Jack stands up abruptly, "Come with me." He said walking away to some dusty corner of the basement. He takes out a book from the drawer of an old chest, puts it on a table and flips through the dusty pages. "Here, read this," I look at the yellowed news article, with a picture of a car crumpled at the bottom of a cliff.

"Ava's mother?" I asked.

Jack nods, "Read it."

"It says that she skidded off the road and down the cliff."

"Through a barrier," I shrug not understanding his point. "It was the middle of the afternoon on a straight road, and it wasn't raining," I straighten staring at him in awe. "Now you're getting it, aren't you? Now look at this picture."

I smile at the obvious picture of Ava's mother, "She's beautiful, her mother … Lillah?" He nods and hands me another picture. "It's her again."

"Pay attention that one was after Ava's father died and two days before her death." The beautiful woman holding her daughter's hand smiles but her eyes are different, the emptiness is apparent, especially in contrast to the other photo. "She died when he died. Those eyes of hers never lived again." Jack said sighing with the sounds of grief still in his heart.

"She committed suicide?" I asked watching his heartbroken nod. "But Ava was only five, how could she give up like that leaving her little girl alone?"

"She was heartbroken beyond repair. Ava is a lot like her mother, she loves deeply and passionately, loyal to the end but her strength comes from her father, a fighter to the end. And I hope it remains that way. Now until you see these eyes." He said holding up the emptiness picture to me. "You have nothing to worry about, her strength has not diminished in the slightest; you're just missing something."

"What am I missing then?"

"I don't know, she's your wife." He puts his book up and waves me to follow quickly back to our spots.

"Maybe you could talk to her?" I asked him.

"Nope, I don't like to get in the middle of folks business," he said. I roll my eyes at him.

Ava walks in, obviously exasperated with the old man as he smiles obnoxiously at her. Neither saying a word however.

"I think I need a drink," he said getting up to get a bottle.

"I don't think you are suppose to drink," Ava said to him.

"Eeehhh," he waves her off. "Sean wants to drink and I can't let him drink alone." I sit up meeting Ava's glare and immediately hold up my hands, defending myself the best way I know how.

"Fine, then I'm drinking too," she said.

"Yeah this is it," Jack said holding out his glass to us. "To a great woman, the love of my life, my inspiration, my reason for being and the best fuck I ever had." He smiles with pride before downing his drink while I choke trying to hold my laughter in when Ava glares at him. We continue to toast to semi-normal things at first but soon they become absurd. Jack stands up again, swaying, "To ...." He stands for awhile thinking. "Oh hell to that horse faced, loud mouth Darleen. Maybe one day I will drink enough to be able to look at her without wanting to vomit my lunch. I look over at Ava as she shakes her head at him but we both follow his lead. Jack rubs his face, "Good stuff," he said wobbling and almost falling.

"Granddad, I think that's enough," Ava said reaching out for him at the same time I do.

"Yeah, kind of tired anyway," he said sitting his glass down and making his way towards the stairs.

"Do you want me to help you," Ava asked him.

"Hell no!"

"Sean could …"

"I can do it myself!" He yelled.

Ava holds up her hands and leans back into the couch, exasperated again. We listen carefully until we hear him stumble his way to bed, both of us sighing with a smile, relieved that the old man made it. I move, sitting next to Ava, "I'm glad he made it because I don't think I could of."

She laughs, "I know, me either."

"Maybe we should go to bed too." I said helping her up, leaning on each other the entire way.

I undress while watching Ava undress too, "Are you getting naked?"

"Why?" She asked stumbling backwards to look at me sternly.

"I just want to know how I should dress for bed. I wasn't sure if you are still mad at me or …"

She narrows her eyes as she walks towards me shaking her shoe at me. I fall back against the bed as she leans in, "You know it's funny that you ask me that, when I remember you specifically telling me that you always sleep naked and I wasn't allowed to do anything but."

I laugh remembering, "That was on our island."

"Yeah that, it's funny," she said walking away.

"You know what's funnier? I only said that so I could keep you naked and touch you all night … naked." I smile proudly when she looks my way. She starts to smile but gets a serious expression on her face before walking back to me again.

"Wait that's not funny," she said causing me to fall back against the bed again.

I look away from her and think about it for a few seconds before looking back at her, "Yes it is."

"Well you know what?" She asked, as I look her over, in her black underwear.

"You are so hot," I said staring at her breasts.

"No, that's not it," I narrow my eyes at her. "On the plane, you know the one that crashed?"

I roll my eyes nodding. *Like there's been more than one.* "I told you, I didn't care about you but actually I stared at you the whole time you slept, daydreaming about being with you."

"I knew it! You are a groupie." I laugh at her, she smiles taking off her underwear and gaining my full attention.

"And now I live with you," she said climbing into bed, my eyes following after her. I climb in next to her naked, as well.

"First off that's not funny either, second you live with me because you're my wife and third …" I pause thinking.

"What's third?" She asked.

"Hold on I'm thinking," I said lying next to her on my side. I lose my balance and fall against her before straightening up again. "Oh hell I don't know." I surrender scooting down into the tiny bed.

We lie quietly facing each other, watching each other's eyes get heavier and heavier. I slowly drift off, getting carried away in my dreams. Ava keeps showing up within them, telling me stupid things for some reason, but always in her black underwear. I finally ask her why and she strips them off entirely pushing me into bed and climbing in on top of me. I grab her hips, rolling her over and sliding inside of her, enjoying the sensations as I listen to her moans. I push up on her against the wall and down on the floor and back in the bed again. I can't get enough.

CRAKHhhhhh!

I open my eyes wide and instantly focusing in on her blue eyes. "What was that?" She asked sitting up to listen.

"I don't know," I said checking out her ass.

"*Hey.*" She interrupted my drooling thoughts.

"What?" I asked lying on my back watching her suddenly avoiding my eyes. I move my leg around her and sit up pulling her close. "Don't worry … I'll protect you," I said brushing my lips along her neck.

"I think I am still drunk, I'm feeling a little dizzy," she said in forced breaths.

"Good, because I am too," I said caressing her.

"I think I should lie down, Sean." I move away from her and wave my hand across her side of the bed. We lock eyes as she lies back slowly. I lick my lips anticipating. She instantly sits back up cradling my face and grabbing my lips with hers.

I take her back down into the bed, maneuvering on top of her as I hold her arms above her head. Feeling her skin with my lips, tasting her with my tongue until I am satisfied, and caressing her legs around my waist. Releasing her arms I maneuver myself directly into her warmth, feeling her wetness take me over. I hover over her eagerly, and passionately moving inside her and seeking her lips whenever the need overwhelms me. Her soft pressing hands wander the muscles in my back, but they never stop encouraging me to keep going. All the while, the bed creaks and clanks like it is a hundred years old. The more we move the louder it is. I try to be softer but the bed still cries out defiantly. I try not to laugh but when I see Ava biting her bottom lip, I break. "Stop laughing," I said avoiding her eyes and burying my face into her hair, listening to her giggle. Neither of us are able to block out the incorrigible bed. "If you don't stop laughing, I'm going to have to make you stop," I whisper into her ear. She holds her breath but starts giggling again. Leaning up, I see her beautiful smile, "Fine, you asked for it." I pick her up and hold her on top of me, working my erection in and out of her, until the moans take over the giggling. The creaking is less but the moaning is becoming louder and more uncontrolled. She sits up tall on my erection, gripping her breasts and moaning her pleasures while letting me hold her in perfect position. Gripping her hips tight, I move her body up and down on my hardened dick, jolting us both into shivering releases. I lay her down gently in the old bed, caressing her lips with mine the whole way down and into the plush softness.

Suddenly the bed cracks loudly and we both instantly stop. "Sean," Ava said looking at me with concern. With an abrupt crack, the bed crashes through the frame straight to the floor. I barely catch hold of the headboard before it comes down on top of us. We lay in the fallen bed frozen until everything stops cracking and smashing into the floor. When all seems peaceful again, we look around us, and both break out into hysterics.

"How fucking old is this bed?" I asked her.

"I don't know. It's been here for as long as I can remember though." I maneuver the headboard away from us and sigh as I move back to Ava.

"Come here and protect me from anything else in your grandparents' house that might decide to attack me," we curl into each other tight and I inhale her dizzying scent, feeling complete again.

❦

The next morning, I awake with the bright sun highlighting the mess we created the night before. *Jack is going to come after me with his shotgun when he sees this. At least we're married, or I might need to make my own funeral arrangements.* He has threatened to kill me before. The first time we met he came at me with two shotguns, one to blow my head off and one to finish me off. I am sure he would have fired a shot at me, if not for Ava standing in front of me with Lillah in her arms. Luckily, by that point Ava had a ring on her finger or I wouldn't have been allowed in the house. However, I still had to sleep in a cot, in the barn, while my daughter and my future wife slept soundly in doors.

Struggling with my hangover, I get up and shower and prepare to catch my flight back to Atlanta. When I walk out into the living room, I see her outside on the patio with Jack, leaning against him as he consoles her.

"He's leaving today?" Jack asked. Ava nods. "And you, when are you going home?"

"I don't know. It doesn't feel like my home anymore," she said and my mouth falls open.

"How can that be?"

"He doesn't trust me, and if he can't do that then there really is no place for me there."

"Are you lying to him?" He asked not even bothering to confirm by looking at her shaking head. "He was hurt, give him some time to heal before you give up on him."

"I hope he heels soon, I miss him," she said mirroring my thoughts about her.

"You know what you need?" Jack asked as she questions him with a sweet smile. "Smoke, he likes you better than anyone else anyway. Maybe you can get that stubborn horse to ride smoother. Go on," Jack urged her while I watch her walk away, wiping the tears from her eyes.

"Did you hear what you needed to know?" Jack said, glancing back at me.

I huff shaking my head, "Enough. I heard enough."

"Good." Jack said getting up and leaning against one of the columns. "And Sean?"

"Yes sir?"

"If you ever doubt my granddaughter again I will kick your ass," Jack said standing tall and straightening his belt. I laugh but his narrowed eyes focus on me hard. "Now what the hell are you still doing here?"

"Sir?"

"You can't really apologize to her from there son."

"Yes sir." I pick up my bag and leave it on the porch before darting off after Ava. I find her already preparing Smoke to ride. She looks up at me with a weak smile, "I'm sorry. I'm so sorry." I said taking her in my arms and pressing my lips to her head, while she holds onto me tight. "I love you so much that it makes me crazy sometimes. Coming home and finding him … it made me insane. I can't even bear to think about another man touching you or hurting you."

"Like Joel?" She said backing away from me to look into my eyes.

I pull her back into my arms, "I wanted to believe you, but I couldn't understand what was happening to you and I certainly would have never considered my friend ever doing anything like that to you. I wanted to kill him, and I nearly did." I said kissing her and holding her tight to my chest. "I will never doubt you again, please forgive me, Ava."

"I do forgive you, I love you too much not too."

I exhale in relief, "So when are you coming home?"

"I don't know. I need to help granddad with my grandmother's things, make sure he has a way to get to places. I have a lot to do, Sean."

"You are coming home … aren't you?" I asked warily. "I don't want to be there if you're not there. I will do whatever you want, kick Rebecca out too, quit the movie … whatever you want."

"It would be nice if she wasn't there anymore but I trust you to do what's best." I nod as her expression changes, "I need some time away though. Kyle is coming up in a few days and he is going to bring Lillah with him."

"Ava please."

She quickly cradles my face, in her hands, "I just need some time away from that, not you. I love you. I will always come home to you as long as you want me to."

"Always sweetheart, I always will want you to."

"It's nice being here Sean, it's freeing, clears my head and gives me a chance to regain my strength and deal with my grandmother's death. And I haven't been to my father's, nor my mother's grave in years, either." I lay my head against hers wanting to argue with her but am unable to. "Give me a few weeks and I will be back in time to play your groupie girl in your stupid movie you tricked me into doing."

"I didn't trick you … groupie." She smiles nodding, as I trace my fingers along her face. "I guess I can deal with that, not happily but I will deal with it, as long as you call me every day and night." She laughs at my ridiculous pouting. "I love you. Don't ever doubt that, no matter how much you drive me crazy I will always love you." I said taking her lips into mine softly. Smoke tired of waiting, pokes his head into my arm. "I'm leaving, give me a minute," I said to him earning a frustrated snort.

"You better go, or you're going to be rushing and I know how you are when you are stressed."

I kiss her one more time, before pulling away. "I love you Ava." I yelled to her as I walk back towards the house.

"I love you too," she yelled back joyfully.

I can't wipe the smile off my face as I race to catch up with the car that has come for me. When I reach the house, I race to the porch grabbing my bag and shake Jack's hand before forcing him into an impromptu hug.

"Okay now, enough of that. Just get on out of here before you piss me off." Jack said waving me on.

"You're a mean old bastard, Jack." I said as he shakes his cane at me. I laugh handing the driver my bag and relaxing back into the car, "Oh Jack, sorry about the bed?" I said knowing the stir I was about to cause.

He scrunches his eyebrows, "What did you do to my bed?"Jack wobbles quickly on his cane reaching the back bedroom in a loud huff. "Son of a bitch!" *I don't know how much it costs to fix an old bed but whatever it is it's worth it just to have this moment.* "You broke my bed!" He yelled walking out fast as we start to pull away, "I'm going to kick your ass, Sean! Where's my gun!" He said turning around and searching for his shotgun. "Knew I should have shot him the first time I saw him," he mumbled as he continues to search.

"Mean old bastard," I mumbled. As we leave, I catch sight of Ava riding Smoke across the clearing, hair blowing behind her, bright smile on her face and the sparkle back in her eyes. I lean back in my seat enjoying the view.

Chapter 18

Rebecca

It is days before I hear from him but my anger has not diminished any. "What the hell were you thinking?" I yelled.

"Shut up Rebecca," Joel huffs back.

"Joel, I just don't get how you could be so foolish."

"I'm still in pain here why are you giving me hell?"

"That's your own fault, you should have shut your mouth and let him get it out of his system rather than piss him off even more."

"I couldn't help it, I enjoyed pissing him off."

"Well you certainly succeeded in doing that."

"Don't lecture me, at least I saved your ass." Joel sighed.

"I believe I actually saved your ass - sweetheart. I did accidently lose your drugs, throw out the mask before the cops arrived and refuse to press charges against you. Without me, all they have is Ava's word against yours. They have no case against you baby, thanks to me." Joel mumbles his praises reluctantly. While I sink down deep into my seat, "Now, I am going to have to become the greatest friend in the world to Sean."

"He's letting you stay in the guesthouse?" Joel asks in shock.

"Baby, he understands that I am scared of you, after all, you did beat me up. Sean loves to protect his women." He laughs nearly causing me to laugh. "Laugh if you want but you need to stay clear of him before you get yourself killed."

"I didn't know you cared?" He smarts off clearly taking a drink in between breaths.

"Well your life insurance hasn't been paid in months, so I don't have much of a choice do I?"

"Touching, I think I will hang up the phone before I get all misty eyed." I laugh at him, knowing he still loves me.

CB&O

Over the next couple of weeks, while Ava is gone, I am able to work my way back into Sean's good graces. I am the perfect houseguest. I have his dinner heated and ready for him every night. Make light conversation about his day and wish him well for the next. And I always make sure to leave early and way before he thinks about asking me to and most importantly, I never push him to talk about anything sexual or even close to. He is lonely and even more so as each day passes but today is the day I make my move. With my killer dress on, I meet him at the set, making sure to take a taxi so he will have to drive me home. Waiting for him in his trailer, I greet him with a vibrant smile when he opens the door.

"Hi," I said lengthening my bare legs out in front of him.

"Hi. What are you doing here?" He said looking around nervously.

"Well you looked a little down last night so I thought we would go out to dinner tonight."

"I don't …"

"I will not take no for an answer Sean. Besides I am dying to get out of that house for awhile and I am already dressed." I said standing up and twirling slowly for him. "Please don't make me go home disappointed in my new dress."

"Rebecca, I don't think I am in the mood, it's been a long day."

"Oh don't act like an old man, take me out for dinner, then we can go home. What's an hour or two of your time going to hurt? And wouldn't you like to get out and eat with other people for a change?"

He sighs loudly, "Yeah, okay, that actually does sound better than going home and staring at the walls."

I clap excitedly, "This is going to be so much fun!"

Sean takes me to a restaurant that knows him well. They greet him by his first name and makes sure we have a private table away from prying eyes. They treat me like a queen and I make sure to act the part so no one will think of treating me any other way.

Sean pulls out my chair for me, "Thank you," I said sitting down and trying to hold back my smile.

"You're welcome," he said sitting down across from me.

"See you look better already," I said.

"I feel better, and I hate to say it, but you were right. It feels good to be out of the house for awhile."

"Wow did Sean Grant actually admit that I was right about something?"

He laughs, "Don't get used to that."

"I wouldn't dare." I said as his eyes wander the room. "So how did everything go today?"

"Good I guess. Your husband showed up today." He glances over at me with a scowl.

"You didn't kill him did you?"

"No, he was smart enough to stay clear of me."

"How does he look? Does he still look like he was run over by a semi ... twice?"

Sean smiles, "I don't know about twice but at least once."

I roll my eyes playfully, "He did deserve it, and I can't say I miss him."

Leaning on the table towards me, his green eyes focus on me, sending amazing sensations through my body, "Why did you marry him?"

"Ummm, well, he was security I guess."

"That's it? Security? You married him for security?" I nod taking a drink. "No perfect romance that caused you to fall deeply in love?" He said leaning back in his chair and pressing his soft lips to his glass.

"Me romance, love? You no better than that." I laugh.

"You don't think you could ever fall in love?"

Looking away from him, "No."

"No? So you have never been in love?"

"I was once," I said concentrating on my food.

"And who was this Romeo that swept you off your feet and destroyed the chances for every other man?" He asked smiling.

"You." I said erasing his smile instantly. "It's true, you're the only one I have ever loved and if that couldn't work out I can't imagine that love is all that wonderful. So I chose security."

"I don't think what we had was love, Rebecca."

"Then what was it, Sean?"

"Two people who were desperate to fill holes in their lives."

"And what hole was I filling?"I ask sharply.

"Your overwhelming need to have all the attention on you," he said. "Don't get mad."

"I'm not mad." He rolls his eyes at me. "So what we had meant nothing to you at all? Wow Sean, kind of wish we hadn't come out to dinner now."

"Don't be like that. It meant something, *you* meant something to me. It tore me up when I caught you and Joel. I even blamed myself for awhile. We had a lot of fun and many great times but at the same time, we fought all the time. And I didn't have enough time or energy to give you the attention you needed."

"Some would have been nice," I mumbled.

He sits back with a rugged exhale. "Are we really going to go back down that road?"

"No, I guess not," I said picking at my food. "We did have some great times though. Do you remember that night we stayed up all night watching movies?" I smiled at him.

Laughing suddenly, "Yeah that was a good night," he said smiling back at me obviously remembering.

"How many times did we have sex?" I asked carefully.

"I don't know, a lot. We had four movies."

"I still can't believe they put the wrong movie in our box and we ended up having sex to that cartoon movie." Sean laughs aloud suddenly. "Those poor dancing bears are probably scarred for life seeing what we did," I said laughing with him.

Sean shakes his head, "They weren't bears; they were raccoons or something."

"Raccoons? You have such a bad memory, they were Koala bears, remember they had an Australian accent?"

He leans back in his chair laughing freely, "Oh yea." He said straightening and focusing as he tries to remember. "G'day! Let's dance," he mimics while dancing in his seat.

I spit my drink out laughing. "I can't believe you just did that."

"I can't believe you just spit all over our food," he laughs.

"Shut up," I look down at my food glancing up at him whenever I think I might catch his eyes. We continue discussing old times and what we have heard about people we used to know. After Sean paid the bill, we head back home. "You know what we should do?" I said lightly touching his leg as he drives.

"What's that?" He asked.

"Get a movie, make some popcorn, and veg. out talking about old times."

He glances over at me with a questioning expression, "A movie?"

"Of course, and popcorn or I'm not interested."

"I think I can manage popcorn and the movie but that's it." He looks over smiling at me, sending exhilarating chills through my body. When we get home, I lean against him laughing as we approach the main house. For the first time in a long while, we are spending the entire night together, just the two of us. If all goes well I will spend the night not only in his house but in his bed too. I look up at his smiling eyes anticipating waking up in the morning with them staring at me the same way.

Sean and I laugh constantly as we prepare for our movie night. Nudging each other, mocking each other's usual responses until we finally sit down in front of the television. I lower the lights and he starts the movie. The movie is a horror film, something I specifically picked out to give me an excuse for being close to him. I gradually work my way closer and closer, until I am nearly in his lap. I graze his neck with my lips and he doesn't move. I encourage him to drink more before I begin playing with his hair. Sean relaxes and I move my hand down his chest. Taking a breath, I grab a blanket and wrap myself in it before removing my clothing. He looks down at me with a suspicious expression before I push my hand down his pants and work to get my hand around his dick. He pulls my hand out and scrambles away from me.

"What are you doing, Rebecca?"

"Come on Sean, you know you want to. Aren't you lonely? You know I can make you feel good." I stand up dropping the blanket and exposing my nude body in front of him. "I know you want me, and all you have to do is take it. We don't have to tell anyone." I push him onto his back and crawl down to his rising erection and trail my tongue down his strained zipper. "Let me stick your dick in my mouth, please Sean. I want to taste it so bad." I grab his hand and pull it to my breasts sliding it down in between my legs before he jerks it away.

"No, Rebecca." He says scooting further away from me. Sean grasps his head, and I realize the drug I gave him is beginning to work. "I need to get some air." He said stumbling to his feet and outside to lean against a wall, struggling to fight the drug.

Smiling happily, I rush into the bathroom to prepare myself for some great sex, and text Joel that I am about to get pregnant with Sean's child. I can't wait to see the look on his mothers face when I have her precious son locked to my side for life. *A miracle baby*, that's what I will call it and Sean won't be able to deny such a miracle for me, not again. I walk out of the bathroom, and see Sean leaning on Ava. *What the fuck is she doing home!*

Sean has his hands all over her, which she laughs off until she sees me. "Sean honey, let's go to bed." Ava said taking hold of his arm and dragging him away. *Oh no she doesn't, I will have him fuck me right in front of her if I have to.* I barely get the idea before Ava suddenly pulls away from him and runs towards their room with Sean chasing after her. Ava stops short of going inside, letting him rip her dress off the moment he reaches her. He follows her down into the big chair outside their room and spreads her legs out wide in front of him. My mind begins to scream for him to stop but I can't get to him in time. I watch him press his proud dick deep inside of her, closing his eyes and groaning happily. He comes like a champion and she enjoys it not caring who hears her.

I grab my clothes and return to the guesthouse defeated and angry. *I hate her.* She has ruined my entire life and I will do everything I can to ruin hers.

Chapter 19

Sean

I wake up with a terrible hangover, and shockingly with Ava lying on my chest.

She wakes smiling at me, "Good morning."

"Good morning, when did you get home?" I asked causing her to look at me with a questioning expression.

Running her fingers through my hair, "Oh baby, you got a little drunk last night and then welcomed me home with a lot of hands and lot of excitement." She laughs kissing me. "But I am not complaining." Ava is forgiving of my forgetfulness and is kind enough to let me try and repeat some of our escapades from the night before. And I am so glad she did.

ೞೋ

Having everyone home together again and happy, motivates me even more so to get this movie done. We are playing catch up now, too many last minute rewrites, interruptions, and cast issues - I being one of them. It did not go unnoticed that Joel was roughed up severely. Not to mention, for weeks my knuckles needed to be attended to before filming and now that he is back on set, he avoids me as much as possible. The intensity on set is starting to get to people. We are all ready to be done but today is different. Today Ava is going to be on set with me and even though she is nervous as hell about it, I am excited about having the experience with her. It is simple but something fun to look forward too.

"Are you ready to go?" I said finding Ava sitting on the edge of our bed looking as if she is going to be sick at any moment. "Baby, are you okay?"

"I think I'm going to be sick," she said falling back into bed and breathing forcefully.

"It's only your nerves, sweetheart. You'll feel better once you see how easy it is."

"But I would hate to ..." She said as I pull her up into my arms.

"It's only nerves. I promise they will pass, besides you don't have any lines." She starts to argue with me but I stop her quickly. "No lines sweetheart, you simply have to kiss me, which I know for a fact," I said leaning down to capture her lips in between mine, "you are very good at." She smiles wide at me. "Come on sexy, let's go." As soon as we arrive, Carol runs up with her clipboard and a stressed smile. "Okay sweetheart we have to be on set here soon, so you need to go with Carol here and she will get you where you need to be," I said kissing her quickly but she pulls me back to her.

"Please don't let me look stupid," Ava whispered in my ear before she lets go and walks off with Carol. I watch her cute ass walk away from me, looking back at me once as she bites her bottom lip.

"You will be fine," I mouth to her. The scene is at a worn out motel bar, in South Carolina, where I am supposed to be staying for the night after doing some crazy stunts, an opening for the main act. The crowd is impressed, especially the young girls in the crowd. Girls are going to be everywhere in the bar, just waiting to be noticed but I am supposed to choose only one for the night - Ava. I have to pick her out of pack of admiring girls and kiss her to make sure she is the one I want. Once I decide she is, I take her back to my room. And that's it. Only a small town stop, impress a group of local girls enough that I can get one to spend the night with me, a supposed routine for my character. It is not suppose to be difficult but my character has yet to become the well-known stunt master as of yet so a local bar is about the best I can get for the time being.

I arrive on set and walk up on Ethan as he looks at me with concern, "Have you seen Ava?"

"Not since we first got here, why?" Ethan shakes his head laughing. "What asshole?"

"You're going to flip your lid when you see what they have her in," he said as I look at him nervously.

"That bad?" I ask.

"I don't know if bad is the right word, let's just say she's going to be easy to pick out of a crowd."

"Wonderful, that should make it interesting," I said at the same time seeing Joel wave at me. *Fucking prick.*

"He sure is being bold today," Ethan said. "I still don't know why you didn't press charges against him."

"I told you, I don't want to force Ava to go through that if she doesn't want too. It is only her word against his now that the evidence is lost. Besides I enjoyed handling it myself," I smile wide at Ethan's stern glare.

"So I assume that since Ava is back home Rebecca is gone?"I give him a quick glance and try to ignore what I expect is coming next. "No? Sean I don't understand why you protect her, you know she's nothing but trouble."

"I do not want to have this conversation with you for the fiftieth time. I have grown tired of it. I promise as soon as I can find her some work - outside of this state, then I will scoot her out the door. I just can't leave her with nothing." Ethan starts to speak again but I give him a stern look before he huffs and walks away. *I feel like I'm on a fucking rollercoaster already today.* I look up and see a group of extras come in for the scene and right behind them is my girl, Ava. *Damn!* She has on some tiny cut off shorts with some extremely high heels and a button down shirt she has tied up in front, showing off her belly button. Her diamond is sparkling, they forgot to ask her to take it out. I shake my head staring at her until she sees me. She looks incredible and I have to adjust myself as she walks towards me. She cautiously tries to balance on her towering heels, tripping as she reaches me. I hide my laughter behind my hand.

"I look ridiculous don't I?" She said pitifully.

"You look hot as hell," I said looking her up and down. "The heels may be a bit much and I don't think girls had belly button piercings back then." She looks down nervously. "Come here," I said carefully removing the diamond. I caress her stomach with my thumb and send us both to a place we do not need to be right now. She starts to kiss me and Daniel sticks his hand in between us.

"Hey kids, how about we save that for the camera?" He smiles making his way through us to pass.

"I just want to get this over with, I can't believe I agreed to do this," she said as I reach for her hand and pull her to me.

I tap the end of her nose lightly until she looks at me, "Don't worry about it." Daniel waves his hands at me, stressed out as usual. "Alright let's go and you can get this over with ... having to kiss me. Oh how horrible." I said smacking her ass, encouraging her before we have to separate. I wait as they touch up my makeup and my clothes, turning my t-shirt's sleeves just right, messing with my hair, and checking my jeans for one final check.

My co-star, Carter laughs at me as he watches them fuss over me. "Pretty boy," he yells at me. I simply wink at him with a smile.

We all take are places and begin the scene. Everything goes well until one of the girls falls. It was not Ava but by the glaring look that she gives Ava, I assume she had something to do with it. We begin again, and again and again. The retakes begin to mount as everyone becomes on edge and Ava even more so. I take the time to reassure her and the next take begins a little smoother all the way up to me kissing Ava, but she faints. I catch her but barely in time.

"Ava sweetheart, are you okay?" I said cradling her to my chest.

"Yes, sorry," Ava said still dazed. An assistant rushes over with some water.

"Is she going to be able to do this?" Daniel asked.

"I'm fine," she said as I roll my eyes at her usual comment.

"Ava?" I said.

"*I am.* I'm fine, I only needed some water," she gets up forcing a smile and walks back to her original place.

Daniel looks at me, "I guess she's fine," I said to him.

Everyone takes their places once again and I glance at Ava one last time while she ignores me.

"Alright people, let's try this one more time. Now is everybody good? No one's thirsty, feeling unstable on their heels, feeling faint or needing to go to the bathroom or something?" Daniel said sarcastically. I eye him and he backs off remembering whose wife he is referring too.

Scene: *TC (Trey Castor)*

I sit at a table near the bar, drinking, and twirling my bottle cap as I listen to my manager go over the details of our successful night. I can hear the girls giggling as they mention my name and suggesting more than once the things they would like to do to me. I ignore them … mostly. Once I am ready to leave, my curiosity gets the better of me and I have to verify their interest by winking at all of them, sending them into a frenzy. My manager, Olin, rolls his eyes.

"So TC which one is it going to be tonight?" He asked me as I smile wildly at the giggling girls.

"I don't know I might have to try a few out before I find the right one. Or maybe, I will take them all."

"Go, before I hate you anymore than I already do," Olin said waving me off in frustrated disgust.

I get up from our table and smoothly walk towards the girls and they instantly get up and run over to me. Five girls pawing at me and pushing each other to get closer to me. I eye them all before checking their table again to look for the sixth. *I know there were six of them.* I search for her and find her sitting away from us on a stool, her gorgeous legs crossed as if she is waiting for me. She takes a drink of her beer and smiles sweetly at me. If she isn't going to come to me, then I of course, can't help but want to go to her. I move away from the other girls and walk up to the bar leaning against it ignoring her, making her wait until she can't stand it any longer. I look her over, before taking hold of her face and pulling her lips to mine. The kiss is deep and suggestive. I pull away from her and she instantly begins to fidget, and bite her bottom lip. She looks up at me still trying to catch her breath. Grabbing her hand, I pull her along with me, winking at my disgusted manager as I take my girl for the evening out the door.

End Scene: TC (Trey Castor)

Once the scene is final, I turn to Ava and kiss her, "You were perfect sweetheart."

She smiles, "Really?"

"Really, you were amazing. That kiss was incredible too. I almost forgot who I was."

"Well it's not like I had any lines, it's pretty easy to only sit there and giggle and stare at you until you kiss me."

"It's not that easy. I mean it had to be all you could do to keep from running at me and pawing at me too." I rub my chest until she smacks my arm, causing us both to laugh. I put my arms around her. "You know if we don't have to do this scene again then we have time to go back to my trailer and …" I grab her ass in the tiny shorts letting my fingers slip underneath. "Ohhhh," I moan burying my face into her hair. "You have to get these shorts off, they are way too small. I'm going to lose my mind."

"Sean," I turn to see Daniel coming towards us.

"Was that good?" I asked him.

"Yeah that was perfect but we are behind so we need to quickly get you two ready for the next scene." I look at him confused, "You didn't get the changes this morning?"

"What changes?" I asked.

"There were some rewrites, with you and Ava in the scene after this one."

I stare at him in disbelief. "Daniel there isn't supposed to be another scene after this one. The scene after this would be us having sex."

"Exactly, everyone feels it will be a great addition …" He looks at me as my anger rages to the surface. "Calm down Sean, read the script. It's not long, shorter than this one even. I promise." He hands the script over to me and walks away.

"Ava we need to get you ready dear," Carol said grabbing Ava's arm as she begs for me to rescue her.

"It's alright baby, I promise I will take care of it." She nods dragging herself alongside Carol. I go back to my trailer and read over the scene, getting more furious by the second when Ethan comes in. "Did you read this shit?" I yelled.

"I did but not until you were already shooting the previous. I checked her contract too and she did not wave the nudity clause. They told her it wouldn't matter since she is only doing the one scene in the bar." I sigh shaking my head.

I slam my fists on the table, "Joel." I said furious. I instantly go to search for him.

"What the fuck are you doing Joel?" I asked shaking the script at him.

"Whoa. Calm down Sean. What's your problem?" He asked.

"This script!" I yelled.

"Sorry, it's been approved," he smiles at me. My fists tighten and I move towards him as a guard promptly takes hold of me.

"You knew I would be fucking ready to tear your head off over this," I snarled at him.

He cocks his head with a smile, "It's my movie Sean and I want to make it better." He raises his eyebrows and smiles. "I of all people know - those breasts will sell."

Lunging for his head, "I will fucking kill you!" The guard struggles to hold me back, until two others come over to help. I calm enough that they let me go but they do not go far. "You can forget it, she isn't doing it."

"I will sue her." Joel said waiting for me to break again.

"Sue her then, but she isn't doing this. You can edit her out of the movie and me too for that matter. Have fun trying to hire an attorney with nothing."

Daniel steps in between us with shaky hands, "Please, please, we can work something out. I am sure we can figure out something else that will please everyone." I look down at Daniel. "Don't worry Sean I will figure out something else, no reason for all this commotion." I nod and agree to work out something.

∞

Entering the set of the motel room I cannot believe what I have to do. I wait for Ava agonizing, and I do not feel any better when I see her trembling and scared to death. She knows and now I have to try and convince her to trust me. I put my arms around her, feeling her trembling to the core. "Ava."

"I can't do this," she says.

"Trust me, we have it worked out. They are going to close the set and Daniel is going to set the cameras at a certain angle and the rest is left up to me. Do you trust me?"

She nods trying to calm down for me. "Okay, now get in the bed with me and take everything off but your panties." I grip her face as she starts to cry. "Trust me Ava, no one is going to see anything." Sighing I take her hand and lead her slowly to the bed glancing at Daniel who seems to be holding up his end of the bargain. I close my eyes briefly before I get in the bed and begin taking off everything for her as tears stream down her cheeks. Stopping at her bra, "Press against me and I am going to hide you. I will pull it off, don't move away from me. Okay?" She nods. "You have to stop crying or it's going to take even longer, follow my lead and it will be over." I kiss her trying to comfort her. Jerking off my shirt, I throw it to an assistant and nod to Daniel to begin. I wipe her tears away, asking for a little touch up but not giving them much room to work.

"Lockdown," Daniel yelled.

"Close your eyes and concentrate on me Ava, I will take care of everything else," I whisper to her. Pulling her face to mine, I kiss her and make sure to cover her from every view point as I simulate having sex with my wife on camera. I moan feeling her, more than I should at this moment. Concentrating on something else I try to calm myself and step back into character slowly. She is apparently incapable of the same, making it nearly impossible for me not to lose my mind. *Damn, I forgot to prepare for this.* Being able to feel her I am hard as hell and she is enjoying it. She has completely forgotten about the cameras with her eyes closed. I don't know where she is, but she begins moaning and causes me to slip and both of us to groan. Trying to hold her still without ruining the scene, I can barely function, not to mention think. I push her down into the bed, making sure to stay against her, purposely putting myself in control of the movement. Ava is lost within it, moaning, and rubbing her hands all over me, driving me completely insane. *Focus Sean. You need to protect her.* I watch her moaning and writhing underneath me. *I'm not going to make it!* I fake an orgasm surprising Ava but at least she catches on quickly.

Once the scene is final, I call for a robe for Ava and myself. Daniel smiles with a nod in my direction as Joel approaches yelling at him. I am sure it is about the scene that he did not write. I wait as Daniel waves me on, assuring me he got what he wanted and what the powers at be wanted as well. Joel is steaming and I smile as he swears at my existence. I take little time in deciding what to do next, I nearly carry Ava back to my trailer. Taking her by the hand I lead her to the bedroom, locking the door behind us. "I love you," I said as I feel underneath her robe. Seeing her, I exhale deeply and brush my lips along her neck, pushing everything off my body before I pull her on top of me on the bed. "I have to feel you before I lose my damn mind, Ava." I sigh blissfully as I find what I am looking for deep inside her.

Graciously, she sits up riding me and allowing me to lay back and enjoy it. She is incredible, moaning, and whispering to me. She handles me perfectly but she suddenly slows, causing me to grow impatient with her, "Keep going. Don't stop!" She relinquishes her control, allowing me to find the pace I desire. I find my peace, raising her legs high and moving my erection in and out of her rapidly until I feel her powerful hold. Feeling her orgasm brings out all that has built up inside me. I push every ounce into her until I am reduced to a shivering, happy man. "You nearly killed me in that last scene, Ava. I was trying so hard to be good and not take you in front of everyone. But you and you're moaning and rubbing. And me forgetting to wear anything to prevent from feeling you rub against me." Her innocent smile says everything. "Uh-huh, yes, you still have an incredible hold on me." I find her lips tenderly. "Just remember what I had to do for you next time you're mad at me."

Ava laughs, "Okay, you get one free pass."

"One! I should get a hundred for that."

"Don't push it," she said narrowing her eyes at me.

"50?" She looks away from me. "25?" She crosses her arms in between us. "10?" She glances at me. "I deserve at least 5 free passes. Hell that's probably only a month's worth anyway.

"Fine 5 free passes, and it's more like only a week's worth," she said giggling as I look at her.

"A week? Damn, I didn't realize I was such an ass."

She wraps her arms around my neck, "No, but you are still in husband training. You're not screwing up on purpose you just don't know any better yet."

"Is that so?" She nods with her smile stretching as far as it will go. I give her a wicked smile in return. "If you're going to be like this to me then I am going to go hang out with somebody else on my break," I edge out of bed but she quickly grabs hold of me pouting. "No, you're being mean to me and for no reason."

"Sean? Baby."

"No, have fun by yourself."

"But Sean," I shake my head grabbing my pants. "I'm sorry," she whispers.

"What's that?" I said holding my hand up to my ear.

"I'm sorry," I get a little closer to her and wait to hear it again. "I said I'm sorry ... Sean"

"Oh, well in that case I guess I can stay and hang out here with you for a little while longer." I crawl in over her, being welcomed in with warm hands and kisses.

"Do you think it was okay? The scene I mean," she asked.

"Yes I do, I think it was better than okay." I laugh at her as she blushes. "We are married now and you still blush, I love it."

"I am still in awe of you."

"Why?"

"I still can't believe you love me, you're supposed to love people like ...," she looks off into nowhere. "I don't know, Rebecca maybe."

"No Ava, only you," I tap her cheek lightly to get her attention. "Only you."

She gets a half a smile before suddenly looking panicked, "Sean move!" She pushes me off her and runs to the bathroom. I hear her get sick before I can get to her.

"Are you okay?" I look at her holding her stomach, shaking her head. "Your parts are over sweetheart, you shouldn't still be nervous."

She looks up at me still holding her stomach and her head. "I think maybe I am sick, this has happened a couple of times the last few days." She said as my eyes widen.

"Ava, why didn't you tell me that?"

"I didn't think it was anything but nerves"

"I'm getting the doctor." I said and quickly calling for someone to come look her over.

CR&RO

I sit barely eating my lunch as I wait for the details, expecting to hear that her nerves are getting the best of her. The door opens and the doctor comes out smiling at me. "She's okay?" I asked.

"She's fine, just fine," the doctor said.

"I knew it, nerves," I said shaking my head.

"No, not nerves," the doctor said.

"Then what is it?" I said getting up to catch her eyes as she follows behind the nurse. "Ava?"

"It's okay Sean, nothing's wrong," she said.

"Of course, you will need to confirm it with your doctor. Without the ability to run the proper tests I can't confirm," the doctor said to Ava.

"Tests? What tests? If nothing is wrong then why are you needing tests?" I asked her.

Ava ignoring me, "I understand, thank you," she says waving the doctor off.

Once they both leave, I take her hand and pull her to me searching her eyes. "Tell me. Why do you need tests?" I ask as my heart beats faster and faster.

"Calm down baby," she said.

"Don't baby me, tell me."

"I will if you will give me a chance to," she said waiting for me to shut up. I sigh and cross my arms waiting. She smiles at me suspiciously, "Sean."

"What Ava?"

"Do you want a girl or a boy?" She said tugging at my shirt playfully.

"What?"

She rolls her eyes, "They think I'm pregnant." She bites her lip as everything begins to make sense to me.

A smile grows across my face, "Are you sure?"

"Well we will need to confirm it with my doctor but I would say it is 99.5% sure." I scream joyfully, picking her up and kissing her everywhere I can. "I take this to mean that you're happy about it?" She giggles.

"Hell yes, I'm happy! Are you kidding? This is the best news I could have gotten. This day just got a hundred times better."

"Good, I'm pretty excited myself."

"Wow does that mean Jack's bed was better than we thought?" She laughs, burying her head into my chest. "Damn, I am going to have pay for that piece of shit bed to be completely restored," I said shaking my head. I look down at Ava's heavy eyes and calm understanding her emotions for the day a little better, "You're tired aren't you?" She nods. "And now we know why," I said playfully. "Go lay down and I will make you something to eat."

I lie in bed playing with Ava's hair as she sleeps in my arms. I smile like a fool staring at my beautiful wife. My daydreams take me to better days until Ethan comes in and signals for me to step outside with him. Kissing her gently I lay her carefully back in bed before I follow him outside.

"Feeling better?" Ethan asked.

I look over and see Ethan sitting in a chair with a stupid grin on his face, "I suppose."

He shakes his head laughing, "I should hope so. Damn."

"Damn what?"

"Sean, the whole fucking trailer was shaking."

I eye him, "No it wasn't."

"Oh yes it was, and by the way the walls are not that thick." I look at him questioning as he laughs harder. "Keep going! Don't stop!" He said dramatically as I roll my eyes.

"You're an asshole you know it?"

He continues to laugh, "Probably but lucky for you I actually heard that when I walked in to talk to you and not from outside the trailer."

"Asshole." I said relieved.

"Well hell Sean, you couldn't wait ten minutes?"

"No! After that scene are you kidding?" I look over at Ethan as he smiles up at me from his laptop.

"It was pretty hot, I have to say. I'm not sure how you handled it as well as you did."

"So what did you think of the scene?" I asked sitting down next to him.

"You were perfect, Sean. Ava was perfect and without giving anything away." I exhale, shaking off the last of my frustrations from earlier. "I have something I need to tell you before your next scene though." I look back at him guarded. "The powers at be, have decided they could save money and possibly make even more money if they use Ava for Aimee instead." When my mouth drops, Ethan laughs. "Good job little brother, they really liked the last scene. So much so, they are making Ava a key part of the movie."

I shake my head with my mouth wide open, "I don't think so Ethan, it's ..."

"Insane ... crazy?" I nod. "Yeah well for some reason they think it's the best idea in the world. Although I do understand their thinking." I raise my eyebrows at him. "Hear me out, it's not as if there are sex scenes only some minor speaking for her but I think she can handle it. It's a small part but a whole lot more meaningful if you relate it to what you two just did."

"Ethan, I am suppose to have a ton of girls in my past not only one that keeps popping up."

"I don't see getting your characters ego or sexual prowess across at this point in the movie being a problem. What isn't evident is why he becomes so *Reckless*, but I think it's clear if she is the one."

"She is only another girl to him," I said.

"I don't think so. She had to be more than that, she was pregnant with his child. He obviously had some kind of connection with her or he wouldn't have believed her when she said the baby was his. At least, he wanted to believe her." Ethan said obviously convinced of the idea.

I lean over resting my head in my hands, trying to get a feel of what it will be like to work those scenes with Ava. The intensity of those scenes with her, pregnant and vulnerable and me the one that holds their lives in my hands. *How easy is it going to be to watch her die, to watch my child die within her? I can't ... or maybe I don't want to know how that would feel? How do you put yourself within a character you don't ever want to be?*

Chapter 20

Ava

Even though I know Sean is somewhere nearby, I do not like waking up without him. I crawl my way to the edge of the bed before I roll back over and crush my face into the pillow all over again. *What's the hurry? I'm done for the day anyway.*

"Hey sleepy head? Are you going to get up some time today?" Sean said grabbing my semi exposed foot, pulling me towards him.

I turn over smiling wide at my sexy husband."No, I think I will stay here, in fact …" I reach up and grab a hand full of his shirt and pull him down on top of me. I suck on his lips and moan my desire for him in hopes to entice him to stay with me this time.

"Ava honey, I cannot do this with you all day," he said kissing me one last time as he gets a hold of me, keeping me at a safe distance from him. "I wish I could stay in bed with you, hell I wish I could take you home to our bed and not leave for days but I can't." His smile disappears with his sigh. "And actually you can't either."

I scoot away instantly, eyeing him, "What? Why?"

Sean reaches out grabbing my hands and pressing his soft lips to the underside of my wrists. I twist my body awkwardly away from him as he tries to pull me to him, "They really liked that last scene sweetheart."

"So!"

"So they want you to do Aimee's part now" *He said it so matter-of-factly it seemed like I should be excited about it but I am not … I'm terrified. She has speaking parts. Acting parts!* "Sean how is that possible, it's two different roles?"

"Not anymore. Now you are the girl that reappears pregnant … with my child. And since we are shown having sex, it only makes since both money wise and flow wise if the script changes in this direction."

"I thought this was a true story, how can it change?"

He laughs at me, "*Based* on a true story. Creative license you know, besides he obviously slept with her at some point who's to say it didn't happen this way?"

"Oh, wow Sean." I grab a pillow burying my face into it.

"I know, but it's really not that much more, only a few lines."

I jump up, "I don't have to have sex with you again do I?"

Sean laughs, "I am extremely hurt by that … but no, not on camera at least."

I crawl into his lap, "Will you help me?"

"Of course, and Ethan said to tell you he will be available as well."

Some little guy brings me a script to go over, my hands shake as I take it from him, unsure of what awaits me. Ethan helps me understand the character and how to approach each scene. It actually is not too much of a stretch for me. A scared pregnant girl unsure if the father of her child will hate her … or support her, sounds very familiar actually. However, things turned out better for me. Sean actually does love me, this guy was in love with another woman at the time. *Damn I wish I could drink.*

CR80

Walking with Ethan and Carol to the set, I am dressed in my new wardrobe of jeans and a well-worn t-shirt that is stretched tight over my fake baby belly. They for some reason were concerned about me looking fat. Daniel the director greets me warmly, putting his arm around my shoulder as he explains things to me. I am glad Ethan pulls me away from him, I am not comfortable with him being that close. It is going to be simple, walk into where Sean will be with all of his crew and his newly declared girlfriend. I have to interrupt him and … tell him. They are in their hometown of Tennessee, working in their custom fitted garage and trying to figure out new stunts for a series of shows they are going to be kicking off in Texas. My name is Aimee, Aimee Barron. *I have to remember to call him TC for Thomas Castor and not Sean. That's going to be hard.* They lockdown the set and on the other side of this door, the others begin their roles. Nerves creep into my body like needles piercing through my skin. *I miss when it was simply sweet butterflies.* I close my eyes and breathe until Carter walks up patting my arm.

"Ready?" He cocks his head to one side sympathetically. I shake my head. "You'll be fine, just breathe, they are going to focus on Sean's reaction to you anyway, not so much you."

We wait to get our cue and Carter takes me to where we are supposed to enter, where we wait again until we are to go. I am glad Carter has to enter before me, introducing me to the scene. I look down at my rounded belly figure and my mind goes a million miles a second. *Calm down Ava or they will make you do it again and again.* I close my eyes and next thing I know ... Carter is pulling me through the door, my security blanket. I follow behind him shuffling my heavy feet along with me. We approach a crew of people, most helping work on the car but a few going over ideas at a nearby table with Sean. *I mean TC! Dear God please help me get through this.* What I wasn't expecting was Tami. *I mean Lacey, Damn! I knew she was playing his love interest in this movie but I was not expecting her in these scenes. I don't know why, she is supposed to be a part of the crew ... his crew. Rambling, I'm rambling to myself and not paying one bit of attention.* I check back in luckily before I miss much, only some general hellos and nervous stares.

Scene: Reckless: Aimee / Ava

"Ummm TC, someone is here to see you," Carter. *I mean Mitch his manager said, fuuuckkk!*

"Really, who's that?" TC turns catching an eye full of me.

"You should go talk to her ... alone I think," Mitch says tapping him on the shoulder.

TC gets up from the table intense and focused, my heavy feet instantly try to carry me backwards. I look away from him, only to see Lacey staring a hole right through me. *Oh God.* I gulp as I match up with TC one on one.

"So you have something to say to me?" He said crossing his arms and glancing down at my stomach before resting on my watery eyes.

"Can we go somewhere a little more private?" I said gripping my trembling hands.

"This is private enough, just tell me what you have to say," he snapped.

I take a deep breath, feeling the tears making their way to the surface, "Do you remember me?" I said softly.

"What?" He yelled.

"Do you remember me? You know from South Carolina, the little town that you stopped in to do your show about six months ago? We met at the bar. I was sitting on a stool and then ..."

"Yeah I know, so what about it?" He stares into my eyes daring me to confess my secret.

The floor becomes my new focus as my back meets the wall, "So you do remember me?"

"I said I did, didn't I?" He snaps at me.

I cringe feeling his anger heat up my skin, "Well I just wanted to let you know that I ..." I force myself to look up at his harsh eyes. "I'm pregnant."

"I can see that. Are you claiming it's mine?" I nod while holding my breath. "Why should I believe that?"

I shake my head. *Breathe!* Tears are flowing down my face uncontrollably and I lose concentration. I close my eyes trying to remember my line but I can't.

End Scene: Reckless: Aimee / Ava

I grip Sean's arm and they stop us.

"That was good Ava," Sean said taking me into his arms. "That was real good sweetheart."

"I couldn't remember my next line though."

"Don't worry about it."

"You did wonderful Ava," Tami said kindly.

"Really?" I asked her.

"Oh yes, you almost made me cry," Tami said patting me on the back before leaving to have her makeup retouched.

"See, I told you," Sean said kissing me on the cheek before he is over taken with people to check his own appearance.

I step back into place. We are to start from Sean's last comment. Sean stares at me with a furious intent for a few minutes before we start, reviving my uneasiness again.

Scene: Reckless: Aimee / Ava

"I can see that. Are you claiming it's mine?" I nod cautiously. "Why should I believe that?"

"Because ..." I said softly. "Because I haven't been with anyone else. Why else would I come all this way Tennessee?" My southern twang easily comes back to me as my emotions get carried away.

"To get money," his says with an assured voice.

I look back at Lacey before finding my secure point on the floor. "Just forget it. I'll figure it out on my own. I knew this was a mistake," I move back towards the door.

TC grabs my arm spinning me back around, "What do you mean you'll figure it out?"

"I don't want anything from you. I only wanted to let you know is all."

"Well who is helping you now?" He said stern but with a softer tone

"No one."

"No one? How have you been getting by?"

"I was waitressing at McKinney's Bar but they don't really like pregnant girls working there so they fired me a few months ago. Now I'm a cashier at the grocery. It doesn't pay as well but I got another roommate to move in with us to help pay the bills."

He narrows his eyes at me, "Us? How many people do you live with?"

"Five, three girls and two boys. It's not much to look at but a pretty sturdy house. It's down the street from the Piggly Wiggly, so I don't have to walk far. I even made up a spot in the basement for me and the baby - it's like our own little place now. I hung up sheets so we can have our privacy and the church gave me a crib. The sheets for it are pink with yellow bows though, but I suspect he won't ever know the difference anyhow."

He is silent and breathing steadily. "He?"

"It's a boy," I shrug with uncomfortable smile.

"Oh, ummm," his eyes wander the room around him before they meet mine again. "You should live here in Tennessee. Stay here and I'll help you with whatever you need."

"Really?" I ask with excitement.

"I'm not about to have my son live in that mess," he said flashing a meager smile.

"So what now?" I asked him.

"I don't know ... I guess we get you moved here."

"I only have this one suitcase and my cousin Jeanie drove me here, so ... this is all I got." I confessed, feeling embarrassed for some reason.

He folds his hands over his head sighing again, "Well that should make it easy. You can stay with me for now." He looks me up and down a couple of times seeming to contemplate something. "Anyway, I have three bedrooms, so there is plenty of room for you both."

I bite my lip, fighting my emerging smile.

End Scene: Reckless: Aimee / Ava

The scene ends there, with us anyway. Sean has to go back and do another with the rest of them. Tami especially, who he now has to tell that I am having his baby and moving in with him. I can't watch this scene, Sean said he is going to get hit and slapped several times by her and I can't handle any more crying by anyone. My next scene is late getting started because Sean continuously refers to me as Ava rather than Aimee in his scene with Tami, which shocks me - he does not usually mess up like that.

❦

My heavy eyes, force me to fall deep into my dreams that is until I feel soft lips on mine. I reach out and hold him to me. "All done?" I asked relieved to see his smiling green eyes again.

"Almost," Sean sighed sinking in next to me, "Only our scenes left now."

"You look worried," I said.

"I am not worried about you, I am worried about me."

"Why?" I asked.

"Ava are you serious?"

"It's only a movie," I shrug trying to lighten his mood.

"Yeah well it's a little too close to home for me. It's …" He lets go of me to rub his face and exhale fully.

"You will be wonderful Sean, I know it," I said.

"Thanks for the confidence but I'm not so sure." I kiss him and lie against his chest listening to his heart beat rhythmically.

For my next scene I am dressed somewhat better than previous scenes. I have on a simple dress that meets my knees and is not nearly as tight, I can actually walk and breathe at the same time. "Are you ready?" Sean asked me.

"Ready to get it over with," I said.

"Me too," he said as I lean against him and feel his heart beating rapidly. "Alright give me your hand," I put my hand in his and he walks me to our spot. Barely a second passes before we walk through the makeshift door of a small town restaurant and bar.

Scene: Reckless: Aimee / Ava

TC holds my hand but barely acknowledges my presence as we walk up to his crew. He greets them with a smile except for Lacey who ignores him noticeably. We sit as far away from her as possible but close enough for them to exchange glances at each other throughout our meal. I do not say much, except when someone asks me a question about the baby but mostly I just sit and watch TC staring at Lacey.

"If you want to go talk to her you can," I said as he looks down at me for the first time tonight.

"I don't."

"It sure does seem like you do. If you like her, I understand if you want to be with her instead. You don't owe me nothing."

He looks back at me angry as he downs his beer, "Why don't you mind your own damn business?"

I look away from him, glancing at her as she gathers her things and leaves abruptly. TC slams another beer on the table and looks out the window to watch her leave. As person after person leaves us, he sits silently ordering another beer and then another.

"Are we going to leave soon?" I asked shyly glancing at the table full of bottles.

"To go where?" He snapped.

"I don't know. Home maybe?"

"Home? Then what." He snaps. "What - you want to play cards or maybe curl up on the sofa together like the beautiful couple we are?" He stares into the side of my head as I squirm in my seat. "What do you want to do Aimee?"

Cringing I feel the tears surfacing again. *I'm getting good at this.* "I'm kind of tired I'd like to go to bed."

He laughs, "Tired? It figures. You're not a whole lot of fun you know that?"

"I'm pregnant, the doctor says that's what supposed to happen."

He rolls his eyes, "Fine." He sits for a few minutes before pushing away his last beer and sighing. "Do you mind if we go somewhere first?" I shake my head anxious just to go. "Come on." He helps me up, walking me to the door casually with one hand on my back and the other holding the door open for me.

End Scene: Reckless: Aimee / Ava

Sean and I wait while they setup our last scene. We are going to be sitting in his convertible now. Sean is already in the car waiting for me when I come in. I sit next to him and he slides me closer to him, focusing in on my eyes and caressing my face.

"What?" I asked him.

"Ava I love you, please don't ever forget that," Sean said kissing my hands gently.

"I love you too. It will be fine baby - I promise." He nods allowing me to lean against him, his heart now imprinting on his shirt it's thumping so hard.

Scene: Reckless: Aimee / Ava

I stare at the stars from his lap, while TC drinks another beer and plays with my hair. "This is beautiful. What made you want to come here?" I asked.

"I just thought you might like it."

I sit up to look at him, "I thought you were mad at me?"

He shakes his head, "I didn't mean to take my problems out on you; it's not your fault."

I move to my side of the car, leaning against the door as I look up at the stars. I smile as I try to imagine something any more perfect than this. TC suddenly leans over and kisses me hard, "What are you doing?" I asked him holding my mouth.

"Damn, can't I kiss you?"

"I just didn't know you wanted to."

"I do, and in fact." He fumbles around in his pocket pulling out a ring. "I want you to marry me." My eyes widened with his casual handling of the ring.

"What? Really?"

"Really, but you have to kiss me right now to get it," he smiles his cocky smile holding the ring out from me like bait. I kiss him happily and he gives me the tiny ring. I put it on my finger and smile wildly at him. He kisses me hard again, barely giving me time to breathe, "I want you Aimee, I want you right now," he said moaning and rubbing my thighs.

"Okay," I said trying to catch my breath.

He continues to kiss me as he undoes his pants. Kissing my neck and sliding his hand up my leg and under my dress. He makes it to my underwear and starts to pull them off when he suddenly jumps to the other side of the car.

"What the hell is that?" He yelled.

"What was what?" I asked confused.

"Your stomach, it jumped at me."

I laugh feeling my stomach, "No it's just the baby kicking." I reach for his hand and place it on my stomach. "I bet he knows you're his Daddy." He stares at his hand and then at me. "It's not a big deal, it happens sometimes," I smile but he pulls his hand away from me.

"I think we should go," he said avoiding my eyes.

"I thought you wanted to ..."

"No, let's go home, you need some rest I'm sure."

I sit back in my seat staring at my ring smiling, "Do you think we can get married in a church? I would really like to start things off right." I asked fantasizing about my expected wedding day.

"Whatever you want," he said in a daze.

End Scene: Reckless: Aimee / Ava

The scene needs a change of scenery and we adjust as Sean closes his eyes with a heavy breath. I grab his hand, rubbing circles with my thumb but he doesn't look up at me he simply waits for the scene to begin again.

Scene: Reckless: Aimee / Ava

I look out at the rode as we drive home. "Aimee?" TC asked. "Yeah?"

"I ... I" He closes his eyes for a second. "I slept with Lacey last night and I asked her to marry me." My mouth drops, but I stay silent as I look at the ring on my finger. "She said no and I thought ..."

"You thought you would ask me since she turned you down?" He nods. "Because you are hurt not because you wanted to." I stare out over the passenger door wanting nothing more than to jump out of this car and run.

"No, I do want to. I mean I love her but she doesn't want me and I know eventually I can love you the same way." Tears pour from my eyes. "I never forgot you Aimee, you were important to me at the time. I just didn't expect to see you ever again."

"No TC!" I yell pushing his hand away from me.

He grabs my face and tries to get me to look at him, "I want to be with you Aimee, please say you want to be with me."

"You only want me because she doesn't."

"No that's not true, she even knows that. That's why she said no." I shake my head pulling as far away from him as possible.

"Do it for the baby, Aimee." I go silent. "He deserves a father in his life," he pleads.

"Are you going to be there? Or are you going to be out running around with other girls?" I stare at him as he tenses his hands on the wheel. "You know you won't be able to stay at home and work a regular job and not cheat on me every chance you get."

"I don't need to get a regular job Aimee, I have a job, and I won't cheat on you." TC tries to convince me

"You already did!"

"I did not!"

"You slept with her just last night."

"So what, that was before I proposed to you."

"But we've been together."

"Together? You live in my house, I have barely touched you since you moved in. How do you figure we've been together?"

"I sleep in your bed with you every night," I cried to him.

"So what, you slept in my bed when I got you pregnant. Did you think we were together then?"

"At the time … kind of."

"Oh please, you are either really naïve or stupid. How many guys have you slept with Aimee? What five, fifteen or is it more like fifty?"

I cry hard, "No!"

"No, then what is it?" I turn from him, not wanting to answer. "You want to talk about me let's hear the truth about you!" He continues to scream. He reaches for me grabbing my arm and turning me around to look at him. "How many?" He yelled staring straight through my eyes.

I cry, "One!" His mouth falls open. "Only one," I jerk away from him again. "TC stop!" I scream.

End Scene: Reckless: Aimee / Ava

We stop and everyone freshens up, including Sean who is fidgeting and pacing. I am just relieved I do not have any more lines. The next part is easy for me, I am overjoyed before seeing the pain in his face. I did not realize how hard this is for Sean. They take me away to redo my makeup, bringing me back to place me at the scene properly, positioning me far away from the tree that the car is now wrapped around. Focusing on breathing Sean gets into the wrecked car and takes one final breath before they start again. Smoke consumes the air around us as he begins to come to life from his now hunched over position.

Scene: Reckless: Aimee / Ava

TC looks around him, "Aimee?" He said searching for me. He gets out of the car, stumbling around it, and yelling for me. "Aimee!" He yells holding his head where it bleeds. He finally sees me laying on the ground after being thrown from the car, broken, bleeding and dyeing rapidly. His cautious breath matches his touch, "Aimee, it's going to be alright. I'm going to go get help. I look briefly at him, struggling for breath as I die in his arms. "No!" He screams at me. He grips me hard trying to find my life but it as well as the life inside of me is beyond saving. He cradles me to his chest screaming and crying. "Oh God no! ……. No. I'm so sorry! Don't leave me, please don't leave me. I'm sorry." His pained pleas continue as he presses me to his chest. He screams furiously, kissing my face as he cries. "I'm so sorry, Aimee. Please don't leave me, I don't want to be without you. Don't leave me like this … I can't lose you both like this. Not like this." He cries out his pain, in a deafening tone as darkness falls completely around us.

End Scene: Reckless: Aimee / Ava

As the scene ends I open my eyes and try to regain my position but Sean holds me so tight against him, I cannot move. The entire set is silent as his whole body trembles, shaking his tears from his face onto mine.

"Sean? It's okay, I'm okay," I reach out wrapping my arms around him and hold him.

Sean kisses me on the forehead and helps me up, "I need a few minutes, Ava. Get cleaned up and ready to go and I will meet back up with you at my trailer."

I search for his eyes but he won't look at me. "Okay." I reach out for his hand before he can walk away and he squeezes mine tight within his before letting go again. It breaks my heart watching him walk away torn apart.

Sean is silent most of the way home. I place my hand on his leg as he drives and he takes hold of it and doesn't let go. *I wish I could say something, anything to make him feel better.* "I am going to make an appointment for the doctor this week, would you like to go with me?"

Shaken out of his daze. "Yes." He said with a bright smile. "Yes, I would like that very much."

I smile at him, "Okay."

CʒBↃ

I can't help but notice him stare at me as if I have some blinking button to show whether I am pregnant or not. I know he is not meaning to but he is making me nervous.

"Sean stop staring at me."

"Sorry sweetheart, I just …" He sighs. "I don't know what I'm waiting for."

"Well even if I am it's going to be a few months before you have to rush me to the hospital. At least wait until then to act like a nutty father."

"I won't be nutty. I was trained to handle all kinds of stressful situations," he said calmly with a smile.

"Oh please, you will be freaking out as soon as you see that little baby inside of me, especially if it's a boy."

Sean smiles so wide his expectations are written all over his face. "Maybe, so will we see something tomorrow if …"

"It won't be much to see right now but you can if you want to."

"I can't wait to be there with you this time, and experience everything I missed with Lillah."

"Everything?" I joked.

"As much as I can, beautiful," Sean kisses me sweetly.

"So you're going to get up for feedings and change diapers …"

"Hey I changed Lillah's diapers and if I recall she was still getting up fairly early when I found out about her."

"And what about watching me get huge and …"

Sean leans over to kiss me, "And? Beautiful you mean, sexy even."

"Sexy, I can't imagine being that."

I look into his smiling eyes, "Ava I saw the pictures when you were pregnant with Lillah; you were incredibly sexy to me. You're carrying my child, what is sexier than that?" I give him a look. "Fine, maybe sexy isn't the right word, but you were certainly beautiful." Sean continues to kiss me everywhere he can until I laugh. "And you will be just as beautiful this time." I grip his hand on my cheek smiling uncontrollably at him. He leans back lost in his happy thoughts.

Sean vibrates the entire car as he drives us home from the doctor's office. "How long are you going to be like this?" I asked him.

"What?"

"You're in a completely different world Sean."

"Sorry I was thinking about some things. I think we should have the room next to Lillah painted and we will need to buy some new baby furniture and …" I laugh at him and he looks at me sternly. "We need to think about these things right? I'm trying to think ahead."

"Oh, well that's good idea I suppose."

"You suppose? Ava your husband is excited about you having his child. Please be a little more excited than, *I suppose.*" Smiling I caress his face gently and whisper my love for him, receiving the same. He shakes his head at me, "So should we tell everyone together or separately?"

"Sean it's bad luck to say anything before three months."

"Really?" I nod. "I don't know if I can wait that long." He said shaking his head.

"It is only six weeks Sean, you can do it."

"I don't think so, I want to tell that guy over there on the corner right now." Sean said pointing to a guy holding up a sale sign for a nearby store.

I laugh at him, "I don't think he would care."

"No?" I shake my head. "How about the girl in the car next to us?"

"She would only care that she isn't the one caring your baby," I said as he smiles wickedly at me.

"Ohhh, jealous again sweetheart?"

"Not at all, I am after all the one that *is* having your baby."

Sean winks at me, "Damn right."

Chapter 21

Rebecca

Joel let me know that the scenes are done, so there is no going back now. I have been replaced by *her. I thought for sure they would change their minds after they saw her. UGGGGHHH! How could they ever replace me with her!* I drive around for hours before ending up at Joel's new place. We barely speak, both of us in a deep rage, however his anger does not even compare to mine.

"This is your fault you know?" I gripe.

Joel rolls his eyes at me, "Well maybe if you were more appealing to people they wouldn't have preferred Ava in the first place." My evil glare does nothing but cause him to laugh. Shaking his head, he walks away from me to make himself a drink. "I talked to the old man today. He wants me to get Sean to do the stunt scene, not a stunt guy or some creative ideas to make it seem as if he did, he wants *him.*"

"But Sean's contract is pretty solid. I don't see how you can …"

"I don't think his contract is the way to go about it, I think I have to convince him somehow. I know he won't listen to me, and there is no way she is going to let him, but there has to be some way to get him so excited about it that he can't say no."

"The only way to get to Sean is if he is pissed off at Ava."

"Well, that bond is stronger than ever, thanks to us," Joel sighed.

"Tell me about it, I'm the one that has to see it every day." I shiver just thinking about it.

"Well, we need to think of something, and quick. There is only so much time left. The stunt scene is saved for the last day of shooting, but it still doesn't give us much time."

"Well, maybe we can come up with something together?" I said with an alluring pose.

Joel immediately starts laughing at me, "You horny little bitch … get your ass over here." He said, eyeing me as he undoes his pants for me. "Now, what was it you wanted me to do?" He said with no sign of a smile.

I pull him to me and lick up his neck to his ear, "Fuck me … and make it hard."

Joel tears my dress up and forces my legs apart with his hips before pounding his way deep inside of me. His wild-man approach always excites me, but even more so when he demands me into positions. My body bounces off the wall and shakes within his hands. Joel suddenly sets me down and pushes me to the bedroom. He bends me over onto the bed so my face is buried into the pillow before I feel his dick slide in from behind. The rapid penetration and the sounds of him pounding harder and harder against my flesh makes me crave him even more. When he takes hold of my hair, he causes me to arch backwards so he can watch my breasts shake in the mirror across from us. Admiring us, he adjusts for better exposure of himself and my ass. He smiles fully, enjoying the visual show. Joel slows his approach as we both reach our ecstasy. He has never matched Sean's skill and build, but he has always managed to impress with his aggressiveness. I roll over spreading out wide for him. "Call me later?" I asked, coyly.

He laughs, "How about you call me?" He hovers over me, showing me everything, "And if you need more of this then you know where I'm at."

"Yes, I do," I moaned, hoping to lounge for awhile but my clothes are thrown back in my face.

Frustrating me, Joel rushes me to dress. "Don't forget to keep me informed of what is going on over there. And just watch, don't do anything Rebecca, you tend to overdo."

"You're one to talk," I said, but Joel doesn't dare respond. He just smiles, gives me a lazy kiss and scoots me out the door.

◌֎◌

Hoping to find Sean, I wander the set until I see Sean walk into his trailer. My only chance to spend time with him without *her* around. I race towards him, but as soon as I get to his steps I am immediately jerked off them. Ethan's intense expression infuriates me. "Ethan, don't you have somewhere better to be?"

"Leave him alone Rebecca."

"I was only going to talk to him." I smile wickedly at him, "You are afraid he will give into me? Do you know something I don't, Ethan?"

"Stay away from my brother."

"Sean, he is still in love with me isn't he?"

"You have to be the most self-centered fool I have ever met."

"What's wrong Ethan, is it *you* that misses me? Your woman not satisfying you at home anymore?" Ethan has always been calmer than Sean on the outside, but it festers inside of him just as much. He would tear me apart right now if he thought he could get away with it. "You know Ethan, if you name the place and time I might be willing. It's been awhile for us, but one Grant brother is better than none." I stick my hand down his pants quickly and he lets go of me, leaping backwards.

"You're pure evil."

"Baby, you haven't seen evil yet, and if you know what's good for you and your sweet little family, you will stay out of my way."

"I'm not scared of you Rebecca."

"Really? So you wouldn't mind if I told my little secret?"

"Tell everyone, I don't care, but I will be damned if I am going to sit back and let you ruin my brother's life."

Sean opens his door, eyeing both of us suspiciously, "What's going on with you two?"

"Nothing," Ethan said as he waits for my response.

"Nothing," I said, smiling at Ethan before walking away.

❧

The morning is bright, too bright for my hangover. I put on my dark sunglasses and my bikini and eventually make my way to the pool. I am pleasantly surprised when I see Sean already swimming. Damn he looks good all wet, muscles flaring with each stroke, hair slick and dark. I sit at the pool's edge watching him finish his laps. He stops, wiping the water from his face and hair before turning to look at me with his deep green eyes. *I am ready to jump in and latch on to his body forever.* "Good morning," I smile at him as I gaze over his body.

"Good morning, Rebecca," Sean said as he pushes himself up and out of the pool.

"Are you done already," I asked, disappointed.

"For now." He towels off every glistening drop clinging to his body.

Ruining my daydream, Ava approaches us holding the child, which is dressed in a swimsuit and some type of exaggerated air puffed, polka dot things on her arms. "Sean, she's ready, but make sure you don't keep her out here too long. The sunscreen only helps so much and keep …"

Sean interrupts, "I got it handled baby. Just go, we will be fine." Ava hands the child to Sean and he kisses her cheek, causing her to giggle.

Ava kisses them both before turning to leave. "Still here?" She asks me with a downward glare. She doesn't even bother to wait for me to answer before she rolls her eyes away from me and leaves - thankfully.

I turn back to Sean as he adjusts the child's sunglasses and hat, cradling her to his chest as he eases back into the water with her. "You're getting back in?" I asked, amused by his indecisive behavior.

"If you want to do laps we can easily stay out of the way, the pool is big enough." He says, not even bothering to look away from the giggling, fidgeting brat in his arms.

"No, I was only curious." I said, watching Ava leave in her Aston Martin. *She doesn't take that car to do errands.* "Where is she going?"

Sean ignores me as he plays in the water with the child. Kissing her cheeks and letting her hold onto him as he floats her around the pool. They are moving too far away to talk to, perhaps on purpose. I get up and dive in, swimming right up next to them. "Can I play too?" I asked, watching Sean's nervous expression appear to my sudden presence.

"We aren't really doing anything other than floating," he said, moving away from me.

"You didn't answer me, Sean."

"About what?"

"Where did Ava go?" He ignores me again and now I know it is on purpose. "I'm going to keep asking until you answer me."

"She went to work."

"Work? You let her go there?"

"I didn't let her Rebecca, I never told her she couldn't in the first place."

"You're not worried about her and Jasper?"

Glancing at me, he is obviously annoyed that I brought it up. "She's not working with Jasper, she's working with Kyle."

I laugh, "That's what she said the last time." Sean instantly shoots me an evil glare to let me know the conversation is over. "Fine." I swim closer to them and they move around me with little recognition. "Why are you ignoring me? I didn't mean to make you mad."

"I'm not mad and I'm not ignoring you. I'm spending time with my daughter before I have to go to work."

"Okay." I trace my finger around his tattoo between his shoulder blades, causing him to spin around quickly.

"Stop it," he said, grinding his teeth at me.

"What?" I ask innocently.

"You know what." He says, glaring at me.

I look him over and notice a new tattoo on his arm. "When did you get that one?"

"I had my guy do it a few months ago, it's Ava holding Lillah."

"I bet Ava loves that."

"She wasn't real happy about it at first. But after she saw it she got so excited she ..." he stops short to look at me. "Anyway, she showed her appreciation for it."

Ugghhhh disgusting. "Got it."

"And Lillah likes it too, don't you sweetheart?" He said to the child.

"Mommy," she said pointing to the picture and kissing his arm.

"Mommy's beautiful huh?" She nods. "You are beautiful too Lillah," he said to her.

"No, I'm cute." She said, causing Sean to laugh.

"Yes, you're cute too," he said, kissing her again. *Uggghhh! It's moments like these that make me glad there are drugs and alcohol.*

I swim to the edge and get out of the pool, making sure to show off my bikini's best parts as I towel my body off slowly. I wait for him to look and I smile at him as soon as he does. *There is, after all, only so much a man can ignore.* I stretch out on the lounge chair and slip my top off before resting my head on my arms.

"Rebecca can you watch Lillah for a few seconds while I go get her some more sunscreen and her floating chair?" I respond with a smile and sit up proudly. Sean's mouth drops and turns the child and himself away from me. "Rebecca! Do you mind covering up please?"

"Oh Sean, don't be such a prude. I'm sure she's seen them before."

"Well I don't think she wants to see yours, and I certainly don't."

"Are you sure?" I ask, knowing otherwise.

"Forget it," he shakes his head, walking away from me.

"Okay, I will watch her and I will put my top back on." I said, grabbing my top and tying it back on. "Happy?" I asked, holding my arms out as he glances cautiously at me.

He sits the child in the lounge chair next to me. "I will be right back," he said as I wave my hand at him. I put my sunglasses on and grab my magazine flipping through as I wait. I look over at the child as she sits playing with some doll.

She turns to me and holds it up to me. "She dirty," she said.

"So clean her off, there's the pool," I said, pointing. She sits at the edge and tries to slip her doll in the water but ends up falling in and struggling to stay above water. *Oh that would be heartbreaking for Ava wouldn't it?* I go back to reading, putting my headphones on and sitting back in my chair with an easy sigh. I barely have a chance to get interested in an article when I feel Sean rush by me and dive into the pool. I sit up, pulling my headphones off. Sean comes out of the pool with the child who is screaming and coughing. "What happened?" I asked confused.

Sean glares at me with an intense fire I have never seen from him. I back up into my seat. "I asked you to watch her!" He screamed.

"I did!"

"No, you didn't. You ignored her and let her walk right into the pool!"

"She said her doll was dirty, so I told her to wash her off."

"You told her to go to the pool?" I shrug. Sean grips the child closer to him cradling her head as if she is helpless. "She could have drowned, Rebecca." The child's hysterical cries surprisingly advance to another level. "It's okay now sweetheart, Daddy's got you," he said, seemingly trying to set me ablaze with his stare.

"How was I supposed to know that she would need help?" I screamed at him. "I don't know anything about kids Sean, I'm sorry. If I had known I would have paid closer attention."

"Stay right there," he ordered before walking into the house. I wait several seconds before deciding to pack up and go back to the guesthouse. I barely get settled before Sean barges in like a bull. "Rebecca?" He screamed.

"Upstairs." I said, eyeing him from around the corner.

"Get your ass down here - now!"

I walk slowly down the stairs, making sure to keep my distance from the giant ball of fire. "What is your problem? I made a mistake I'm sorry."

He huffs at me as he tightens his fists, "Rebecca …" he said as his body shakes with intensity.

"I'm sorry Sean, I didn't realize she could be in danger."

"Her name is Lillah! Say it! You never say her name, you never say my daughter's name - why?"

"Lillah - there are you happy? What does that have to do with anything? I made a mistake and now I know better."

"Rebecca - she is two. And besides that, I asked you to watch her, not put your headphones on and bury yourself in a magazine."

"I didn't …"

"No! I don't want to hear it, you are, and in fact you always have been the most self-absorbed, spoiled, disgusting woman I have ever met."

"Excuse me?" I step forward.

"Ava was right about you the whole time, and I defended you because I felt sorry for you." He puts his hands on his hips, staring me down. "You really did put Lillah out with the dogs and then blamed it on Ava, didn't you?"

I narrow my eyes at him, "You have lost your mind, I would never do …"

"Shut up! Don't even try to tell me anything different. I am sick of your lies and your aggressive jealousy."

I look him up and down with a strong stance of my own. "I don't know what you think is going to happen between us, but no matter what happens with Ava and me, *you* and I will never happen again. I can't stand you. I feel sorry for you, but I can barely tolerate your presence. Thank God Joel felt the need to steal you from me. And thankfully my brother convinced me how much better off I was or I might have gone back to you. Hell, I thought all that time that it was my fault you cheated on me, but it didn't have anything to do with me … you're just a slut!"

I smack him hard across the face, "I am not! And it is your fault. If you hadn't of ran off, screwing who knows what, I would have never been persuaded by Joel. Hell, you were sleeping with that bitch that lived next door to us but I took care of her. I bet she never got near another man again, especially someone else's."

Sean stares at me hard, shaking his head. "You know what, I don't know what I did to get so lucky with Ava, but thank God I did."

"Oh Ava, your precious perfect rose, the one who lied to you, the one who is probably fucking her old mentor right now?" He glares at me as if he wants to kill me. "Oh, you know it's true. That whore is probably screwing everyone behind your back, Sean. She's in it for the money and nothing more."

"You better stop, Rebecca."

"Why? The truth hurt? Your perfect Ava, not so perfect?" I huff at him. "Hell, you might want to get a paternity test done on Lillah and any future offspring," Sean leaps forward at me, wrapping his hand around my neck and cringing as he slowly releases me.

"Rebecca!" He yells as I stand wide eyed and stiff. "I feel so sorry for you. You automatically assume that every woman is as desperate as you. No one wants you, and you are too stupid to realize you did it to yourself." He shakes his head, stepping away from me. "I want you out of my house by the end of the week."

"Where am I going to go?" I snap back.

"I don't know and I don't care."

I start hitting him. "I hate you! You're an asshole!" He grabs my arms and holds them out from him as he stands silent. "You are going to regret doing this to me."

"I doubt it, but if you go near Ava or Lillah or even the boys while you are here, I will make sure that you regret it." I look into his intense eyes and stand back from him, working up as much hurt as I can throw at him. "Do you understand me?"

"I understand you."

"Good. Actually, stay away from me also. The thought of you coming near me makes me brutally ill. You know, I have a slight recollection of you coming on to me a little too strong on our movie night. I would be willing to bet that I didn't drink too much after all, did I?" He pauses, looking me over. "You're disgusting." Sean said reaching for the door.

My revengeful self quickly surfaces, "You know, I did lie to you!" I said, staring a hole through the back of his head. "And not about what you think."He looks back over his shoulder at me. "About the baby, the one I said was yours."

"It wasn't mine?"

I shake my head.

"You fucking bitch!" He huffed turning for the door again.

"No, but it was a Grant baby." I said, relaxing into my confession.

Sean pauses before facing me harshly. "Do you expect me to believe that? Ethan can't stand you."

"Only because he is so afraid that his pretty little wife will find out that he was fucking me while they were dating." I said, watching him back off. "I changed the date of the abortion papers so that you would think it was yours, but it was after you were gone." Sean looks me over silently and I smile wider. "While you were filming in California, you sent him for some more of your things and while he was visiting *her*... Well, it turned out Ethan had a slight substance abuse problem himself back then. His guilt over it is incredible. I shared whatever I had with him and he would keep coming back, even after he would drop his perfect Abbey off after their date. Your brother, Sean, was something else. Always trying to be the perfect son, the perfect brother, the perfect actor, he just couldn't handle anyone seeing him vulnerable. Except me, that is. He would pour everything out to me, losing himself in whatever drug I gave him and fucking me in all the same places you and I did." I said, smiling at him as his fierce eyes burn into my skin. "You two are really similar, you know that?" Standing on my toes, I stare right into his eyes. "You both fuck very much the same."

"You're lying!" He hissed.

"Really, then why did Ethan pay for the abortion and continue to send me money all these years to make sure I kept my mouth shut?" I casually find my file full of copies of checks and hand it to him. "See for yourself."

"No, you probably faked these just like you did with the abortion papers."

I laugh, "Ask him then. He's the one that decided to stop sending me checks. He has been so nervous since I have been here. I was sure I could get more money out of him, but apparently he is a man of principal now."

"I'm not listening to another word of this, and I want you out tonight." Sean demands.

"But I don't ..."

"Tonight! If you are not out by the time I get home I will have the police escort you out." Sean walks out, slamming the door behind him.

Chapter 22

Sean

I was dazed the whole way back to the set, unable to put what Rebecca said out of my mind. I don't want to believe her. The problem is, it all makes sense. Memories of Ethan not looking me in the eye every time he got back from New York, and I disregarded it, thinking he had lost his mind over Abbey. *I need to talk to Ethan.* By the time I finally find Ethan, I am already steaming over my memories and thoughts. I approach him stiffly, but I am thrown off when Daniel races towards me from the opposite direction.

"Sean, can I talk to you for a second?" Daniel asked.

"Sure, what about?"

"Well, about the stunt scene. I wanted to make sure that you still weren't interested in doing it yourself?"

"Daniel I already told you no. Ava would have my head."

"I know, but with all the safety precautions we have added, it really wouldn't be that dangerous."

Ethan suddenly steps in front of me and interjects. "Daniel no, I told you he isn't going to do it. Now back off and from now on come to me with these things."

"You told him?" I asked.

"Yes, it's too dangerous for you." Ethan tells me like he is my father.

"Who says?" I snapped.

Ethan looks at me strangely as Daniel looks on confused, "We discussed it Sean and it's not something you should be doing."

"We did? I don't remember discussing it? Not with you."

"Sean, you're not doing it. Why are you acting like a spoiled child suddenly?"

"Who are you to tell me anything?"

"You're not doing it and that's final." Ethan said.

"Fuck you, Ethan!" I yelled at him.

"What is your problem?"

"You! You're always bossing me around like I'm still a little kid."

"Well, maybe because you act like one." I glare at him. "Sean you need to listen and let me do my job."

"Why should I listen to you?"

"Because, baby brother, I might just know something a little more than you."

"You don't know shit Ethan, and I'm sick of listening to you. I'll do the stunt Daniel."

"Okay," Daniel said awkwardly.

I leave them both to return to my trailer.

"Sean!" Ethan yelled. Ethan storms in soon after me. "Do you mind telling me what the hell is going on with you today?"

"You and your lies Ethan. I thought, of all people, you would be the last one that would ever lie to me." He looks completely lost. "Rebecca told me everything." His expression changes instantly. "Oh, so it is true."

"Sean it was …"

"What Ethan? It was what?" I yell at him as he cowers away from me. "I can't believe you got my girlfriend pregnant."

"I was not exactly in the right state of mind then."

"No, apparently you were getting high every chance you got."

"I felt guilty for not helping Mom after Dad died … for not being there when he did die."

"You were filming, he understood."

"Did he?" Ethan screamed through his pained face. "I loved him so much, Sean. He gave me everything and I couldn't even catch a flight out to be with him? I couldn't turn down that one possible Oscar winning role to help him for once?"

"You were perfect in his eyes Ethan, it didn't matter what you did."

He laughs at me, rubbing his hands over his head. "You're making a mistake Sean."

"It's not a big deal Ethan, they are going to go over everything with me. They have already been training me to drive. I know I can do it, and honestly, I want to do it."

"Do you? Because if you can't and something happens to you… well, you're leaving behind an awful lot."

"Nothing is going to happen, worry about your own family."

"I would never hurt Abbey or my kids."

"No, you just cheated on her."

"I… Damn it Sean, it wasn't like that!"

"Then tell me Ethan. What was it like?" I yelled as Ethan stands silent. "You know what, I have heard enough." I walk out, leaving him standing alone and silent. *My brother, my so-called idol, is nothing but a fraud.*

Chapter 23

Ava

The day is going fairly smooth, and the thoughts of Sean finishing his movie soon are making my mood even lighter. That is, until Ethan calls, wanting to come over and talk to me. Sean's anger with him is too intense for me to feel comfortable about talking to him behind his back, but I am not about to let this quarrel between them continue much longer. I put Lillah down for her nap and Ethan shows up soon after. His solemn face tells the story, even if I didn't know anything. I hug him, knowing how it is when Sean is angry with you. "Are you okay?" I asked him.

"I guess Sean told you," Ethan smirked.

"Some, he's not real good about sharing things he's not ready to talk about."

"That sounds like him."

"I have tried to talk to him but ..." Ethan shakes his head stopping me.

"I know, but that's not why I'm here. I'm here because I assume Sean hasn't told you that he's doing the jump tomorrow?" Ethan said, awaiting my expected response.

My mouth drops, "He said he wasn't going to do it."

"Initially, but he decided to get back at me by agreeing to do it."

"No, he promised." I snap.

"He is going to be even angrier at me for telling you, but at this point I don't see how it can be much worse."

"But Ethan, he's going to get hurt."

"He doesn't seem to think so. That's what he's doing today, he is learning how to make the jump work. Learning how to control the car and ..." Ethan shakes his head, walking away from me. "He has convinced himself that they have taken every safety precaution into consideration and that he can do the jump with no problem. He's invincible, you know?"

"He's crazy," I huff.

"That's what I told him, but he won't listen to me. If anything, I only fuel the fire."

"So you want me to talk to him?" He nods. "I don't know that he will listen to me either."

"Well, you have more power over him than anybody else, that's why he hasn't told you about it."

"I will talk to him but he's going to know you told me."

"Like I said, what difference does it make now?"

CRWO

There is no way I am going to get much work done now. *I curse the fool for ruining my good mood.* All throughout the day, the images of the stunt appear in my head. Only this time, Sean is getting into the car, driving up the ramp on the back of that semi and jumping clear from one end to the other, all the while trying to outpace the semi to safety.

That's the biggest obstacle. The semi does not have enough time to stop and keep from crushing the car, or my husband, if anything goes wrong. Much like it happened the first time the stunt was done. I am not even sure if he can get hurt in the practices they are having today. I have not heard from him all day, and the more I think about it the tenser and angrier I get. By the time Sean arrives home I have managed to work myself into a complete wreck. As soon as he walks through the door I grab the nearest thing to me and throw it at him!

He barely ducks quickly enough for it to miss his head. "What the fuck Ava?" He screamed at me.

I run up to him, jerking at his shirt furiously, "What the hell is wrong with you Sean?"

"I don't know what you're talking about." He holds out his arms innocently.

"You know damn well what you are planning to do tomorrow, and you said you wouldn't do it. You promised, Sean!"

He rolls his eyes, "Who told you?"

"It doesn't matter, just tell me you're not going to do it."

"Ethan. It was Ethan, wasn't it?"

I look into his eyes, crossing my arms and standing tall. "I knew it, fucker can't keep his mouth shut."

"Sean!"

"What Ava?" He grips my arms moving me out of his path.

"Don't you do it."

"It's too late Ava, I have already committed to it. It's tomorrow, and there is no time to change my mind now."

I fist his shirt, jerking it wildly. "You promised me!"

Sean grabs me, throwing me over his shoulder and carrying me to our room. He puts me down on the bed, crawling on top of me to hold me down. "Stop it, Ava."

"Let go of me," I yell, trying to release my arms from his hands. "Not until you calm down."

"I'll calm down when you tell me you're not going to do that jump tomorrow."

"Well, that's not going to happen." He said while I squirm, trying to free myself. Sean looks me in the eyes calmly, "Stop." I break down crying when he finally lets go of me and takes me into his arms. "I'm sorry I didn't tell you and I know I promised you, but this is something I have to do."

"No you don't," I whimpered.

"I do. I know you don't understand, hell I'm not sure I even understand, but I want to do this. I want to succeed at it where he couldn't. I feel like, if I can do it, then maybe I can somehow feel good about this whole damn movie again."

"You don't need to risk your life, Sean."

"I'm not risking my life, baby. They have every precautionary measure taken care of. Besides, he was drunk when he did the stunt. He lost control of the car, or at least that's how it seemed. I think he purposely let that semi smash into him. On the set it's not even going to get that far, we are filming me making the jump only. We already filmed the semi crushing the car." His eyes plead with me. "I know I can do it Ava."

"Please don't do it," I cried while he sighs.

"I have too. I love you, but this is something I have to do." I shake my head as he cradles me, stroking the back of my head. "Where's Lillah?"

"She is with your mother. She and Bobby wanted to take her and Collin to the aquarium tomorrow."

"You didn't say anything to my mother did you?"

"No, but I should have."

Sean pulls my face up to look at him. "You don't need to worry about me. The car has me well protected, and the stunt crew is incredible. Nothing is going to happen to me, I promise."

"I can't live without you Sean," I cried trying to plead with him one last time.

His expression changes suddenly, "You can live without me, you won't have to, but you can."

"I won't!"

His sudden angry expression shocks me, "Ava." He said through his teeth. "I don't want to ever hear you say that again!" He yelled at me. "Do you hear me?"

"Yes," I whimper, slowly falling into full hysterics.

Sean pulls me back into his arms, "Please don't cry, I didn't mean to yell at you, but I don't like you talking that way. I forget about the hormones with the pregnancy. This is not a good time to upset you." I hold onto him tight, crying as he cradles my head in his hand. He gives me time to get it out of my system, not overreacting or getting impatient with me at all. When I cry myself out, he leans back trying to look at my face. "Better?" I shake my head causing him to laugh, "I think you are. Come on, I'm hungry." He helps me up and I walk with him, clutching his hand with both of mine. I do not let go of him all night. I was sure he was going to get annoyed at some point but he never did. He held my hand, rubbed my back, kissed me as much as I could desire for him to, until he finally left me to take a shower. I waited in our room as long as I could without him, and then I slipped inside the bathroom to watch him shower. I watch the steaming water run down the back of his neck, over his broad shoulders, and down his long muscular back before curving over his perfectly rounded ass, easing his tense muscles and arousing me. I slide my clothes off and open the shower door, stepping in as he turns to watch me get in with him. His expression of shock easily changes to understanding and acceptance. Taking my hand, he pulls me to him, searching for my lips as soon as I get near. Leaning me against the shower wall, I feel his wet, strong body press against mine while his arms grip the wall beside my head. His hands slide down off the wall to my body while his mouth glides down my neck, my breasts, licking the water off as it flows down my skin. Lifting me up, he holds me against the wall, encouraging me to wrap my legs around him. With a slight tug of my body he gives me what I want and I relax, letting him in completely. I beg him for more, running my hands over his body, memorizing every steam-soaked muscle and enjoying his tight-fitting erection inside me. With one hand he holds me up, and with the other he fondles me with desiring groans. When our eyes meet, I want to tell him to never leave me, but all I can do is kiss him. I take in his soft lips until my body is taken over by wave after wave of pleasure. I hold tight to him, resting my head against his as I listen to his moans coming harsher and heavier. My body is pressed so hard against his I can feel his heart racing. With a harsh moan he releases, caressing my thigh and gripping my ass until he finishes completely. That passionate encounter may have ended, but the seduction continues to an even more wild abandon. His kisses remain on me as his hands glide over my body. His eyes watch me carefully as I do the same for him. Slowly and meticulously, our hands caress through the steaming water and along our heated skin, lathering each other for our own pleasure. Resting my back against his chest, I welcome his hands on my breasts, sliding down my arms, reaching for my hands, and placing them against the wall. He encourages me to lean towards the wall and push my ass out to him. His movements are swift, assured, and I feel him throbbing inside of me again. His groan roars while I fight for breath. Leaning his head against mine he enjoys the position he holds me in - to the very end. "I love you, Ava."

"I love you more than I can even tell you Sean." I said, falling against his chest as my tears fight to return.

As soon as he gets into bed, I curl up into his welcoming arms, falling asleep sooner than I would like to.

CRER

The morning is bright and warm as I awake and smile, remembering the previous night. However, it quickly diminishes when I realize he is gone, having left a note at the bedside confirming an early departure he claims was for my sake.

Ava,

I love you, but I think it's best I leave before you awake and get upset again by having to watch me go. Don't worry, and I will call you as soon as we are done. Last day, baby, and then I'm all yours again. Get the shower ready for me tonight because I can't wait to repeat last night. You don't know what you did to me, I dreamed about you all night. You were so incredible, you are incredible. Don't worry, everything is going to be fine. I will see you tonight, I promise.

I love you,

Sean

The immediate sadness he was hoping to avoid takes over me. I had hoped that I would have had one last chance to change his mind, and apparently he knew I would try. *I don't know how he expects me to sit here all day, waiting. There is no way in hell I'm doing that.* I don't hesitate going to the set with plans of stopping him. I call Ethan to warn him, and he greets me as soon as I arrive.

"Sean is not going to like you being here, are you sure you want to do this?" Ethan said, hesitating to walk me in.

"I'm not changing my mind," I said, to his obvious disapproval. As we walk towards his trailer, there is a definite mood that develops between the two of us. I am not sure exactly what it is, fear maybe, or worry. Whatever it is, it is obvious Ethan and I are in the same place. We walk cautiously to Sean's trailer. Ethan is leading the way, and suddenly I am not so anxious to come face to face with Sean as I thought. Ethan looks at me one last time before he opens the door and enters. I step through, seeing Sean sitting with Dillon, laughing. Sean's expression changes instantaneously and dramatically, his eyes narrow as he alternates between Ethan and me. With a sudden rush, he slams he fists down on the table scaring poor Dillon right out of his chair.

"Now Sean, just calm down." Ethan put his hands up trying to shield me.

Sean stands up and moves towards us. "Why the hell would you bring her here Ethan?"

"It's not his fault. I came on my own!" I yelled at him.

"Ava, I thought we went through all this shit last night?"

"Last night didn't change my mind, Sean."

Sean raises his hands in the air, grasping his face as he looks up. "Ahhh son of ..." he stands away from me, silent. "No. No Ava. Go home." He turns to me suddenly, pointing towards the door.

"You can't tell me what to do Sean."

"You want to bet?" His eyes harden towards me.

"I won't leave!" I yell, holding my stance.

"Ava, either you leave on your own or I will have security escort you out."

"Sean, don't you think that's a bit much?" Ethan asked, placing a hand on Sean's chest to hold him back from me.

Sean glares at him, "I don't care what you think."

"She is your wife," Ethan said.

"My pregnant wife," Sean sounded out perfectly for everyone to understand.

Ethan, wide eyed, looks back at me. "You didn't tell me that."

"Of course she didn't," Sean huffed.

"What difference does it make, whether I am here worried or at home worried?"

"It makes a big difference Ava. Here, you're seeing it and it looks a lot worse than it is." Sean said, crossing his arms and projecting his strong resolve in my face.

"I'm not leaving, Sean," I said, lifting my chin up to him and crossing my arms. With a tense smile, he grabs my arm and drags me out of the trailer, both Ethan and Dillon following closely. "You're hurting me Sean." He doesn't slow down, he simply changes from my arm to my hand - not that it is much better. I can barely keep up with his pace, stumbling and falling into his side, until Sean finds Randy, who looks confused at the display coming at him.

"Get her out of here, now!" Sean yelled at him.

"Calm down Sean. What's wrong with you?" Randy asked, glancing over at me.

"I don't want her here today, so make sure she gets home." Sean slowed his words, emphasizing them rudely.

"I will take care of it," Randy said, repeating Sean's rude behavior.

"Thank you."

Sean kisses me on the head. "I will see you when I get home," he said, walking away in a huff.

"Sean, she is your wife. Don't you think you should treat her ..." Dillon started, getting in front of Sean but swiftly diverts when Sean stares him down. "Alright, be an asshole then."

"Dillon, you don't know what the hell you're talking about so just stay out of it!" Sean yelled at him.

Dillon raises his hands to him, "Fine, I'll stay out of it." Sean walks away, leaving us all speechless and exhausted.

"Can someone please tell me what's going on?" Randy asked.

"Sean is pissed that Ava is here to see the jump today, and I don't really blame him Ava." Ethan said with his hands on his hips.

Really sick of the Grant brothers today. "I don't see the difference Ethan," I said.

"Ava, you're pregnant. You shouldn't be here. I wish you had told me, now I feel responsible if anything happens to you."

"Nothing is going to happen. I wish everyone would leave me alone and talk to my husband. He's the one doing something foolish."

"It's too late for that. Besides, Ethan and I both tried to talk to him again this morning and all we got was his usual relentless determination." Randy added.

"I'm not leaving," I said, crossing my arms and focusing away from all of them.

"You two are so perfect for each other," Ethan huffed.

"I tell you what, let me go and talk to him and see if you can at least stay in his trailer until it's over," Randy said.

I look up at Dillon, who is scratching his head. "I'm sorry, Dillon, that you were put in the middle of this."

"I'm not sure what I'm in the middle of exactly."

"Sean promised me he wouldn't do this dangerous stunt, and he expects me to sit at home and wait for him to call."

"I don't know why he is shocked to see you then, if he promised not to do it." Dillon looks me over, reaching for my arm that Sean had a hold of. "How is your arm? He had a pretty rough grip. Believe me, I know how that feels."

"It's okay, nothing to make a fuss over."

"I think I saw a place we can get some ice for it."

"No really, I'm okay."

"Are you sure? I think it might help, although no one will probably be able to find you there." I look up at him as he winks at me. I nod, following him with a smile.

Dillon sneaks us into a catering truck, helping me up on a counter as he gets me some ice. "Here we go," he said, placing some wrapped-up ice on my arm.

"Thank you Dillon, but it really is fine."

"Well, Sean is probably going to want to kill me, but it's not going to be the first time, huh?"

"No, I suppose not."

"You know, I came down here to show Sean the promotional pictures and hoped to catch some of the movie drama. I didn't realize I was going to get the 'behind the scenes' drama too."

"Yes, well Sean is really good at overreacting to things."

"Especially when it comes to his pregnant wife?" Dillon asked, giving me a sideways glance.

"That doesn't help," I admitted with a soft sigh.

"Well congratulations, you must be excited?"

"We both are. There has been a lot of drama at our house lately, so we haven't gotten a whole lot of time to enjoy it yet. As soon as he is done today, hopefully we can put it all behind us."

"I'm sure you will, you guys are the perfect couple."

"I don't know about perfect."

"I do. I have never seen two people so in love in my life. I was talking to him about you right before you walked in. He completely lights up every time he talks about you." I shake my head. "He does. He told me how you met, and how torn up he was when you were separated for that time. He said he never wanted to know pain like that again, and the first chance he had to get you back he took it and didn't look back. That man is crazy in love."

I smile at him as he peels an orange, pulling the slices apart and eating them. "You are really sweet, do you know that?" I said.

Dillon narrows his eyes at me, shaking his head. "No, don't say that. Sweet, uggghhh. You might as well say I have a nice personality."

"You have that as well," I said, laughing at his disgusted expression.

"Oh, now you didn't have to go and say that." He cringes.

"It's true," I said, egging him on.

"Ava, please stop."

"And, you're incredibly hot." With that, his eyebrows raise and his masculine stature unfolds to its full height.

"Yeah?"

"Oh yeah, you're the whole package Dillon. For sure, if I was a little bit younger and there was no Sean I would be all over you," I laugh as he struts around.

"I knew it." He nodded, smiling all over himself. "But it's probably best you stick with Sean though."

"Why is that?"

"Because I'm a heartbreaker Ava, and I like you. I would hate to do that to you."

"A heartbreaker?" I ask, laughing at him.

"Yeah, you know, I just can't help it. Girls constantly falling in love with me, and I try to stick with one, but then she goes all crazy on me. I find another one and it ends up the same way. It is sad really, but that's my life I guess. It's a curse being so desirable sometimes."

"Oh, I'm sure," I laugh at him but he isn't as amused. "So you broke Taylor's heart? I thought for sure you two were…"

Dillon interrupts quickly, "Damn, you and Sean spend way too much time together. I think you share a brain or something." I laugh even harder.

"So?" I asked.

"So what?"

"How is Taylor?" I cock my head, waiting for his answer as he glances up from his remaining orange slices.

"She's fine, I guess." He mumbled.

"You guess," he glances up at me to confirm.

"No, it is good thing actually. I mean, I support her fully. I didn't tell you, but she has this really great voice, so I helped her get this job at a club to sing."

"That was nice of you." I say, causing a slight smile on his face.

"Yeah, she really loved it. And I loved going to see her except … well now she has signed a contract and is off to LA to record her first album."

"Oh. Well, maybe you can go with her." My response causes him to laugh as he explores the shelves and drawers.

"No, she isn't going to have a whole lot of time to see me, so no sense quitting my job and moving. Besides, Jalen is going to be with her every step of the way since they are now writing partners." He sighs as I suddenly realize his troubles.

"Oh Dillon, I'm sorry. You fell for her hard, didn't you?"

He shrugs. "Fall for her? I don't know… I am not sure I know what love is, Ava. I have really only been in love once. She was my best friend from the time we were twelve until we were eighteen. She lived right next door, and our bedrooms were right across from each other. We would stay up for hours talking and dreaming about our lives when we grew older. I didn't see her as anything but a friend until … well anyway I fell hard. And she said she felt the same."

"What happened to her?"

"Her father moved her away. He really hated me. I guess he convinced her to feel the same because I never heard from her again. Promised myself I would never feel that way again about anyone."

I hug him. "You know, I thought I would be alone forever after I went through some horrible things, but then came Sean. Sometimes you just have to be patient."

"Well, enough of the prying into Dillon's crazy and disturbing life please."

I nod in acceptance.

"Do you want anything else? I saw a bunch of great food over here," Dillon said, snooping and filling his pockets.

"No, I'm good. Do you know when Sean is due on set?" I asked him.

Dillon glances out the window. "No, but it looks like they are starting to gather. We probably still have some time before Sean is ready. And boy are they frantically looking for you! Sean must have thrown another fit when he found out they lost you."

I roll my eyes, "I wish he would just listen for once."

Dillon laughs as he bites into a pre-made sandwich. "I suspect Sean is not one for negotiations."

"Ummm no, I don't think he will ever get to that point."

"Your daughter is in trouble or should I say her boyfriends are in trouble. He's going to scare the hell out of them."

"Maybe not ... maybe he will calm down and be understanding and patient with them," I said, barely able to contain a smile.

Dillon doubles over with laughter. "That's funny. I bet he is going to either severely injure them or kill them if he ever catches them touching her. If I were you, I would build a room to lock him up in with only a view window. When she brings the guy over, put him in there and let him see the guy but make it sound proof so the poor kid can't hear him threaten his life. Make sure to keep him in there until after the date is over." I laugh, picturing his crazy idea. "No, forget that, no view window. He will hunt the poor kid down. Tell Sean she doesn't date at all until he's so old he can barely move."

"Well hopefully we will have grandchildren by then."

"Grandchildren? You better hope you have a boy then, because that's about the only one that's going to be allowed out of the house." Dillon said, shaking his head.

"Did you ever have a girl's father scare you?"

Dillon bites into an apple, "Ummm, there was this one girl whose Dad ... he was *crazy*. He thought I was a smartass punk - at least that's what he said to me. He told me he would shoot me if he caught me near his daughter. I wouldn't have taken him seriously but he brought the gun out and loaded it right in front of me. Crazy son of a bitch."

"So you stopped seeing her."

"No," he said casually.

"No?"

"No, she was hot. I snuck into her room that night. I climbed up a tree in the back, right into his daughter's bedroom. We did it while the old man sat out on the front porch waiting for me."

"Did he ever find out?"

"Do I look dead?" He said, holding out his arms.

"Do you always do the opposite of what people tell you to do?" I asked.

"That's enough about me. It looks as though your husband is going to be called here soon."

I jump off the counter and kiss Dillon on the cheek, "Thank you Dillon, for making me feel better and taking my mind off of things." He winks at me.

"Whatever you need, but can I ask one favor?"

"What's that?"

"Can you kiss me one more time?" He leans down with his other cheek facing me. I smile and reach up to kiss his other cheek. "Perfect."

"Are you going with me?" I asked him.

"Yes, but hold up. Let me grab some of these rolls and oh, and a banana." He said, stuffing his pockets with more food.

"When was the last time you ate Dillon?"

"I just had lunch with Sean in his trailer, why?"

"Where does it all go?"

"Where does what go?" He asked, biting into another sandwich.

"Never mind," I said as the surprisingly fit Dillon shrugs and follows me out.

We both walk cautiously while trying not to be noticed. Dillon taps me on the arm and points towards Sean. He is dressed in a driving suit that fits him snugly, showing off his body perfectly. He takes my breath away as I cower at Dillon's side, hiding from him.

"Did you come out here to see me baby?" I turn to see Joel's evil smile.

"Stay away from me," I said to him.

"So that's how it's going to be now?" Joel said, trying to look surprised.

"Joel, you attacked me in my own home." Dillon straightens instantly, eyeing Joel as he moves me to his other side. Joel doesn't even hesitate to move towards me. He brushes his hand through my hair before grabbing the back of my neck and pulling me towards him, "I have a feeling you might change your mind soon. I promise I will be the best you've ever had." He crushes his lips to mine.

"Hey, get off of her." Dillon said, pushing Joel off me.

"Settle down kid, were old friends."

"I think you better get away from her before you get hurt," Dillon said, stepping in between us and daring Joel to try anything.

"Ava, you certainly have an interesting ability to get men to run to your rescue."

"I don't need rescuing from you Joel, I handled you just fine on my own."

"You sent your dogs after me." Joel huffed.

"Don't you have somewhere to be? Where is your wife anyway?" I asked him.

Joel laughs and starts to walk away, but suddenly yanks me off my feet and crushes me to him. I scream as he holds my face to his and begins groping me.

"Get the fuck off of her!" Dillon screamed at him, taking hold of Joel's shirt.

Suddenly, Joel is ripped away from me and I am flung into Dillon's arms. I look down at Joel on the ground, struggling against Sean.

"Sean stop!" Randy yelled, running over to pull him off Joel.

Joel sits up, wiping the blood from his lip. "Don't you have a scene to do Sean?"

"Touch her again and I will kill you." Sean said, struggling against Randy's grip.

"Get over it Sean, it was just a kiss."

Sean jerks loose from Randy and grabs Joel by the collar, "Don't ever touch her again." He punches him one more time, sending him hard to the ground. He eyes him for a time as he slowly backs away and pulls me away from Dillon, guiding me away with his hand on my back. "I thought I told you to leave?"

"I thought I told you I wasn't going to." Sean stops abruptly, causing our new entourage to scramble to keep from running into each other and us.

"Please Ava, I don't want you here"

I grip his hands, biting my lip as he softens towards me. "I'm not leaving you Sean." He stays connected with my eyes, waiting for something.

His hands leave me abruptly, "You stubborn ass! I swear, I wish you would listen to me for once."

"Sean they're ready for you," an assistant yelled to him.

"I will be right there." He turns back towards me, "Are you going to leave or are you going to make me be mean to you and have you escorted out? And I don't mean by the soft-touch boys behind you. I will have security do it, and they don't care who you are."

I shake my head.

"No what, Ava?"

"No, I'm not leaving," I said crossing my arms.

His eyes burn as he breathes heavily, "Fine, but remember you forced me to do this." He waves his hand at some nearby security men who sprint over to us.

"Sir?"

"Please escort this woman off the set immediately," Sean said with no hesitation in his voice.

"Sean, don't you think you're being a bit harsh?" Ethan yelled at him.

"She can sit in your trailer or something," Randy tried to step in.

"Get her out of here," he looked right into my eyes as he gave the order.

They take my arms, "Come on Ms.; don't make us get rough with you."

Sean walks away. "Fine, I'll go. Just let go of me." They both release me and I run back at Sean grabbing hold of him. He turns around trying to release my hand from him.

"Ava!"

"Sean please don't do this stunt. Have someone else do it please!" I cried as I gripped him harder.

"Ava, go!"

"Sean don't, I have a terrible feeling, please."

The men take hold of me, ripping my hands from him. I fight them as they throw me around while Sean watches the whole struggle. When they throw me to the ground, I scream out in pain as they jerk my arms behind me to put on handcuffs.

"No wait!" The men fight me to get me up and on my feet. "Let her go," Sean yelled, running towards me.

"But you said…" one of the guards said.

"I know what I said, but I don't want her hurt either, and apparently she is going to make sure that happens." Sean said, looking at me disgusted. They take the handcuffs off of me and he takes my hands. "Why won't you listen to me?" He sighed.

"I don't want you to do this Sean," I pleaded with him.

"It's too late Ava." I shake my head at him furiously. "I don't have time for this. At least don't watch." He leans in and kisses me before darting away from me. I watch him get ready and Ethan stands in front of me, as does Randy, shielding me from the view. Dillon hugs me as I cry in defeat.

"I'm so scared Dillon."

"I know, but he should be fine. They have all these people who know what they are doing. Tell you what, you look away and I will watch for you?"

"Okay," I whimpered, burying my face into his chest. We stand for a while, waiting for the whole thing to get setup. You would have thought they would have been ready long ago. *I mean how long does it take to get someone into a car? If they can't even get that right* ... Suddenly the loud engines rumble, startling me back into reality.

"They're starting Ava, it will be over in a few minutes." I hold Dillon tight, trembling. Closing my eyes, I leave the whole scene not wanting to hear the loud noises anymore. I never imagined I could make myself go deaf, but fear forces you to do unimaginable things.

When I feel Dillon tense and stop breathing, I rush back to reality. "He did it!" I lean away from him, watching his joyful face. "Damn that was cool as hell!" I turn to look and see Sean's car closing in on concrete barriers ... fast, and with a giant semi chasing. *It's not over.*

"Get out of the way Sean!" Randy yelled

"Sean stop!" Ethan screamed.

My body goes numb as I watch his car turn way too fast, crashing into a barrier and causing flames to shoot high out of his car.

Everyone reacts, seemingly too slow. "Get him out!" I screamed. "Sean!" I yelled trying to run to him but Dillon holds me back.

"Ava, no. They're getting him, see they're getting him." Dillon said, fighting to hold me back. I scream for Sean hysterically until the world around me goes silent. They pull him out and onto a stretcher, and as they come closer with him, I struggle to get to him. Ethan's eyes are intense as he runs beside him. He glances up at me with a look I don't understand, then shakes head before rushing away with Sean. I barely got to see his face as they whisked him away into an ambulance.

I am his wife and I didn't even get to leave with him.

Randy walks uneasily towards me. "He's unconscious, but breathing." I have no control over my fear as I watch his car become indiscernible as it is taken over by flames.

"Ava, you need to calm down." The images of him being pulled out of that car, lifeless, take hold of me. "Ava!" The screaming and chaos surrounds me, then everything goes dark and quiet...

Chapter 24

Rebecca

"Rebecca, where are you?" Joel yelled, interrupting my tranquil escape.

"Taking a bath if you must know." Joel walks into the bathroom and despite my cucumber obstacles I can still feel his eyes on me. "What do you want?" I sighed.

"You know, when I said you could stay here, I didn't realize you were going to take over the whole place."

"Can we talk about this later? I am releasing my stress." I hum, easing down deeper into my bubbles.

"*Stress?* What stress?"

Removing my cucumbers, "Don't you have somewhere to be or something?"

"No, this is my home."

"That your Father pays for," I emphasized.

"Either way my dear, it is still not yours."

"Your point is?"

"My point is that you have no right to go out and spend my money, buy new furniture, new draperies and new ... what the hell is that on my bed?"

Exasperating. "A duvet. It's a duvet with decorative pillows to match the new draperies. This place looked drab and boring Joel. It needed a little uplift and, I must say, some style."

"And what's with all those Bloomingdale bags in the living room?"

"I needed some new clothes. Do you expect me to run around this place in the same outfits all the time? It's not as if it's coming out of your account. Your father is paying the bills lately."

"For now, until he finds some other reason to be disappointed in me. I am taking away your credit cards and your bank card."

I instantly jump out of my bath water. "You can't do that!" I screamed at him.

"I can and I will."

"What am I suppose to do all day?" I demand to know.

"Oh I don't know, why don't you try relieving your stress?" I glare at him and his mocking tone. "Or how about you act like a wife and have my dinner ready when I get home. Maybe even be ready and naked in my bed so I can relieve some stress of my own."

"I will hire a cook, and don't push it."

"Why? Because you're saving it for who … everyone?"

"At least I can get whomever I want into bed." I smile triumphantly, sitting back down in my bath as Joel strolls towards me.

Sitting on the edge of the tub he runs his fingers through the immense bubbles. "Not everyone you want. I do believe you missed out on one particular person." He said, flicking the bubbles remaining on his fingers in my face before walking away with an obnoxious grin.

"No thanks to you, prince charming!" I yelled after him. My tranquility interrupted and ruined, I get out in a huff. Joel sits at his desk working on something, frantically making notes as I sit comfortably; watching his odd behavior for something to annoy him with. "Are you actually working or are you too high to realize that you're not writing anything important?" I do not even wait for his response before starting on my nails.

"Were leaving next week" He said matter-of-factly and still writing.

"For where?"

"L.A. Dad has me helping out on another film. He bought us a place in Long Beach."

I jump up, leaping to his side. "Oh Joel, I can't believe it! Are you serious?"

"Yes, but I do need you to be good to me or I will find a new wife."

I pull his chair around to face me and straddle him with a purpose, "How's this?"

"A lot better, but I expect to see a lot more respect and a hell of a lot more dedication from you in the future."

I swirl my fingers up and down his chest, moaning his name and feeling him heat up with every passing second. He undoes his pants, pulling them down enough for me to lower down to meet his throbbing erection. My mouth welcomes any and all stress he needs to release and Joel welcomes my respect. He watches me work and moans appreciatively. I finish him off in perfect fashion and earn one of my credit cards back.

‹3≈0›

It's the morning of the stunt and Joel is in an exceptionally good mood. I watch him set his fully packed suitcases at the door, preparing for our departure to L.A. "Ready to leave already? So should I assume you are giving up on your quest to get back at your old friend?" I asked him.

"Not quite," he said with a peaceful smile.

I'm intrigued. "Isn't today the last day of shooting with him?"

"Yes and the day of the big stunt, which he finally agreed to do, earning us a huge pay out from my father."

"Do tell, my newly successful husband, what do you have in mind?"

"I'm not sure you want to know Rebecca, it is not going to be pretty."

"Will you stop playing games and tell me already?"

"You are so impatient." I cross my arms blocking his exit. "I manipulated Sean's brakes. They should become completely inoperable about the time he needs them the most."

I gasp, "Joel, you're going to kill him."

"Does that concern you?"

I think about it for a second, "Actually, no. It might even be nice to see that redheaded bitch struggling to live without him." I smile eagerly. "Oh it would be even better if she is so heartbroken she can't hardly go on, get fat and wrinkled and terribly pathetic. Waste away like a complete nothing." I flick my fingers to emphasize her dismissal. Joel shakes his head at me. "What? Well at least I'm not killing her."

"No, you prefer a life of misery as opposed to immediate destruction. I'm not nearly as cruel."

I shrug, "Although, I would have to go to the trouble of checking in on her to get any real pleasure out of it. That will be a pain in the ass."

"Hire a detective to take pictures for you." Joel said, walking around me and exiting easily.

"No, I can't do that." I follow after him. "It's no fun if she doesn't know. I have to invite her to a good-will lunch, a charity lunch even."

"You know, you keeping tabs on Ava might be a good idea?"

"Really, why?" I asked curiously.

"Because, by the time Lillah is legal, I will be ready for a younger model anyway. And, as hot as her mother is… Well, she is looking more like her every day." Joel smiles, raising his eyebrows at me. "I can't wait to handle that."

"Funny," I said, narrowing my eyes at him.

"Who's laughing?" Joel walks past me and out the door with an obnoxious smile.

"Have a good day dear!" I yell after him.

"Be naked and ready when I get home honey," he yelled back. *The things I have to do to live suitably.* I pout briefly before remembering the credit card he gave back to me. *If he wants to celebrate, by all means I will make sure he has the celebration of his life.*

CR&

Shopping is so tiring sometimes, thank goodness they have valet at this mall. The boy drives up in my newly rented Mercedes, I get in and drive off without acknowledging his outstretched hand. My only decision now is, do I go to another store or home to take a breather before Joel comes home? I'm thinking shopping, but my feet are telling me otherwise. *Damn the dilemmas in my life.* Before I can make a decision, Joel calls. If I tell him I'm on my way home, maybe he will leave me alone. But, what if he is already home waiting for me? Then I can't go shopping and now I really want too! "Yes, my love, I am going home now."

"No, I need you to go to the hospital and find out about Sean for me."

"Oh I forgot about that, did he …?" I ask, feeling a strange twinge inside.

"I don't know. They carried him out of here so fast I didn't get much of anything. Then all the drama with Ava."

"Ava? Why was she there?" I ask rolling my eyes.

"To try and talk him out of it apparently. She was an absolute wreck. She screamed so loudly, I think she busted my eardrums and I wasn't anywhere near her."

"So, how is sweet Ava now?"

"No idea, but she is at the same hospital so check on her while you are there. Call me as soon as you find out something." Joel abruptly hangs up the phone before I can refuse.

"Why sure dear, I will be more than happy to run all over town for you." I mumble to myself. "Maybe I have something real important to do, but please don't bother yourself by asking."

I walk into the hospital undercover: a hat, sunglasses and my hair twisted up. No sense causing any attention to myself while I'm here. I carefully search for someone that can give me some kind of information. It is nearly impossible to find anyone to help me, but after wandering to a nearly deserted part of the hospital, I manage to find someone. *He has to be in a private room somewhere.* I approach, smiling sweetly at a happy young thing who seems to be working diligently.

"Hi, can I help you?" She asked at a level I could never reach, even if I was happy to see her.

"Hi, I was wondering if you could help me find a friend of mine?"

"I will do my best." She chirped. *She needs some Valium.*

"Great, well, he was brought in recently from a movie set nearby."

"Really? Here in Atlanta? Like an actor or something?"

I stared at the wide-eyed moron. "Yes. Well, he may not be under his real name, but could you give me an idea of where someone like that might be taken?"

"Ohhh, I don't know."

"Maybe you could just tell me about the people that have been admitted in the last hour," I asked.

"Well let's see," she said, typing away as if she got laid at lunch.

"Okay, it seems we have only had five people admitted since this morning."

"Great, so can you tell me about them?" I ask, ready to move in the right direction.

"Like what?" She asks.

"Like their names, age, anything would help?" I huff.

"Oh, I don't know."

"Well what does it say?" I emphasized my words carefully.

"I don't think I can tell you specifics."

"Then tell me what they were admitted for." Slipping her a hundred her eyes widen and a smile spreads across her face, "Any information you can give me would be helpful and appreciated."

"Oh, well, there was a lady admitted for kidney stones. "

"No, not her." I sigh.

"And there was a gentleman admitted after a car accident."

"What about him?"

"Ummm… Oh, he died." She says with a pitiful pout.

Straightening my posture, "How did he die?"

"It says here it was a massive trauma after a head on collision." She shakes her head. "He was drunk. And so early in the day too." She ticks her tongue, as if he can hear her disapproval. "But I think his death was more due to the metal rod that came through his windshield and into his head, not the car accident."

Oh dear God. "No, that's not him."

"Okay, there is another car accident, a pregnant woman who fainted and a man who fell out of his wheel chair."

"Where is the other car accident at?" I wait, watching her smile up at me - motionless. "Are you going to tell me?"

"I can't"

"Why not?"

"Because it says private."

"But I have to get him his special medication or he might not make it without it."

"Oh no, that's terrible," she pouts.

"I know, so can you give me the room number," I asked hopeful and handing her another hundred.

"I can't sorry."

"Why?" I snap at her.

"Because it says private."

"Just call the room and ask if I can visit," I pleaded.

"I can't, it says private so no number is listed to call."

"Why didn't you just say that in the first place?" I cringe, wanting to strangle her perfectly tanned neck.

"I did."

Absolutely exhausting, "Well, do you have any idea where they might have a private room?"

"No."

"Can you tell me his status at least?"

"It says … private," she said, smiling happily at me.

"Can you tell me anything about him?"

"Ummmm … No."

Rolling my eyes, "Thanks for all your help," I mumble. Taking out my phone, I start to call Joel but then remember something else important.

"Ummm…" I search for the chirpy girl's name tag, "Casey."

"Yes ma'am?"

"Could you tell me about the woman? The … pregnant woman. Where is she?"

"Oh, the Jane Doe?"

"The Jane Doe?" I ask, confused.

"Yeah, that's what we call people when we don't know their names." She said, nodding as if it were some big secret.

"Yes, thank you. How is it no one knows her name?"

"Don't know exactly, because her I.D. says her name."

My eyes widened, "You have her I.D.?"

"Yes, all of her things were with her when they put her in the room down the hall. I accidently dropped them all over the floor when I was trying to get her settled in. It was such a mess. Her things went everywhere, and I was carrying that water and that went everywhere. I didn't think I would ever …"

"*Casey*… Dear… Can you just tell me which room exactly that she is in?"

"Oh sure, because she certainly isn't marked private but …" I mock her own smile and hand her what money I have left. "She is five doors down on the left."

"Thank you, Casey. You have been *very* helpful."

"You're welcome. But, if you are going to go see her, please be careful. The doctor told me to make sure she rests and is not upset in any way. She is in a delicate condition right now," she said, nodding with a motherly glare.

I turned away from the girl and stroll towards the room down the hall. Before walking in, I search for any sign of persons that might not welcome my presence. I giggle at the sight of Ava laid up and attached to machines. Her eyes are closed, but she is seemingly alright. I glance around the drab room, which is clearly not meant for her. They really did screw up. If Sean finds out, he will be irate. I toy with her machines, deciding what to do with my new information, again eyeing the room before turning back towards her. "Ava?" I brush her arm to see if she will awake. Her eyes flutter. "Aaaavvvaaa." I sung as her eyes open slowly, and looking obviously confused as to where she is.

"What are you doing here?" She asked rudely.

"Just thought I would visit you and express my condolences."

She looks away from me, trying to sit up. "Leave me alone, Rebecca."

"Okay, if you want it that way, but I thought I would at least check on you since no one else will."

"What are you talking about?"

"Well, since you're the reason Sean wrecked the car..." Her eyes rise to mine again. "You really should not have distracted him so. It is just terrible how things happen sometimes." I sigh, pouring some water into a cup and looking at her sympathetically over the rim as I drink.

"Leave, Rebecca," she insisted.

"Well, I am sorry to hear about Sean and ..." I pat her arm. "And your other little loss. But, I am sure you will find a way to go on." Her expression intensifies and I have to fake my shock. "Oh dear, they didn't tell you?"

"Tell me what?"

"He died, Ava." Her eyes focus on me. "Sean died shortly after he arrived at the hospital. Massive trauma, they said." I turn away from her to hide my smile. Such a tragedy."

"I don't believe you."

Gathering my sad, sympathetic expression again, "Don't. But I would think the lack of guests and this pitiful room should tell you something." She shakes her head and turns away from me. "They hate you Ava. You caused his death. His brother and his mother are distraught beyond belief. They are cursing your name to anyone who will listen. You know how they are, they have to have someone to blame. And on top of that, now you have lost Sean's baby too. The one chance they had to replace him, not that Sean could be easily replaced." I shake my head, pursing my lips.

"I don't believe you at all, Rebecca."

Nurse Casey hops into the room and none too soon. "How are we doing in here?" She asked, fussing over Ava.

"Umm, nurse Casey?" I asked.

"Yes," she said.

"My friend here is the wife of the man that was brought in earlier. You know the car accident victim."

"Oh, the one with massive trauma?" She turns to me, hovering her hand over her mouth, perfectly.

I nod, looking concerned, "Yes...that's the one."

"Oh no! So that's why you got so upset, huh?" She asked Ava.

"Can you tell me how he is?" Ava asked her.

The nurse makes a concerned face as she pats Ava, "Honey, he is going to be looking down on you every day from heaven I'm sure."

Immediate panic takes over Ava, "No. No, he can't be dead."

"I am afraid he died soon after he arrived honey, but it's going to be ..."

"No! No!" Her screams increase with every word. *Joel was right, she can scream.*

The nurse tries to calm her, but quickly realizes she has lost control of this situation. "Please, calm down. I probably should have had a doctor talk to you first. Please calm down. Oh, I am going to get in so much trouble. I am sure everything will work out just fine for you."

"I want to see him! Find him now!"

"Oh dear, I don't think that's allowed. I'm sure he is down in the morgue already." I have to bite my lip to keep from laughing at the simple-minded girl making it worse. Ava begins ripping out her tubes and needles as she pushes her way out of bed. She steps to the floor, swaying and holding her head. "You can't do that. Please stay in bed or I am going to have to go get a doctor."

"Get whomever you want. I'm leaving!" Ava screamed at her as she grabs her clothes and gets dressed in a drunken manner. Casey runs out of the room in a panic.

"Where are you going Ava?" I asked her calmly.

"I'm going to find him." She said, putting her shoes on.

Before she can reach the door, I grab her arm. "She just told you where he is. Must you torture yourself further?" She grips her face with tears forcing their way out. "I tell you what, you can come and stay with Joel and I for a little while. At least, until you can find a decent place of your own." She stares at me blankly. "He is excited to see you again."

"I have a home Rebecca."

"Not anymore, Ethan is making sure of it. You know how ruthless he can be. He is planning to take everything, including your daughter...the only child you have left now. He is using your recent drug indiscretions to get full custody of her." I sip my water, shrugging at her.

"He would never do that," she said, looking at me pitifully.

"Ava, look at this room. There is no one here and Ethan did recently see you completely gone, as did everyone else for that

matter. And now! You caused his brother's death. Your husband…
you *killed* him! You don't think Ethan hates you for that? Not to
mention, you lost his brother's child in the process." I mock the
sweet nurses ticking of the tongue. "You have nothing. No reason
for him to care about you at all. Sean is dead. Your unborn child is…
Well, it is too sad to discuss I suppose. You know, Ethan and his
wife have always wanted a little girl, so now they have yours and no
reason to have anything to do with you at all."

She slips down into a dark corner of the room, retreating within
herself. "No he can't be…" I get out of my chair, watching her sink
deeper into the darkness. "I can't live without Sean. I can't!"

"Well, he's gone now, thanks to you, and so is your home, your
daughter and everyone else you have called family since you met
him." She begins to shake violently. *Wow she is going to go crazy right in
front of me.* "He's dead Ava. Face it!" I said, stomping my way into her
face. "You're going to live the rest of your life without him!" I bend
down to her level, caressing her face until she focuses on me. "Sean
is dead, did you hear me? Sean is never going to come back to you
again and it is … all …*your*… fault. You couldn't just stay home and
let him do his job could you? You had to distract him." I screamed at
her. I stand back up, watching her squirm in complete hysterics.
"He's dead, Ava. You're all alone!" She grips her head, fisting her
hair so tight she is pulling it out. Her crying is so hysterical that she
goes silent in her screams. I pace around her, trying to decide how far
to go. "How does it feel, Ava, to kill your husband and your child, all
in one day? How does it feel to be all alone again? Do you think you
can find someone else like Sean? Or, maybe another Spencer will
come after you. Without Sean around, you are vulnerable again.
Vulnerable to be taken back to that isolated house. Back to that dark
room." I keep screaming the devastating words at her, getting more
and more insistent. "And no one will care, because Sean is dead
because of you." She fights towards the wall, climbing it away from
me. Away from my words. Away from her worst fears, which are
coming so painfully true to her. "Oh Ava, you deserve everything
that is coming to you. You fucking bitch, you killed the only man I
ever loved." *You took him away from me and now I am going to make sure
you are left with nothing.* I grab her face and force my words into her ear.
"Payback is a bitch, Ava. Now live with it … *alone.*" She screams,
falling away from me and seemingly giving up her fight.

"What the hell is going on in here?" A young man comes running in towards Ava. "Ava, what happened? We have been looking for you!"

I back away, realizing he knows her and was obviously sent to find her.

"He's gone, Dillon." Ava mumbled, completely broken.

"What?" Dillon asked, glancing up at me suspiciously.

Suddenly the hospital staff comes rushing in to Ava, fighting her and trying to get her hysterics under control. *Good luck.*

I walk out of the room calmly, smiling as I walk away. I glance back, expecting to see Ava's friend Dillon come after me, but instead I see him run in the opposite direction. *He knows where Sean is. Maybe I should wait here a bit longer.*

Chapter 25

Sean

They have me strapped in to the point I can barely move. I force Ava's image out of my head so I can concentrate, it won't be the first time I have to do it, not that it is easy for me to do. The engine roars and I smile, feeling the excitement of it all take hold of me. I wait for the signal and I take charge, adrenaline flowing through my veins from the start. I hit the ramp and feel it, it is perfect. The adrenaline races as I feel the success of it. I pump the breaks to slow down to make my turn away from the semi but nothing happens. I keep pumping as the car speeds with no response to my attempts to stop it. *Fuck!* Thinking quickly, I make a decision to aim for the barriers. I turn the car just before impact so I hit from the passenger side. The car flips upside down, crumpling and jerking my restraints from the car. Pain instantly shoots through me as the world begins to burn around me. I can't tell what is happening, or even see where I am. It is all a massive nothing, except for the screaming. Deafening screams. Ava's screams. My sudden recognition to her stirs me to try and find her, but I am unable to fight off the heaviness keeping me from her.

⚮

There is a pacing noise echoing around me. My eyes open as I move towards the noise. "Ahhh Shit!" I cringe.

"Stay still Sean, you cracked some ribs." Ethan said, hovering over me.

I grimace and hold my head. "My head is killing me."

"I will see if they can get you something for it," he said before leaving the room. I adjust my bed to better search the room. "She's not here," Ethan said, entering with two pills and some water.

"She who?" I asked, downing the pills he retrieved.

"I am assuming you're looking for your wife? Or did you hit your head so hard you forgot all about her?"

"No, I didn't forget about her, but I am surprised she isn't here. Is she that mad at me?" I asked, a little worried about what kind of wrath I will encounter.

"No, she has a room of her own." I look up at him. "She became hysterical when she saw you crash and passed out. They rushed her in soon after you."

I fall back into the bed, grasping my face with my hands, "Damn it. I told her! This is why I told her to go home." I punch the bed forgetting about the pain. "AAAggughh!"

"Yeah you told her alright, you both have issues of stubbornness."

I roll my eyes at his unnecessary comment, "So is she okay?"

"I don't know," Ethan said, avoiding my eyes.

"What do you mean you don't know?"

"They rushed you both in and somehow they have lost her somewhere." My confused expression must have begged for more explanation. "She was supposed to be in a private room next to you. Somehow they have misplaced her somewhere else in this place and no one seems to know where she is. It's incredibly frustrating, to be honest, but we're looking for her. They told Randy, when they brought her in, that they thought she would be fine if they could get her to rest."

"I feel better after hearing that, but would still like to confirm it. So when can I leave here?"

"Not for a few days at least, you have a concussion and they are taking it pretty seriously considering the stupid stunt you just did." I glare at him from the corner of my eyes. "So you're talking to me again?"

"No, get out," I said, leaning back into my bed.

Ethan laughs, "You know you would miss me."

"I can't if you are always around." Ethan leans back in a chair, his smile pissing me off even more. "Are you just going to sit there all day?"

"Mom told me to stay with you." He says, waving his hands innocently.

"Mom told you? Great, now you become the obedient son."

"You know what prick? You really need to get over it!" Ethan yelled at me. I try to roll away from him but my ribs scream at me to stay put. "I am sick of this. I understand you being angry for a while, but it's reached a point of absurdity. Yes, I screwed up and I am sorry for that. It's not like Rebecca is important to you anymore."

"I don't even care about Rebecca." I snap.

"Then what is it?"

"That you didn't come to me. You didn't come to me and tell me that you were having problems." I said, looking away from his judging eyes.

"I didn't want to get you involved. You were dangerously close yourself to crossing a line if I recall. The last thing you needed was being around me and both of us falling deeper into trouble. I didn't talk to anybody, Sean. I was scared and I didn't want to be judged."

"I would have never judged you, and I would have listened to whatever you had to say and helped you, however I could."

"I know that, Sean."

"Then why did you hide from me?"

"I didn't hide from you, I thought I was protecting you."

"Well maybe you should stop protecting me and let me help you."

"That's just it Sean, no one could have helped me - but me. If it wasn't for Abbey kicking me to the curb, I might have never snapped out of it."

"Abbey broke up with you?"

"Yes, she did. Worse day of my life, she didn't even look back. She told me she never wanted to see me again because she didn't want to be with someone that couldn't respect himself."

"What did you do?"

"I did what we Grant boys usually do, I assumed she was the crazy one and that I didn't need her." I laugh, and he follows. "Yeah, I lasted about a week before I went back to her begging. It never worked of course. I finally went to Mom to get her to help me and she told me no. I couldn't believe it. She sat us up and she wouldn't even help me get her back?"

"Judging from the ring on your finger and the two kids, I assume you came up with something."

"I checked in somewhere to work out my issues. Hard as hell, but I finally woke up and realized it's not all about me."

"It's not?" I mocked him.

"No smartass, and it's not all about you either. You and that stupid stunt, you didn't think about anyone but yourself."

"I needed to do it."

"No you didn't, it didn't make the film any better. You only wanted to be able to say you did it, that you are the official badass of Hollywood. I knew you wanted to do it from the beginning, and then

I stupidly challenged you on it and you forgot all about your wife, your daughter and your baby on the way."

"I knew it was going to be okay."

"No, you didn't, and it didn't matter if you did. Because no one else did."

"It was an incredible adrenaline rush though," I said, watching Ethan shake his head at me.

"Well enjoy it, because when Ava gets a hold of you I'm pretty sure you will be groveling for the rest of your life." He nods, feeling good about his prediction.

"It's not going to take that long," I shrug. "Ava gets mad but she doesn't hold onto things like that. She probably has already forgiven me. I am injured. She will be so happy that I'm okay that she will forget about her anger."

"Oh, I'm sure."

The door to my room opens and my mom walks in carrying bags. "Oh good, the fool is awake," she said.

"Mom?" I snap at her as she comes over to kiss me on the forehead.

"I went out and bought you some pajamas, and a toothbrush and …"

"You did what?" I said, looking at the things she is laying out on my bed.

"Now Sean, you are not going to stay in this hospital in that. All these girls are drooling, just waiting for you to get out of that bed and show your ass to them."

I laugh, "But Mom, I have a damn nice ass."

"Don't curse at me Sean, I'm your mother."

The door opens again and Randy comes in with Dillon following close behind. With food and drinks in their hands, they both come in and sit down. Immediately they adjust a table and some chairs so they can eat comfortably. "Just come in and make yourselves at home boys." I hold up my hands looking at Ethan.

"Thanks," Dillon called out as he chomps on some chips.

Randy leans towards me in his chair, "So Sean, I heard the jump looks incredible."

I sit up, excited. "Really?"

"Yeah, aside from you crashing the car into a million pieces and it bursting into flames, it was a complete success. But that part was pretty cool too." Randy nods happily.

My mother snaps her fingers at us and we both take notice. "I do not want to hear anymore talk about that damn stunt! Do you understand me?" She yelled at us, tensing her fists on her hips.

"Yes ma'am," Randy cowered from her.

"Sean?"

"Okay mom, settle down."

"Good, now I am going to go help Abbey by picking up your daughter and taking care of your dogs too." She kisses me as she tries to straighten my hair. I look over at Ethan as he fights his laughter. "Now you put those pajamas on I bought for you Sean, don't make me come back here and dress you myself."

"When did I revert back to five years old?" She glares at me. "Fine mother. Thank you."

She kisses Ethan as she does me, straightening his hair too. "You need a haircut Ethan."

"Yes mother." I look away at Randy and Dillon, who are biting their lips trying not to laugh. Luckily, they are next. She approaches Randy and Dillon, finding something to straighten or fuss about each one of them. When she finally leaves, we all laugh at each other, moving our straightened-up selves back into dishevelment.

"Your mom does realize were out of grade school now, right?" Randy asked.

"I don't think so," I said, sinking back into my bed.

Ethan gets up, and digs into the bags she left. "Okay Sean."

"Okay what?" I asked him, eyeing him suspiciously.

"Let's get you changed." He holds out pajama pants in front of me.

"Are you serious?" I laughed.

"Yes, I'm serious. You know she will come back and do it herself otherwise, and that won't be pleasant."

"Fine," I said through my teeth. I struggle out of bed, feeling the pain in my ribs. Ethan holds out the pants, low enough for me to step in. "Lean on me and step in," he said as I glared at him.

Randy and Dillon immediately begin laughing uncontrollably. "This is stupid Ethan!"

"What do you want me to do?" Ethan said huffing.

"Give them to me and let me put them on myself," I said jerking the pants away from him.

"Alright, I am only trying to help."

"Don't," I said, struggling to try and put them on myself, but my ribs are taped so tight I can hardly move.

"Nice ass Sean," I look back at Randy winking at me.

"You would notice, bitch." I said, shaking my head.

"Hey, this is cool, I always wondered how a celebrity puts on his pants. Apparently it's with his ass out." Dillon laughs.

"Dillon!"

"Yeah Sean."

"Why are you here?"I asked him.

He shrugs, "My flight doesn't leave until tomorrow morning, so I thought I would hang out with you until then."

"Well go somewhere else, you're starting to annoy me."

"Where do you want me to go?" He asks.

"Dillon," I cringed.

"Why don't you go see if they have located Ava?" Ethan interrupted my frustration.

"Why are any of you here bothering me, when you could be looking for my wife, who you managed to lose?"

Dillon and Randy get up, still snickering to themselves. I wait for them to leave before I try to get dressed again but Randy pokes his head back in. "Hey Sean?"

"What?" I sighed.

"I like your jammies," Randy laughed before running out.

"Fucking assholes, I swear. I'm the one injured and they're laughing." I mumbled. "Shit!" I can't get it.

"Do you want some help now?" Ethan offered, smiling when I hand over the pants.

"Yes, but not a word of this to anyone." He snickers as he holds them for me. "Ethan."

"I promise, Sean." He stresses, but I know he is fighting laughter.

When I finally get dressed I crawl back into bed, trying to relax.

"Do you want to watch TV? I want to catch the stock reports," Ethan's voice fades into the background as I close my eyes drifting off easily.

Cས8

Bam! My door slams open, nearly startling me right off my bed.

"Sean!" Dillon screamed at me

"What!" I said annoyed.

"It's Ava. I found her and she's not good."

"What do you mean she's not good?" Ethan asked him.

"When I found her, some woman was screaming at her and Ava was all balled-up in the corner of the room, hysterical."

"What woman?" Ethan asked.

"I don't know who she was, but I think she told Ava that you're dead," Dillon said.

"She doesn't believe that?" I breathed.

"I think she does, Sean. I asked her what was wrong and she just kept saying… 'he's gone'."

I jump out of bed and make my way to the door. "Where are you going Sean?" Ethan asked, grabbing hold of me.

"She thinks I'm dead, Ethan."

"I will go and talk to her," he said.

"I don't think that will work Ethan. She is beyond consolable, her eyes are just so … empty," Dillon said.

I eye Dillon as his words cut right into me. "Ethan, I have to go find her." As we get closer I can hear her terrified and broken screams. It scares the hell out of me.

"That's her room," Dillon said, pointing to her door as we round the corner. "And that's the woman who was yelling at her." I look over to see Rebecca smiling at me.

"What did you do?" I glare at her.

She shrugs happily, "Sean. You are alive. Oops, my mistake." She giggles, hiding her smile behind her hand.

The only thing that keeps me from strangling her is Ava, who runs out her door and away from me. "Ava!" I screamed to her. She stops but doesn't look at me. "Ava!" I yell again and she falls against the wall gripping her head and slipping down to the floor shaking.

Ethan immediately runs after her, "Ava, it's okay, Sean is fine."

"I'm so sorry Ethan! I'm so sorry!" She yells, gripping his shirt wildly. Ethan picks her up, looking as worried as I feel.

Ethan carries her to me. "Ava," I said, running my fingers through her hair. She jerks away, looking at me obviously frightened. "Ava, it's okay, she lied to you." Shaking her head slowly, she looks me over silently as Ethan sits her on the floor. She is a mess. Her eyes are just as Dillon said - dangerously empty. Looking at her, I see nothing but the same image of her mother after her father's death. I reach out for her, brushing my fingers across her cheek to push her hair out of her face. Her hand rises up to me, trembling. I watch as her fingers shake their way towards my chest. I take her hand and hold it to my face, her breathing instantly becomes erratic. She grips my shirt hard and holds it tight before crashing into my sore ribs and crying out. Wrapping my arms securely around her, I try to console her as best I can, but her response to me ... is not Ava. "Ava, look at me," I said, lifting her chin up to me. "Everything is going to be okay. Come back to me, Ava." Her eyes flutter, for a second.

"No," she cried. "I don't understand." She twists in my arms until she finally looks up at me on her own, regaining some life again.

"I'm not dead, everything is okay," I said to her, cradling her face in my hands.

"Sean?" I nod with a slight smile. She smiles back at me and I begin to relax, bringing her hard into my chest despite my own pain.

"Damn Ava, you scared the hell out of me," I said but she begins to go weak in my arms. "Ava?" I pull back, watching her contort as if she is in severe pain. "What's wrong?"

"Doctor!" I look up, noticing an entire staff of nurses including Pamela watching us. "Sean we need to take her now!"

"What? What's going on?" She pulls Ava from my arms, rushing her away from me.

"Sean ..." I look over at Ethan as he stares at the floor. I follow his gaze to the spots of blood.

"Oh God," I whispered, watching Rebecca smile joyfully before she prances away.

"We will make sure she gets what's coming to her, but now is not the time." Ethan tries to reassure me. *I don't understand how she could be that evil ... and I never saw it?*

∞

The pain in my head is minor compared to the fear holding me hostage right now. "Sean," a soft voice calls out to me. I lift my head from the darkness of my palms as Pamela grasps my hand and leads me down one hall and then another, down an elevator and then through a deserted hall to an empty room. She faces me with a concerned expression and I begin to shake. "I wanted to tell you first," she said with a warning exhale. "Ava is going to be fine."

I nearly smile but quickly realize that's not why she brought me to this secluded place. "And the baby?" I asked, feeling my worst fears cut me to an unfathomable depth.

Pamela looks at me saddened, shaking her head silently. "Ava doesn't know yet." Clinching my eyes shut, I fist my hands into my eyes.

"You lost a child, there is nothing worse than that." I try to hold it together, but her words send me to my knees, releasing the pain with a deafening scream. Pamela's warm hands try and comfort me. "That's it, let it go. She's going to need you to be strong when you see her." I bury my tear soaked face into her shoulder. "Yes, you lost something wonderful, but you still have something beautiful and wonderful waiting for you. She loves you very much." She said, pulling my face to look at her. "You need to be there for her, she is going to feel even more pain than you can even imagine. It's her body that lost the child. She's going to feel responsible."

"But it's my fault. It's my fault, not hers," I cried out.

"It's no one's fault, Sean. Neither of you could help what happened."

I continue to cry in her arms, releasing the pain from every part of my body until I can't cry anymore.

"Are you ready to see Ava?" She asked me.

I shake my head at first, but change my mind when I think about her. *I need to see her, I need to hold her.* I clean my face up and take a few deep breaths before I follow Pamela back up to the room adjacent to mine. Her new room echoes. I hesitate to approach her, gazing over her as she faces the window opposite the door. They have her cleaned up in fresh hospital clothes, her hair brushed to softness and her face fresh and beautiful. She twitches when I touch her. "Ava," I whispered.

She shakes her head, "Don't." She faces me with tears already built up in her eyes, "Don't say it, Sean; please don't say it." Holding her face to mine, I close my eyes, feeling her tears run down my cheek. "Oh God," she cried. I struggle for comforting words that never come. All I can do is take her into my arms and curl up in her tiny bed with her. She cries for hours against my chest, and I release tears I didn't know had left. When that numb feeling finally overwhelms us, the silence becomes our only form of communication.

Exhausted, I close my eyes, listening to the rhythmic sounds of the rain and feel her heart beat against my painful chest. No one bothers us, no one even tries. The rain continues to fall as the rhythmic tapping on the window sets the pace of our breathing and the darkness becomes darker.

☙❧

I am not sure who I hate more, the snake or the rat that lead her here. Ava continues to work, and with me home she spends even more time at the office. Although it is a relief from our deadly silence when she is home. All we have these days are conversations with one-word answers and a complete avoidance of anything that might provoke much more. I watch her drift from one room to the next with no emotion towards me, breaking my heart into a million pieces from neglect. Every night we lie beside each other and despite my attempts to touch her, there is never any response in return. Her hands are lifeless against my touch and her eyes continuously shift away from mine. My guilt grows and I am not sure how much longer I am going to be punished. With Lillah's birthday fast approaching, Ava might break our silence, or at least I hope she will.

It is late and Lillah is already in bed. Ava has her reading glasses on and is stretched out reviewing details, as she calls them. I sit nearby, desiring her more than I realized. I almost forget to speak as I fantasize about her. Her eyes lift, catching mine and startling me out of my trance. "So what are we going to do for Lillah's birthday this weekend?"

"Oh, I thought we would keep it simple. Just the three of us … maybe."

"Ava, you know my mother is going to want to be here, and what about Abbey and Ethan. And Lillah will want Collin here. They have watched Lillah, I don't know how many times, we should at least watch Collin for the night. And Kyle will want to be …"

"*Fine*, do whatever you want," she snapped, looking back down at her paper work.

Watching her ignore me again, the anger builds up inside of me. "You know, it's one thing for you to shut me out but it's another when you shut everyone else out."

"I don't know what you're talking about!"

"Are you serious? Ava you are a walking zombie. You are completely void of any life at all. I understood for a while, but now it's… "

"Well I'm sorry! I didn't realize how much I was bothering you Sean."

"That's not what I meant."

"Sean," she yelled at full attention.

I meet her stance, "What Ava? What is it? Talk to me for God sakes, talk to me! I can't take much more of this." I yelled, shaking my hands at her.

I refocus on her face and her tear-filled eyes, "I'm so sorry. I am so sorry, Sean" she said before throwing everything in the floor and running off. Weak and unsure, all I can do is fist my hands and crumble.

CBℰO

Ava and I barely speak over the next few days, outside of the, "I don't cares" and "whatever you wants." I barely hear from her but despite her avoidance I am able to pull a nice party together for Lillah's birthday. Everyone is coming over, I hope it might help Ava come out of her shell some. I didn't bring out the circus but I do have it catered and a pony ride setup because that's what Lillah said she wanted when I asked her. I enjoy watching Lillah's face when the pony arrives. My joy overtakes me when I watch her ride the pony so in awe, she cannot even close her mouth.

"Three years old and a pony?" My mother said as she approaches me from behind.

I smile at her, "And your point is?"

"A little spoiled don't you think?"

"Not in the least, you know damn well Dad would have done it for her if he had been here."

Mom gives me a glancing smile, "Well you are just like him so I guess I shouldn't be surprised," she said laughing when Lillah waves at us, squealing happily.

"Now how can you say no to that face?" I asked her.

"I couldn't but I don't have to, I'm grandma, I'm supposed to give in."

"Ah, and what did grandma get her?"

"I got what every three year old needs"

"Which is?"

"A car."

"A car? Mother you didn't?"

"Not a big person's car, a little jeep battery car she can ride around outside, a silver one to match her mother's car." I force a smile as I turn back to watch Lillah. "How is Ava by the way?"

"I don't know, she won't talk to me."

"It will get better"

"I don't think so mom, she ..." I shake my head. "She is intent on punishing me."

"Punishing you? What did you do?"

"Please mother."

"No Sean, tell me, what did you do to cause any of that to happen?"

"I brought them into our lives for one. I did the jump to cause her to be in that hospital, I put her and my ..." Breathing heavily I look up to the sky to regain composure.

"Sean, none of that has anything to do with what happened. If it wasn't for that woman you two would be looking forward to your life with a newborn right now."

"She would have never come near Ava if it wasn't for me."

She grabs my face and forces me to look at her, "Sean you listen to me, what happened is not your fault and it's not Ava's. You will overcome this, both of you. You only need some time, some understanding, and a lot of communication."

I laugh, "Well communication is not happening mother; she barely looks at me."

"Don't worry about that, it will happen. I'm sure of it," she smiled kissing me on the cheek before returning inside.

Lillah played all day, overjoyed by the attention. The biggest joy for me was watching her open presents and blowing out her candles. She claps for herself as she looks at Ava and me for approval. She and Collin take turns riding on the pony, both laughing and being so cute that none of us could stop laughing at them. Even William with Ethan's help, sits on the pony for a bit, or at least until he tries to eat his mane. By the end of the day, we have to put Collin and Lillah to bed, neither making it to their beds before falling asleep. I help Ava clean up, smiling and feeling pretty good about the day when I notice Ava watching me. "What?"

She shakes her head and smiles, "Nothing."

"Okay," I mumbled.

"Sean?" I am shocked to hear my name come from her mouth. "You're an incredible father, Lillah couldn't ask for any better."

I stare at her astonished, "Thank you."

"You really are, I watched you today, and you handled everything perfectly. I wish I could ..." She walks away before finishing and I am not about to push her.

Ava steps out of the shower and crosses my path. Sitting on the edge of our bed all I want to do is make love to her. Taking off my own clothes is a task in itself I am so overcome, ignoring her naked wet body is something else entirely. She comes to bed running her hand down my back and if I hadn't noticed her before I suddenly become abundantly aware of her presence.

"Your bandage is gone, are you feeling better," she asked softly and seemingly seductive in my state.

"I went to the doctor and they said I was fine."

She works her fingers through my hair, "Your head and all?" My eyes roll back in my head.

"Yes," I said roughly.

"That's good."

"Uh huh," I don't look at her and I hold tight to the edge of the bed as her seductive breaths echo in my ears. She is silent and I think maybe she is going to bed but she reaches out to me again. Her touch so soft and warm I can barely breathe. It has been almost two months and I am distressed and hungry beyond words.

"Sean?"

"Uh-huh." *Oh please let her...*

"I don't blame you, you know? Your mother said you blamed yourself but it's not your fault," I sit silent vibrating with want. She slides closer to me, her warmth radiating, "I'm sorry, I have treated you the way I have. I didn't mean to be that way to you, I never wanted to hurt you," she said reaching for the back of my head caressing me. My desire exceeding my ability to control, I turn around to look at her sweet face smile innocently at me and that is all I can handle. I grasp her face finding her lips and sucking on each of them as I pull her down onto the bed. In an instant, I pull her shirt off, sucking on her breasts and feeling my way up her thighs to pull off her remaining piece of fabric. I rip off my pants and underwear in one move and without moving from her. Pressing my lips to her soft skin, grasping for her body to be closer to mine. I move up to her mouth again and hesitate long enough to look into her tear filled face. "Stop Sean, please stop," she says as I stare at her and my stomach twists into pieces.

I breathe hard as she sobs underneath me. I move off her to crouch at the edge of the bed. "Fuck! Damn you Ava!"I yell grabbing the nearby pillow and tossing it across the room. "I don't get it. I don't fucking get it!" I stand up staring at her, unmoved by her sobs. "I need my wife Ava, I need you to get over it already!" I scream at her until she looks up at me.

"Fuck you Sean!" She screamed at me. "Fuck you!" She approaches me smacking me anywhere she can reach and I take every hit. Her anger increases and I continue to take it until she collapses to the bed in front of me crying and screaming. "I'm so sorry," she said shockingly. "I'm so sorry Sean, I don't know why I did it."

"What are you talking about?"

Teary eyed and drained she looks up at me, "I gave up; I gave up. I don't want to be without you and she said they were taking Lillah, and they all hated me and blamed me for you and for the baby, that I thought I had already lost. I gave up once the nurse confirmed it. I know you said not to, but I did," suddenly her eyes meet mine. "I'm so sorry Sean it's my fault, it's all my fault. I didn't want be without you and I thought it didn't matter anymore. I thought I didn't matter anymore." Her broken demeanor crushes my soul.

I take hold of her focusing in on her eyes, "Ava it's not your fault. You were lied to and ..."

She shakes her head, "It is, and you know it. I have seen it in your eyes every day and I hate myself for it, more than you could ever hate me Sean. Please believe me, I hate myself more than you ..."

"Ava damn it, listen to me. I don't hate you, and it's not your fault. Your focusing on things that aren't real, you need to start focusing on what is, what you have now." I stare at her fuming, "Like your daughter! Like me! Damn it Ava. Your friends, family that all love you. You have thrown all of us away because you feel sorry for yourself." She looks back up at me as I scream at her. "Have you considered anyone else at all? Or have you only thought about yourself? You fucking bitch! It's not just you in this Ava. It is not only you suffering a loss." I let go of her, gripping my head. "Damn you, I have needed you so much and you let me suffer alone because you hurt. Do you not think I feel the loss? That I don't feel the pain you feel?" I throw up my hands, "You know what forget it. I'm sorry

I …" I shake my head and grab my clothes and shoes darting towards the door.

"Sean don't leave."

"Ava, what do you want from me? I can only do so much for you."

"I only need some more time."

"More time? Wow does that sound familiar." Her eyes hardened as she refocuses on me. I lean down into her face. "You know what Ava? You are just like your mother and that scares the hell out of me."

"My mother? What do you know about my mother?"

"I know plenty, I know she didn't have a simple car accident like you said," she stares at me with a confused expression. "Don't tell me you don't know what I'm talking about? Your mother Ava! You know the woman that committed suicide because she lost her husband. She killed herself leaving her sweet little girl behind like a coward. Your mother couldn't handle it, because she was weak and pathetic." Ava smacks me hard, her face changing instantly to horror and I know right then … *she really didn't know*. "Ava I … I'm sorry I thought you knew." Falling into bed she hides her face from me. "Ava, I'm sorry. I shouldn't have said that."

"Get away from me!" She screamed pushing my hands away from her.

"Ava?"

She pushes me again, "No get away from me."

I sit away from her, my head in my hands while she cries hysterically. After I swallow the huge lump in my throat, I leave, driving for hours, waiting for her to fall asleep.

Chapter 26

Ava

I lay in bed staring at the ceiling, missing him from the moment he left the room. It only took a few minutes spent with his mother to realize that I had been unfair to him. Mary has never been one to mince words. Her harshness towards me in privacy, although shocking was understandable. I have been horrible to her son. It took me awhile to recover from her brutal attack but I showed no signs in front of anyone else, especially Sean. When I watched him all day with Lillah and Collin, I was in awe. His smile was joyful and wonderful towards each of them and they loved him. Both of them grabbing hold of his neck and arms anything to be near him. He obliged their every want to be near him, even carrying both of them at one time as he spun them around in the yard. Their laughter should have been mine but my guilt overshadowed any possible joy I could have. And now to know the truth about my mother. I suspected but never questioned out of fear. Sean struck hard and deep and not realizing how deep he was striking me. I don't want to be her. As soon as I hear him approach, my heart beats hard against my chest. I close my eyes and pretend to be asleep, waiting for him to get into bed. He curls in near me, careful not to touch me. I look up at him slowly as he lies on his back.

"I thought you were asleep," he said glancing my way.

"I can't."

"Maybe you should … hell I don't know what you should do."

"I can't sleep until I tell you one thing, make one promise to you."

"Which is what?"

"I'm not my mother Sean, I am stronger than her." I said watching him turn towards me with a comforting hand to my cheek.

"I know," he whispered.

✿

After a long night, I am anxious to get a shower, my body feels tight and sore. Once in the bathroom I realize why, the bruises on my body are the imprints of Sean's hands. In his desperate attempt to reconnect, to awaken me to his fears, he was unaware how forceful he was with me. I was unprepared for his eagerness, I can't imagine what he must have been going through waiting for me to come back to him. I step into the heated shower trying to find strength within the pressure beating down on me. At the end, I wrap in a towel and walk out immediately running into Sean, causing me to stumble backwards. He catches me and I grab hold of him releasing my towel to the floor.

"You okay?" He asked holding me securely.

"Yes, thank you," I said reaching down for my towel but he stops me. I shy instantly as he examines body.

"What happened to you?" I shake my head ignoring his question. "Ava?" Sean let's go of me stepping back as he continues to gaze over me before raising his hand to my waist, matching his hand perfectly. "Oh God." He stumbles backwards staring at me wide-eyed.

"It's not a big deal, I barely felt it." I said to try and ease his obvious guilt.

He raises his arms over his head fisting the back of his hair. "I didn't realize what I was doing to you." He said continuing to back away from me, "I can't believe I would do that to you."

"No Sean it's …" He turns away from me running towards the other side of the bathroom vomiting.

I watch him hurt and beaten down, and I want so bad to help him. I go to his side with a cold cloth washing his face and his neck. "It's okay, I'm okay I promise."

"It's not okay," he said pulling away from my arms.

"Sean it is, you didn't hurt me, and certainly not nearly as much I hurt you." I cradle him to my body. "I know you didn't mean to handle me so roughly. Please don't push me away Sean."

"You did that already."

"I know that now, just don't …" I look down fighting for the right words. "I love you so much and I thought you blamed me."

"Why would you ever think that?"

"I saw it in your eyes, you were disappointed in me."

"Ava you were attacked and under pressure like no one should ever be, especially in the condition you were in. I should have never put you there."

"No, I should have never been there."

Sean shakes his head, "Ava I should have known that you would have been and I should have honored my promise to you. It's my fault …"

"Stop!" I yelled at him causing him to jump. "Stop talking about whose fault it is, apparently neither of us is perfect. Can we just put it behind us?"

Sean looks me in the eyes, "Are you sure?"

I nod, "Yes, I am. I don't want to feel guilty anymore and I certainly don't want you to feel that way."

His eyes soften as his hands creep up my arms to my face, "I love you, and I want you to be happy. But Ava if you need something more than me to get through this, please tell me."

"Maybe. Maybe I do, and I will get it, if you will stop blaming yourself?"

His eyes are so strong and reassuring. "I will do that. Let me know if you need me to go with you?" I nod. "Good," he said reaching down for my hand, kissing it softly, "Maybe when I get back from L.A. in a few weeks we can go to Ireland and get away for awhile?"

"I would like that very much," I said wrapping myself around him completely.

 C3 ››

Sean is arriving back from L.A. at noon and I am there at ten to wait for him. We are supposed to leave for Ireland tonight and I can't wait. My therapy sessions were helpful and after finally admitting that I am scared to get pregnant again, scared to lose another child, that's when I realized why I have been pushing him away. I smile anxiously when he catches sight of me. He instantly rushes to me with the warmest of embraces. His smile is wonderful, and his arms around me, deepen my joy. I crush my head into his chest as Ethan and Randy pass by, both calling out my name. I wave them on, not wanting to move from Sean's arms.

"Are we good Sean?" Randy asked before leaving.

"Yes, be sure you check in with Ethan and both of you let me know how it goes."

"We'll let you know," Ethan said exasperated with him.

"Ethan, I'm serious let me know the minute it's all done."

"We will let you know the minute it's all done. And I will break out the victory cigar with you from …" I feel Sean motion to him and I look up at Ethan as he eyes me smiling. "Don't worry Sean, it's handled. Your big brother, always has it handled." Sean rolls his eyes while Ethan laughs. "Just let me handle it. You know it will be my pleasure to."

"I know but I kind of would like to handle this one myself."

"You have more important things to worry about. Besides we both know its best you are nowhere in sight," Ethan said back to him.

"What's going on?" I asked watching them both talk secretly to each other. Sean looks down at me pulling me closer to him, "Ava don't worry; it's only a couple of business issues that we are taking care of." He kisses me, "Let's go home."

I nod walking with him to the car. "You will never guess what I did today?"

He smiles, "What's that?"

"I bought some new things for the trip, some things I think you are really going to like."

"Really?" Sean raises his eyebrows as I smile even bigger. "I can't wait to see them," he winks at me.

CREW

We arrive tired but happily when we see the beautiful old cottage restored perfectly. My design of the old place was rough but a few visits here with Kyle gave me enough information to create what was needed and still hold true to the original design that we loved so much. It was our home that helped pay our small firm's way for awhile, so it is even more pleasing to see it done spectacularly. I wondered why Kyle seemed so silent before I left, he being the last one to see it completed. With every step towards our home, I become more excited. It is gorgeous, welcoming and posses a charm like no other. Our first night we acclimate the boys and Lillah to the new surroundings. The boys easier than Lillah, they chase the geese instantly upon seeing them and other wildlife, announcing their presence to all. Sean and I sit out on the porch watching the boys run wildly, as Lillah fall asleep in my arms with Sean's arm stretched out around us protectively. The first night is easy, calm and with no expectations. It is the next day I feel the pressure.

I watched Lillah play all day, chasing birds and laughing at the boys chasing the geese. This was our time together and it is my job to make sure she is too tired to interrupt us tonight. Sean is spending most of the day out golfing with some of our new local friends while I spend the day preparing for our night alone. As nervous as I am, I am even more anxious for it to begin. Dinner is on the table, candles light up the room and my soft white dress hugs my body gently enough for me to feel comfortable. I look down at the boys after reviewing my setup one final time. "So what do you think? Over the top or just right?" Barely moving from their lounge positions they both give me an acknowledging cock of the head. "Yeah, right. It really doesn't matter does it?" The sound of Sean pulling in makes my heart skip a beat. *Just breathe.* I rapidly search the room for the right place to be when he enters. *How ridiculous, I don't know where to be, how to be, how could I have not considered that?* Like a fool I choose to hide as if I am suppose to jump out and yell *surprise* at my own husband for no damn good reason. Hovering around the corner and embarrassed by my own stupidity, I wait for him - hoping, praying tonight will go smoothly. I hear him enter the house and make his way into the dining area, pausing silently for longer than I would have expected. I walk from around the corner and his eyes find me instantly. "Surprise?" *Ugh - idiot.*

Sean laughs and my nervousness intensifies as he reviews my appearance. "What's this?" he asked.

I shrug, "I thought we would have a night alone together."

"Lillah in bed already?" He asks with an emerging smile.

"Yes, she has been playing very hard today."

Hiding his wide smile, Sean nods, "So what's for dinner, beautiful?"

I smile rushing over to uncover the massive preparation, "What do you think?" I said excited about sitting down with him finally and having all the pre-drama out of the way. It must look somewhat inviting because the kiss I receive from him causes my legs to go weak.

We talk through dinner without effort. His smile lighting up everything I want to feel. As dinner comes to a close I begin to feel the tension within me again, watching him lick his lips and eyeing me from the edge of his wine glass. *This is what I wanted. It's going to be perfect, it has to be perfect.*

Sean sits watching me walk around him to pick things up off the table. He reaches over playing with the bottom edge of my dress between his fingers, his lips full and wet from his tongue. I focus on him as he pulls away and gazes over me, "Thank you for dinner, it was wonderful." Our eyes connect with an exhaling breath. "I will start a fire while you're cleaning up," I nod. "Don't be too long," he winks before leaving the room.

I walk seductively to greet him but forget my wine and have to run back to retrieve it before entering the room at a gingerly pace and somewhat out of breath already. Sean has the fire going in the fireplace and seems just as anxious as he lounges on the sofa. I smile as he calls me over to him. Sitting in his lap, I curl into his welcoming arms as he takes my glass and places it nearby. My heart begins to pound and I can feel his doing the same. I watch him carefully, waiting for his eyes to meet mine and when they do, I melt. Feeling his lips and his hands caress me is all that I have been wanting. I return his affection, meeting his lips one for one and his tongue lingers with each matching touch. My legs shift and I sink deeper to his side as he grips my face and my body, breathing heavily into my mouth. All of him, his hands, his mouth, it all feels so good against my skin. His hand glides slowly up my bare leg, under my dress and to my ... *every day wear.* This is supposed to be perfect and not every day, I pull away from him.

"Sean wait!"

"Why, what's wrong?"

"I need a minute," he exhales closing his eyes as he releases me. "No, I promise I only need a minute."

He helps me up but doesn't look at me, "Okay." I look back once as I rush to get my perfect lingerie on for him. His sinking posture is defeating but I smile knowing he is going to be even happier once he sees what I have for him. I rush to get my clothes off but before I can get my outfit on I hear him leave. I look out the window watching him in the rain with his coat on and walking towards his car. I throw my dress back on and with my fancy lingerie in hand I hastily run through the house and out the door.

"Sean!" He stops, not facing me. "Where are you going?" I yell confused by his actions.

"I thought I would give you time," he yells back.

"But I said I only need a minute."

"Yeah well, I assume that means you're not ready at all. So before I hurt you again I'm going to go get a drink somewhere else."

"Don't you fucking leave me!" I scream at him.

"Ava - what do you want from me? I can't sit here and look at you and not want you. All I want to do is ..."

"That's what I want too."

He turns around, "Oh really? Then why did you stop me?" I stare at him in silence. "That's what I thought. You know what Ava you really need to get some help. I can't take this anymore. I love you but this is getting to the point of … well I am worried about you. You need to get some help, some real help because whatever you're doing now isn't working."

I scream and his stance stiffens, angering me even more. "You stupid ass," I cried as he stares at me. "I was changing into something better for you." Still he is silent. "Sean, I was trying to make it perfect for you." His stubborn resistance makes me crazy so I throw my fancy lingerie at him just missing his face as he catches it.

He looks up at me furious "What the hell are you doing?" He yelled.

"I wanted to make it perfect for you, so I went to change into that. Into something sexy … *for you*." I cried as I push my rain drenched hair from my face.

Sean looks down at his hand with the lingerie. "This is what you were doing?" I nod. "Why? You were perfect the way you were."

"I wanted it to be better."

He sighs, "I'm sorry, I thought …"

"I know what you thought and thank you for giving up on me."

"I didn't give up on you, Ava."

"You sure as hell did, walking away and saying what you said."

"Ava, I didn't understand and I was angry." He glances over me as the rain continues to soak through to my skin. "Let's go inside, it's cold and you're soaked."

"No," I said strongly.

"Ava your dress," he holds out his hand to me. "Your dress is completely see through now, and you have nothing on underneath."

"What do you care, you were leaving remember?" I look up at him and his eyes focus in on my body. I look down at the drenched white dress pasted to my body, showing everything. Before I can find him again I feel his hands on me. I wrap my arms around his neck, holding onto him and meeting his heated eyes silently. Unzipping his pants I feel for his erection, causing him to grunt in shock. "It feels like you want me pretty bad. If that's true - then show me," I said stroking him while his strong eyes seduce my every being.

He shakes his head slightly, "It's cold and raining, you need to …"

"I want you now Sean, I want to feel you inside of me ... right now." I press my lips to his ear and breath, "You always said it was good in the rain, prove it." He groans as his hands glide down my dress, gripping the edges and sliding it up my body before massaging my bare ass deliberately. I moan as he takes me in his arms and holds me up against the wall, lifting my legs and ripping my dress half off. His erection meets my center hard and wanting, feeling the hardness press into me so tight that I have to call out to him. His sweet kiss caresses my lips and revives my desires. "I want more Sean, don't stop, I want to feel all of you.

One big thrust and my head falls back, "Is this what you wanted?" Sean asked me forcefully, controlling my body with his wide palmed hands.

"Yes," I said forcing my breaths.

"Do you know how sexy you are right now? This thin dress clinging to your naked body, showing me everything I have been wanting. You didn't need anything else." I feel his words against my ear, making me even crazier. I am shivering in the cold rain, making his warmth that much more welcoming. I can't get enough of him. "Do you want to keep this up? Shivering and fucking in the cold rain? Or do you want to go in and do this right?" I can't speak, as I shake uncontrollably feeling a mixture of extreme pleasure and intense steel cold pain. "You're freezing Ava, I'm taking you inside," Sean pulls out of me and takes my hand, escorting me in front of the warm fire. I watch the water drip down his face as he tries to warm me with a towel and a blanket. I push them both away, push off my rain soaked dress and stand naked and wet in front of him, daring him to make a move. Within seconds, he rips off his clothes, being sure not to take his eyes off me for more than a second. He kneels in front of me, gripping my body as he kisses his way up one side to the other, tasting and feeling his way to control. Wonderfully powerless, I get down holding the back of his head and sucking on his bottom lip, pulling him down on top of me. He follows willingly, sucking off the remaining droplets of water off my skin. His strong hands hold me in his desired position, pulling my legs up around his waist, while he thrusts deep inside me again causing us both to gasp. Words cannot express the raw seduction between us. Both of us searching for every last droplet of water glistening on our bodies. My hands trace his muscles along his back with pressure - up and down to his rounded ass, squeezing him deeper inside of me. The pleasure intensifies each time causing my back to arch and pushing my hips into him even more. The harmony of our bodies move gracefully with our heated breaths echoing in the room around us. Enticing his lips back to mine, I feel the overwhelming bliss rush through my veins from my center to the tips of my toes, moaning the whole way. Sean groans watching me writhe underneath him. His control only sustains until after I release, I am weak and heavy when his force becomes focused. I watch the fire cast our shadows against the wall, dancing with our every move, his every move, with every last push of desire from him until he surrenders in my arms. Sean groans in my ear causing my smile to increase with each vocal release. He wanted the control and I never considered attempting to change his mind. One final exhale and I watch his green eyes smile at me, bright and beautiful, kissing me with a rich appreciation. When the fire goes out, we sprint to our room and he goes straight to bed, and I go to the bathroom to brush out my wet mangled hair. I look down at the drawer as I put my brush back and see my birth control. *Oh, I forgot.* I pick up the case to take the pill I forgot to take this morning and hesitate putting it in my mouth. I stare at it with overwhelming feelings.

"What are you doing?" Sean asked wrapping his arms around me as he looks over my shoulder. "Oh," he sighed. "Back on the pill, huh? I guess I didn't think about it."

"With all the things I wanted to do today I forgot to take it this morning."

"So are you going to take it now?"

"I don't know, I'm scared not to," I said watching his reflection in the mirror, wanting his support and hoping he's where I am.

"About what beautiful?" His reflection serious and concentrated.

"What if it happens again? I don't know I could handle …"

"It's not going to happen again Ava."

"How do you know?" I asked gazing into his secure eyes.

"It's not going to happen again. I promise you." I close my eyes sinking deeper into his arms. "I promise it will be different next time sweetheart but it's your decision, I will support you either way." I open my eyes to see his strength and confidence pushing me to make the decision I want to. Holding my hand over the sink we lock eyes as I let go of the pill and turn on the water. Sean holds out his hand and I hand him the rest, watching his smile form at the corners of his mouth. And with a flip of his wrist, he flings the remainder into the trash and picks me up and carries me to *our* soft, warm and oh so welcoming bed.

C3&O

I wake up surprised not to see him by my side. Leaving our room I wander silently and find him suspiciously sitting with his phone in his hand and a cigar lying on the table beside him. Within seconds his phone rings. "How did it go?" He answered quickly.

"That's your greeting?" Ethan said over speaker.

"Ethan," Sean said through his teeth.

"Break out your victory cigar little brother and light it with me," Sean reaches over and tears open his cigar, lights it and leans back with an obnoxious smile.

"I'm lit how 'bout you?" Sean said.

"Smoking this sweetness happily," Ethan said relaxed and confident

"So everything went smoothly?" Sean asked.

"A few minor hiccups but nothing we couldn't handle. All things considered it went better than we could have ever hoped for. Oh and Randy got the puppy too. You would not believe how excited he is, the guy who was scared to death of dogs now can't live without one. At least now you don't have to worry about him stealing Rondo and Prince from you."

Seam laughs, "Thanks Ethan."

"No thanks necessary, we all wanted this one, hard to say who wanted it more actually. Just make sure you take care of that family of yours and I will see you when you get back." Sean picks up his phone and speaks softly. Briefly I wonder if he realizes I am behind him but when I touch his shoulder he jumps reassuring me that he isn't purposely keeping something from me.

"Hey baby, I thought you were asleep," Sean said pulling me into his lap. "Okay Ethan we can talk more when I get back, alright, thank you."

"What was that all about?" I asked enjoying his bright smile.

"Ethan and I managed to succeed in a really nice deal today. Still waiting for the final details but the bulk of what we wanted has been … ummm … agreed to." He said looking suspicious all over again.

"Are you lying to me?"

He laughs at me, "No, why?"

"It seems like you are hiding something from me." I said holding his face still so he has to look at me.

He continues to smile and laugh at me, "You are so beautiful." He said trying to kiss me.

"Oh now I know you are up to something. And what puppy did Randy get?" I asked as he sits back sighing.

"Randy adopted a new shepherd, he's young apparently but in excellent health, he named him Hollywood after the shelter he got him from." I smile but wonder, *why is Randy in Hollywood - without Sean?*

Chapter 27

Rebecca

As I pull into our new home in my new convertible, I can't help but feel unstoppable. Joel and I are on top of the world now. A big beautiful home in the hills, a selection of luxury cars at our disposal, and servants for our every need. Joel's renewed appreciation from his father has earned him his trust fund back, plus other accolades that I appreciate. My husband has finally managed to give me the lifestyle I sought when I first pursued him. Most days I drive around in my convertible, shop at the best places and eat at the best restaurants, just because I can. Always making sure to turn my nose up at anyone who had previously written me off. I have no time for those people who I once begged for opportunities, and now they want to befriend me again? *Let them beg.* I stroll into the house, discarding my things as I walk in the door, knowing someone will pick them up and put them away for me.

"Is that you baby?" Joel called out.

"Yes," I walk into the large white living room and all its pristine glory…and stop. "What is that?!" I yell, pointing with disgust.

Joel smiles up at me innocently, "A puppy."

"I can see that Joel, why is it here."

"I went and got him this morning, isn't he great?"

"No." I huffed, crossing my arms and stomping my foot.

"Oh come on, his blood lines are some of the best. He's going to be way better than Sean's."

I roll my eyes, "Are you serious? Idiot! Sean does not live here or anywhere near, why the hell would he care? Why the hell would he care if he did live here?" I throw my hands up in frustration.

"He might not, but I do. I want to outdo him in every aspect and now that I have the money to do it, I am going to make damn sure I live his life, only better, and throw it in his face every chance I get."

"Well, if you think I am going to produce some of those whiny little brats for you, then you better seek professional help." I huff at him as I make myself a drink.

"Oh my beautiful girl, I wouldn't dream of it … we can adopt."

"No!"

"Why not?"

"Because then I will be expected to … deal with them or something." Upon seeing his obnoxious smile I realize he wasn't serious. "Real funny."

"I thought so," he said, returning to the whimpering puppy.

"So, you are still planning on screwing Sean over somehow?" I said, sinking down into my chair feeling only half-way interested in the topic.

"I don't know, I still wish I could have gotten Ava to leave him, something, anything to push him over that edge."

"Well, I am sure you will think of something, but right now I'm hungry. What are we doing for dinner?" I ask, falling into his lap and trying to take his attention off the puppy.

"I made a reservation at that new restaurant. They have an opening for tonight and only the best people will be there, so I knew that would be where you would want to be." He says, smiling wide when I jump up shaking with excitement.

"What should I wear?" I contemplate for a few seconds. "Damn you, Joel!"

"Why?"

"Because, you should have told me earlier so I could have shopped for something today." He rolls his eyes. I run to my room to start getting ready. "And you better make sure that mutt isn't wandering the house while we are gone!"

CB&ED

I sit reviewing the invitations for tonight while Joel mindlessly looks out the window of our limo. "So how did you get these invitations?" I asked, admiring him in his new suit.

"I didn't, they sent them to us by courier."

"Really, why?"

"Sucking up to us, I'm sure. Face it my dear, we are sought after now," he smiles.

I pull out my sunglasses as we drive up to the bright lights of the entrance. Joel steps out first, holding his hand out to me as I gracefully exit. Bulbs flash and I smile expectantly as we enter the restaurant. We are seated in one of the restaurants prime spots and order some of their finest wines. Just as Joel had said, it is the 'who's who' of Hollywood here tonight. We drink our wine, toasting to our perfect life while I eye everything, covertly trying to judge possible opportunities to meet the right people for my career.

"Well, look who's here," I look up at the obnoxious smile of Mary Grant.

Joel and I both sigh. "How are you, Mary?" Joel asked halfheartedly.

"Oh wonderful, have you met my boyfriend Bobby?" She asked, gesturing to indicate the distinguished gentleman with her.

"No." Joel tensed nervously as he nodded at the gentleman.

"He's a doctor in Atlanta."

"A psychiatric one I hope, for your sake," I said harshly.

"Ahhh Rebecca, looking as desperate as always," she said, smiling her sinister smile that I remember well from when I dated Sean years ago.

"Ahhh Mary, you look just as old and washed up as always. I bet your sons are proud." I said with attitude.

"How sweet of you to ask about my boys."

"I didn't," I said taking a drink, hoping to make her disappear one way or another.

"Well, either way you will be happy to know they are both doing wonderfully."

I thought I could hear a growl come from Joel. "Really? Please sit and tell us all about it," Joel mumbled. I assumed he was joking but she sits anyway. "You can let them know we are doing great as well."

"Oh really? Rebecca's corner picking up in business?"

I snarl at the wicked witch.

Joel clears his throat, "No, we have a new home in the hills, several expensive cars, and money coming in at will. And please let Sean know, I even grew to have his same affection for German Shepherds. I picked up a puppy this morning, best papers I have ever seen."

"Is that so?" Mary asked, still possessing a wicked smile.

"It certainly is. Let him know he is welcome to come over any time since I am training him to attack on command. I use a picture of Sean as a training reference," Joel snarled back at her.

I laugh and catch Mary's evil glace, "I will be sure to let him know, although he and Ethan have been so busy lately working on their new deal."

"A new deal?" Joel asked.

"Oh yes, it's going to be huge. They both are so excited about it. It is a huge investment, but well worth the money apparently. A business magazine is expected to interview them both once the deal goes through. 'Talented and brilliant' they are calling them both for orchestrating the deal."

"You don't know anything about this so called big investment?" Joel huffed.

"Not much more than a name… HT Acquisitions, I believe it was. Really doesn't matter, in a few days they will be in L.A. signing the final paperwork to take it over."

"Well good luck to them," Joel said with a forced smile.

"Thank you, I will be sure to tell them you said so."

"Honestly, I really don't care," Joel said.

"No?" She eyes Joel more seriously. I straighten in my seat. "No, I guess you wouldn't, considering what you did to Sean."

"And what did I do to Sean?" Joel asked with a half a laugh.

"I know you're the one that tampered with his breaks and I know your low-class wife harassed my daughter into a miscarriage."

Joel leans back in his chair, "Well it sounds like you have it all figured out, Mary."

"No, not completely. I am still unsure what your father will do when he finds out what you did."

Joel laughs aloud, "No need to worry about that, he was the one encouraging it. Whatever makes him money - Sean doing the jump, Ava naked onscreen, and hell, if Sean had died during the making? Wow, would that increase ticket sales or what? But that's all … *if* we had anything to do with any of it."

"You really are a family of low-class losers, aren't you?" Mary asked, pursing her lips.

Joel angers instantly, getting in her face, "Listen here you old bat, what you think of us is irrelevant to me. Your sons will be constantly chasing my shadow from now on."

Her smile increases, "It's sad that you think so, but no matter. You will be hearing about their huge success when they take control of their new company. And then sweetie, maybe if you beg they will toss some change in your direction after you fail miserably." Mary and her silent escort get up, smiling as Mary tosses a quarter on the table at us. I eye it before looking back up at her departing figure.

"I hate her," I said, gripping my glass harshly.

"Don't worry baby, I have all I need to make sure to turn things around on them," he said as I watch his eyes dance with gratifying determination.

CℨБↃ

Within a couple of days, Joel comes home screaming in excitement. I search for the maniac to see what is going on. "There you are, *victory* my dear!"

"Victory?" I ask him, searching for more answers to his obvious psychotic episode.

"I did it! I bought that company right out from under those losers."

"You bought … the company Sean and Ethan were after?"

He picks me up, twirling me around and confirming my question. "Oh, it was so incredible. I wish you could have seen me. I wheeled and dealed like a pro. I wouldn't let it go until they signed everything over to me. Now if those two fuckups want this company they have to go through me."

"Wow, I can't believe you pulled it off."

Joel, finding his favorite drink to celebrate, looks at me in shock. "I can't believe you would doubt me."

"I didn't doubt you. I didn't even know what you were up too."

His glorious smile is overwhelming as he crashes into the sofa, "It's going to be so wonderful when those two show up tomorrow. I can't wait to see their faces when they come face to face with me and I get to tell them they are too late. So sweet, sweeeeeet…!" He yelled.

"So how much money are we talking about here? I mean, are we really obscenely rich now?" I ask, trying to understand what is really important.

"Well, not yet. We haven't earned from the company yet, plus I used everything we had available to buy the company."

"You did what?" I snap.

"Calm down, it will pay off quickly. I was assured that we would make our money back three times over in the first few months."

Sighing. "But Joel, why didn't you go to your father and get a loan or something?"

"I can't go to him, I had to do this on my own. He would have taken too long to decide. I only had a few days Rebecca. Besides, once I start bringing in more than he does, he will be even more impressed with me. It's the biggest day of my life, don't ruin it." He grabs my hands pulling me to him. "In fact, let's celebrate."

"Celebrate how?" I asked.

"Our favorite way to celebrate baby," He smiles perfectly as he takes out his phone.

By the time the sun begins to edge up over the horizon the following day, I lay on top of the bed naked and floating freely, while our celebratory drug still lies out across our table. We fucked everywhere and enjoyed the hell out of our night. I can barely hear that annoying puppy bark and cry anymore from his cage.

I wanted to go all night, but Joel wanted to be ready to go the next morning. He doesn't want to miss his big moment to show up his adversaries. We didn't clean up, we didn't even wipe the white dust off our face, slamming into the bed naked and free of any and all concerns. I slipped away, deep into my own fantasies.

"*Bam! Bam! ... Boom!*" I struggle to open my eyes as the loud noises seem to increase towards me.

"DOWN ON THE GROUND!" Men screamed at me.

"What? I stammer, still struggling to comprehend what is going on. I look around at all the people in my bedroom, and before I can say anything else I am pulled out of my bed and thrown to the ground. Joel lies next to me, handcuffed and nose in the floor. "What's going on?" I screamed.

"You're under arrest."

"For what?" I ask, still in disbelief.

"Possession."

⌘

I am not sure how much time has passed since I arrived to this gray cell. I am dirty, disgusting, and even worse, I have to wear this stiff, oversized jumpsuit. I am so relieved when I am bailed out. I expected Joel or his father to be waiting for me, but there is no one. I wait for whoever it is, but I finally have to beg for some money for a cab home. When I get there, I have to step over the pieces that they left behind.

They went through everything, taking our computers and all of our files, they even took the dog. I assumed Joel would be here waiting, or at least be right behind me, but after several hours there is no sign of him. I take a thorough shower before deciding to go to bed, exhausted. When the phone rings I answer it quickly.

"Rebecca." Joel said with sigh.

"Joel! What is going on? Where are you?"

"I am still in jail, I need you come down here and bail me out."

"How am I supposed to do that? They impounded all of our cars, I have …"

"Just shut up and listen, you need to go to my Dad and get the money."

"Do you think he will give it to me?" I asked him, trying to figure out how I will ever approach him with this.

"He bailed you out didn't he?"

"I don't know who bailed me out."

"What do you mean you don't know? Fuuucckk, I assumed it was him. Well it doesn't matter you have to get him to bail me out."

"Why can't I just come down there and …"

"No!" He is silent for a second after screaming. "No, I used all of our savings to buy that company and then most of our ready cash on the drugs."

"Joel, what are we going to do? I need a lawyer and I want a good one. I'm not going to jail over this bullshit."

"Just get my father!" He yelled, hanging up harshly.

I prepare myself and make a call to his father. It wasn't easy and far from pleasant, but at least he agrees to go see Joel with me.

When we arrive, it is obvious that his father is not going to bail Joel out for some reason. I wait impatiently, feeling stressed with each passing second until they finally call us in and I see Joel come in on the other side of the glass, like a common criminal. Joel's increasing anger is obvious as he realizes he isn't getting bailed out. His father picks up the receiver. "Well Joel, this couldn't be worse timing." I can hear Joel screaming on the other end. "You can yell at me all you want, but there is nothing I can do. And I mean there is absolutely nothing I can do. The government has seized all my accounts and has charged me with tax evasion, fraud and list of other things. It's a fucking mess, Joel." My eyes widen as I watch his father sweat for the first time since I met him. I look over at Joel's frozen figure for some kind of solution. "Listen son, I came down here to tell you in person, but I have to get the hell out of dodge. I wish I could help you but I have my own problems. I hope it all works out for you, good luck son." His father hands me the phone and walks out, while my mouth plummets to the ground.

"What do we do now?" I asked.

"Check the files on the computer, see what we have. Maybe there is money somewhere?"

"They took it Joel. They took everything, even the dog!"

He slams his fists down, "Fine, then sell everything."

"Like what?"

"EVERYTHING!"

I jump back, Okay, I will get right on it."

"And you better get my puppy back, I don't care how many of those precious shoes of yours you have to sell to do it."

"But Joel, I tried, I went with your dad to get him, thinking it would help ease your stress when you got home, but he's gone already."

"Gone?"

I nod.

"How is that possible? They can't give him away in one day. They need my consent to do that."

"I don't know. They said someone came in with all the right paperwork and made a sizeable donation ..." holding my hands out to my side, I try to defend myself, "and then they left with the puppy."

"Who came in?"

"I don't know Joel!"

"They didn't get his name or what he looked like?" I watch his eyes dart from side to side rapidly as his mind struggles for explanation.

"All they said was that he was a large black man." Joel's face freezes. "What?"

His angered expression intensifies suddenly. "That fucking asshole!" I shake my head as he stands up screaming at me from the other side. I am not able to make out what he is saying before the guards take him away.

CX80

Long horrible day, the second in a row, and I don't think I can handle much more of this. I walk into my house throwing my things off to the side, not caring that we don't have anyone to clean up after me. I head straight for the bar to make myself a drink - a huge drink. Mixing hastily, I guzzle down all that I can at once while gathering more to pour.

"Bad day?" Startled, I look up at the figure resting on my sofa.

"Who's that?" I turn on the light and my mouth drops.

"Nice house, Rebecca."

"Get out of my house, Ethan!"

"Oh, don't be like that. After all, my brother had you as a guest for some time, surely you can give me a few minutes."

"What do you want?"

"Nothing much," he comes towards me and makes himself a drink, making me even more nervous. "You know, I was shocked to see your place in such disarray. I would have thought you would have at least cleaned it up by now." He laughs as he sips his drink. "I guess it is a little overwhelming. You have to give those guys credit, they sure are thorough."

"Get to the point, Ethan, and get out!"

"Okay, calm down. I'm here to make you an offer." He sits back down, stretching out confidently.

"What kind of offer?"

"I guess you could say a get out of jail free card offer."

I straighten instantly, "And how is that?"

"It's easy. You confess everything you know about Joel and I will help you stay out of jail."

"What about Joel?"

"No. No, I can't help Joel, he's done for, trust me." His confidence sends chills up my spine.

"So why should I believe that you can help me?"

"Good question. Well, I don't know if Sean ever told you much about our father but he handled money for some fairly powerful people. People who would do anything for my father and his family." Ethan smiles as he relaxes, waiting to see if I will respond, but I stand frozen, unsure of how deep the water is I am swimming in. "You see Rebecca, I, or even Sean for that matter, can find out just about anything we want to know. Legally, of course."

"Oh, I am sure," I snarled as he laughs at me.

"For instance, let's say if I wanted to find out how much money you made and if you paid the right amount of taxes on it," he smiles at me as he watches me carefully. "Or, if money was being made that was never getting reported, money being made fraudulently. With one phone call, I could find all that out and then share it with some well placed friends in the government."

My eyes widen instantly, "You are a fucking asshole Ethan!" I throw my glass at him, missing him entirely.

He laughs, "Wow, and Sean said I would need to explain it to you. I guess you're not as stupid as he thinks you are. You should be happy. I know how much you like proving him wrong." I glare at him as I make myself another drink.

"So tell me, did Joel mess with Sean's brakes?" His smile immediately disappears.

"I ... I don't know."

"Oh come on Rebecca, you do too. Now don't screw with me, tell me what you know and I will do what I can to keep you out of jail for this horrible drug charge you're facing."

I close my eyes hard, "No, Joel just bought a huge company, and we will be bringing in plenty of money soon. I don't need your help."

"You mean HT Acquisitions?"

"That's the one. You know, the one you and Sean were so desperate to get yourselves." I cock my head at him in defiance.

"Neither Sean nor I ever had any interest in HT. We bought one of their acquisitions, which they had to sell since they are going under."

"No, your mother said ..."

"My Mother?" Ethan laughed. "Wow, I'm not sure what my mother said, but Sean and I purchased what we wanted days ago, one of the last remaining parts. All that's left now of HT Acquisitions is ... a name. The employees took what they could and the owners cut their losses and moved to Miami." I eye him, trying to decide if he is telling me the truth. "Basically, all you and Joel own is a name and some old computer equipment, maybe, if the employees didn't steal them on their way out," he chuckles.

I shake my head, hoping it is all a dream, a bad dream. "That can't be right, they would have told Joel that ..."

"Tell him what? That they weren't worth what he was offering them? Not likely. Hell, I would have taken what he paid, for the small part Sean and I bought. I still can't believe he didn't go to his father first, but I guess Sean was right on that one." Ethan said, stirring his drink methodically.

"This was all a setup?"

"I don't know what you're talking about." He smiles wide. "Never would I have imagined you guys would have such a victory party. What, the other hundred people couldn't make it?" His amusement sours my mood even more. Ethan suddenly gets up looking at his watch, "Well it's getting late and I have an early flight tomorrow. Nice seeing you again Rebecca, I guess we won't see each other again for what, at least ten years?" He nods at me before making his way towards the door.

"Ethan wait!" He pauses, sliding his hands casually into his pockets as he seemingly waits to see if he is interested in what I have to say. "Joel did mess with Sean's brakes."

"Why?"

"Because he hates him, he is so overly jealous of him. He wanted to get rid of him or at least ruin his career. He didn't care what happened really, as long as he lost everything, including his wife. That's why he tried to get Ava to sleep with him, anything to hurt Sean."

"But Ava didn't sleep with him." Ethan asked.

"No, he even tried to force her ... a few times."

"What else?" I look up at him, confused. "Did he drug Ava too?"

I laugh, "Oh yeah, I forgot about that – no, he didn't do that."

"You did, didn't you?" Ethan asked, shaking his head at me.

"Yes, but it was harmless, I only wanted to get her out of the way for awhile."

"And the hospital?"

I huff at him, "I didn't do anything there."

Ethan approaches me angrily, grabbing my arm and looking me dead in the eyes, "The hell you didn't!"

"You're hurting me, Ethan."

"Tell me what you said."

"I said that no one wanted her anymore, that everyone blamed her and that you were planning on making her pay by taking her home and her child and anything else that mattered to her."

"Blamed her for what?"

"Sean's death and losing his baby. She had no idea and it was easy to convince her since she was in that horrible room and none of you were anywhere in sight. Pretty pathetic really, how easily she fell apart."

Ethan lets go of me and promptly walks towards the door, "Have a nice life Rebecca."

"Wait Ethan, aren't you going to help me?"

He turns around looking me up and down, "No ... I changed my mind."

"ETHAN!" He continues to walk out while I chase after him, but I am stopped when another man walks in.

"Ma'am, I am here to take possession of all household items to pay back taxes on behalf of Mr. Butch Castor."

Ethan laughs at me, squeezing out behind the gentleman and his henchmen as I run to save what I can. I lay in the floor crying, holding as many of my handbags and shoes with one hand and my dresses with the other, while all of my furniture is gone, my rugs, my dishes, are all taken away. The house echoes as the men exit to post a notice to vacate the premises. Tears well up in my eyes as I focus in on a dusting of white powder on the floor.

Chapter 28

Ava

According to Sean, time is flying by. According to Sean, that is, but he isn't the one carrying a bowling ball or been unable to sleep for the last eight weeks. This baby is nearly ready to be born and Sean is even more protective of me than usual. I try to be patient with him and his overprotective ways, but I am becoming anxious and I need to get out of the house. I need something to distract me.

I pull out the mail to find some magazines or even some junk mail to read, and stuck in the middle of it all is a letter addressed to me. I don't recognize the handwriting, but I am curious and bored enough to not care.

My Dear Ava,

I have to say I am quite surprised that you haven't come to visit me and gloat, but then again you do still have some time. Anyway, I would actually love to see you if you ever get a chance. I want to apologize. It has been hard to come to terms with what I have done, but I promise I am truly remorseful for what has happened. Ethan said at one time he could help me stay out of jail, I assume that he can also help me get out. My attorney said personal references could go a long way. If you could get them to make some calls for me, I would be so grateful. I promise I will never bother you again or ask for anything else ever again.

Please Ava, it is so scary here and they have taken everything from me. Even when I get out I am not sure what I will do. My career is surely over and Joel is not expected to get out for some time. His father is long gone and all of Joel's money with him. I have nothing and will have even less when I get out, but the thought of staying here any longer is so terrifying. I have been threatened and beaten, I don't know how much longer I can survive in here. I am so frightened. I would call, but Sean threatened to make things worse for me if I ever contacted any of you. I had to try something, though. I hope this letter finds you well and that you are able to find it in your heart to forgive me before it is too late. If I do not survive before I am able to speak to you again, please know, I don't blame you. I do believe you to be one of the kindest and most sincerely wonderful people I have ever met. If nothing else please visit me and let me apologize properly to you.

Best Wishes,

Rebecca

I twist the envelope right and left until I see a prison stamp. Rebecca must have assumed I would know how to get a hold of her, but since I don't, then obviously Sean must. Anger and fear course through me as I try to remember everything he said, Ethan said, the actions of the both of them including short trips to L.A. I never thought to question.

"Okay, I got you a little bit of everything since I wasn't sure what you would want," Sean says, walking in with several bags of groceries. I stare at him intently as he approaches. "What?"

"I got a letter today," I wave it at him until he takes it from me. "What is going on Sean?"

"That fucking bitch! Don't worry about it, I will take care of it." He slams the letter to his side cursing under his breath.

"What did you do Sean?"

"I didn't do anything, now relax and forget all about it."

"I don't understand. Rebecca is in jail? For what? And Joel? I don't know what is going on, but I am pretty damn sure you and Ethan do and at the very least have some responsibility for it."

"Baby, calm down."

"No! Not until you tell me what that letter is all about."

I can see him contemplating, but he eventually sighs and looks at me with his hands on hips, "We set them up."

"Set them up how?"

"We hung out some bait for Joel to take. He took it and spent all of his money on a failing business."

"Why would he do that?"

"Because he thought he had outsmarted Ethan and I, buying it before we could. Then he decided to celebrate." He begins to laugh. "Although *celebrate* doesn't do it justice. I never imagined him buying that much." He glances back at my irritated face and straightens. "He bought a lot of drugs and other things he shouldn't have. I had a feeling he would do something like that, so we made a few calls and had his house raided and surprise, I was right."

"And?"

"And they were arrested and that's that."

"No it isn't, I know better than that Sean. I'm not stupid and that letter said Joel's father took off. Why would he do that?"

He rolls his eyes, sitting at the edge of the bed. "That was more of calling attention to his own stupidity. The man was making a ton of money and not paying any taxes on it. So they convicted him, of all kinds of charges, things we didn't even know about so they liquidated as much as they could to pay back his debt. In the meantime, he took off to hide what little he managed to save."

"What about the movie?"

"It was sold."

"To who?" He smiles at me. "You?" He nods.

"Ethan and I both, since it was our company that bought it. We are working on getting it back on track, hoping to get it released sometime this next summer - early fall at the latest."

"And Rebecca and Joel are serving time on drug possession charges?"

"Yes, and no. Ethan also got Rebecca to confess to some additional charges, crimes that she and Joel both committed. Such as, tampering with my breaks, drugging you and attacking you several times. We didn't do anything illegal, we simply know the right people to call and the rest was betting on them being themselves."

"How did you set the bait?"

"You don't want to know."

"Yes, I do."

"Mom." My eyes widened with shock. Sean laughs, "I have to give her credit; the woman still has it. We sent them tickets to a restaurant opening that we knew they couldn't refuse and Mom went with Bobby, making sure to run into them *accidently*, baiting them perfectly."

"Oh, I don't want to know." I said, hiding my face in my hands.

"The only surprise was that stupid Joel bought a puppy. We knew that wouldn't sit too well with you, forcing another puppy into the pound."

"Hollywood?" I asked, already knowing the answer.

"Yes. We got the paperwork needed for Randy to go in there and pour on the charm, and he walked right out of there with no problems. Of course, we also made a sizeable donation so they would not think to call anybody about it. He barely got out of there before Rebecca showed up. We shouldn't have bailed her out so soon, but who would have ever thought she would ever think to rescue the puppy?"

"I'm not going to ask."

"Probably best. When we got back from Ireland I went to check on them both. Joel was ready to tear me apart - I enjoyed that immensely. Rebecca was more subdued. She made small talk for a few minutes, then started yelling at me to help her, that I owed her for helping convict Joel on more charges. Then she calmed again and started asking about you, which pissed me off, so I told her if she ever came near you I would find a way to make it worse for her. And now the stupid bitch goes and writes you. I swear … Ava don't fall for her bullshit. Nothing has happened to her. Hell, she sits in her cell all day watching TV and being a snob to anyone that tries to talk to her, well except for the guard that she is sleeping with to get extra privileges. No one has threatened her or done anything to her, I promise. Trust me, she is fine. Now don't worry about anything else, both of them are out of our lives for good. All you have to worry about is taking care of yourself and having my baby."

CB80

I wake up to the bright sun beaming through the window. "Good morning," my overjoyed husband said while rocking our newborn son.

"How is he?" I asked.

"Perfect," he said, walking over and putting Jayden in my arms. I nuzzle my son while checking all his fingers and toes. "They're all there, I checked," Sean said.

The door slowly opens and balloons drift in, "Can we come in?" Mary asked.

"Definitely. Come meet your new grandson." The whole crew comes in, each of them taking their turn to come over and kiss me and look over Jayden.

"Another beautiful baby Ava," Kyle said while kissing me, tears already streaming down his face. I grip his hand and he nods before having to go hide his face in Michael's shoulder.

"I love you," I said and he nodded, burying deeper into Michael's shoulder.

Ethan walks over and kisses me. "Well I don't know what all the crying is about, the boy is only another fine Grant boy, just like his uncle." I hand him Jayden, much to Ethan's surprise, but he takes him anyway. "Definitely a Grant, too handsome not to be. So what did you end up naming my nephew," Ethan asked, cradling Jayden as Abbey plays with him at his side.

"Jayden," Sean said, watching Ethan carefully.

"Jayden, that's a good name," Ethan said.

"Jayden … Ethan … Grant," Sean said confidently with a smile. Ethan looks up in shock, already showing watery eyes. "Well you got Dad's name, so we took the next best."

The brothers' bond is unbreakable, no matter what life throws at them. No one can get to one without having to get through the other first. Their father always told them, "You can accomplish anything in life but together you can accomplish everything."

Epilogue

Sean

I can't take the silence anymore, I don't care if she is mad at me for being here. "So what are you going to say?" I asked.

"I don't know for sure," Ava said, still dazed by the landscape passing by.

"Then can you tell me again why the hell we are doing this?"

"*We* weren't supposed to be doing anything. But for the tenth time today, I want to see her and verify on my own that she is truly not remorseful about anything."

"And you think you are going to know that by seeing her?"

"I do, actually." She said. I shake my head, disbelieving that it could be possible.

"I don't care what you think Sean. You got your closure - I didn't."

"I know Ava, but …"

"But nothing. I deserve this as much as you did." She yells at me as I pull in and escort her inside.

They are allowing us to talk to Rebecca during off hours so we can have privacy from other visitors. My mind is racing, watching everything around me as I hover over Ava, wanting to grab her and carry her out of here as quickly as possible. This is the exact reason I never told her anything about it in the first place. *Damn she's so fucking stubborn.* "You know our plane leaves in two hours?" I said, earning her typical shut-up-Sean expression. I fidget tirelessly as we wait for them to get Rebecca. "It's going to take us at least forty-five minutes to get to the airport and we should try and get there early so …"

"Sean!" She snaps at me. I put my arm around her shoulders mumbling under my breath, but sit up straight when the door opens. Rebecca comes in casually and smug at first, then she eyes us with a sarcastic grin. *I already want to strangle her.* I take notice of Ava's fists balling up tighter. There is no glass, or barrier of any sort, blocking her from us, only a room-length counter with barriers in between each guest section. I am not sure if I am more worried about Rebecca trying something or Ava, although I probably will not stop Ava.

"Well if it isn't the couple of the year" Rebecca said, sitting down in front of us, glancing in my direction but concentrating on Ava. "So what do I owe this visit to?"

"I wanted to talk to you, of course. I would have sooner, but I didn't know you were here until I received your letter," Ava said.

Rebecca looks hard at me with a slight laugh, "Of course you didn't, because you two are so open and *honest* with each other." I roll my eyes leaning into Ava and ignoring the witch across from us.

"Sean did what he thought was best for me at the time, Rebecca," Ava said.

"Oh that's right. I heard congratulations are in order. A boy, is that right?"

"Yes," Ava said.

"And how is he doing?" Rebecca smiled her meaningless smile.

"He's perfect, and none of your damn business," I snapped at her.

"I'm not here to talk about us Rebecca," Ava said.

"Well, then why are you here darling Ava?"

"Like I said I got your letter, and now I am here as you requested. So you tell me, why am I here?" Ava said as I glance at Ava suspiciously.

"Really? Oh Ava, if you help me I will be forever in your debt. I didn't realize you were going to be so kind, I thought you were here to gloat. I am sorry, but you can understand my harshness. I always knew you had a good heart despite your husband." She said, glancing my way while I laugh at her. "You just wouldn't believe what they have done to me here. They took everything from me, my home, my clothes, my jewelry and my cars. It's been horrible and now I am in here with all these scary people. It's torture, pure torture." Rebecca wells up with tears.

I shake my head at the rotten actress. She continues for some time, talking about her routines and what she has to do and what she has to eat. She rambles on and on forever about the same things. I keep glancing over at Ava to see when she is going to stop her but she never does. "Ava this is ..." I said to her before she hushes me.

Rebecca smiles at me under her hands clearing her watery eyes, "So, you're going to help me Ava?"

"Even if I wanted to help you get out of here Rebecca, I couldn't. My husband made that demand before I came out here, and he is the only one that can. There is nothing I can do and I am certainly not going to make him do anything he doesn't want to do." Ava spoke so smoothly and so calmly, I wonder if she isn't about to shoot Rebecca between the eyes at any moment.

"You bitch!" Rebecca stands up and I follow suit, hovering over Ava protectively, but still Ava remains calm. "You act like you are so self-righteous but all the while you only wanted to come out here and rub it in, watch me suffer. You deserve everything I did to you!"

Ava stands and leans around me, "All I wanted - was the apology you promised me." Ava walks out with her head held high. I look back at Rebecca's shocked face, happily.

I escort Ava back to the car, kissing her with pride, "I have never been more proud to call you my wife." She smiles at me, "I thought for sure you were going to give in to her."

"She hasn't changed at all. She still blames everyone else for her problems. No matter what I think about what you and Ethan did, you didn't force them to take the drugs or even lose all their money." She sighs, "I wonder if Joel is the same, maybe we can ..."

"Absolutely not!" I yell, enforcing my demand. "Not even close to the same situation Ava, Rebecca is crazy but Joel is on a whole other level. He's angry as hell, and in way deeper trouble than he was originally. I will save you the trouble, I am sure he is blaming everyone but himself. And he certainly has no reason to be nice to you and even less reason if I am there." She nods and I am relieved that she settles into her seat calmly and without arguing with me any further.

◌୫ଓ

Our flight was right on time, both of us anxious to get back home, me even more so. My mother is taking Lillah and Jayden for the night, allowing Ava and I some personal time together for the first time since we brought Jayden home. My mother is suppose to wait until we get back so we can see them one last time before they leave and then it will be only us and I can't wait. I have been staring at her all day, her breasts, her legs, her lips, they have all been torturing me throughout the day. Ava nearly runs inside to see our children before they leave. I am not far behind her, preparing for Lillah as she leaves her mother's arms to run and jump into mine. My mother hands Jayden over to Ava and she quickly nuzzles our son like she hasn't seen him in weeks rather than hours. It is wonderful to see, especially after everything she has been through. I kiss Jayden on the head, then swing Lillah around in my arms causing her to giggle but as soon as I round the corner I see Dillon sitting comfortably, too comfortably as he munches on some of our food.

"What are you doing here?" I asked him.

"Hey Sean, how's it going?" I stare at him confused and a little annoyed.

"Dillon, so good to see you again." Ava walks over to hug him as he smiles his goofy smile at me over her shoulder.

"I'm good, thank you. I thought I would come see the new addition and I must say he is one good looking boy. Obviously gets his looks from his mother." The bastard said, winking at me.

"Thanks for stopping by Dillon, it will save us the time in sending you an announcement but I am sure you have a flight to catch?" I wave him on.

"Nope, I'm good," He said, sitting back comfortably.

"Well then you must stay for dinner," Ava said as I glare at her.

"I would love to," Dillon said happily, nodding in my direction.

"Wonderful. Now if you will excuse me I need to go feed my son before he goes." Ava said before leaving the room.

"Sure," Dillon watches Ava walk off until he finally meets my eyes, smiling at me a little too much.

"Sean, let me go get Lillah ready to go while you spend time with your friend," my mother said as she picks up Lillah from my lap.

"He's not my friend," I said after her. "Did you tell her we are friends, is that how you got in here?" Dillon puts his hand over his heart, seeming shocked by my response. "Don't play that game with me."

"Damn Sean, I make an effort to stop by and see you and this is how you treat me? You really need to work on your friendship skills," Dillon said, continuing to munch and relax.

"*We* are not friends!"

"Sure we are, with everything we have been through together. You like me. Don't lie, I know you do." I cringe, rubbing the sudden pain in my head. "So does Ava breast feed?" My eyes narrow at him. "That's hot," he nods, smiling.

"Do you want me to hurt you?" I asked him.

"I'm just saying. And damn Ava got her body back quick, well except the," he makes a motion toward his breasts. "They seem a lot bigger, that's got to be a plus, huh?"

"Are you suicidal Dillon?"

"No, why?" His confusion makes me worry about his sanity.

"Don't you have a girlfriend or something in New York to annoy? Why are you here bothering me?"

"I don't know."

"You don't know?"

"No, I mean I ..." He sighs, looking perplexed suddenly as he leans forward and hangs his head. I hesitate to say anything, not knowing if I really want to know or not. "Sean, I ..."

"What?" I finally said, impatiently.

"Damn your worse than a girl, just spit it out already," I said, checking behind me to make sure I don't get myself into trouble.

"I need your help, Sean." I look back at the suddenly intense form avoiding my eyes.

"What did you do? Do you need a lawyer? Because you can't afford the ones I know."

"No, I don't need a lawyer."

"You got Taylor pregnant, didn't you?" I assumed.

"Who? Oh, no. I just..." He stands up, pacing around the room, gripping his head and sighing. "Hell, I don't even know why I am here. This was a stupid idea. I'm sorry Sean, I don't know what I was thinking." He grabs his coat and starts out the door.

"You already told Ava you would stay for dinner. If you leave now, she's going to think it's my fault. So, at least stay until after that so you don't get me into trouble." He nods and sits back down, silently and solemnly.

We all said goodbye to my mother and the kids... even Dillon. I suddenly feel like I have adopted him or something, the way my mother fussed over him. Dillon makes polite conversation throughout dinner but is noticeably stressed. I get many concerned glances from Ava, but all I can do is shake my head as I study him for any clue as to his problems.

"Well, how about I clean up so you boys can go and talk in the living room?" I shake my head at Ava, dreading that possibility.

"Thank you, but I really should probably get out of your way here. Thank you for dinner. Are you sure you don't need any help cleaning up?" Dillon asked.

"No, I'm good, but Dillon if you don't have a flight out tonight you are more than welcome to stay here."

"Thank you, but I really need to go," he said.

"If you need to," I said rushing Dillon out of his chair.

"At least let me wrap up some food for you to take with you." Ava insists.

"Okay." Dillon halts instantly at the offer of free food.

Ava jumps up smiling as Dillon leaves to wait in the other room. I help her clean up and then feel a smack to the back of my head. "Ow! What was that for?" I asked her as she gives me a dirty look.

"Go talk to him," she said.

"I tried, but he doesn't want to talk about it."

"Yes, he does Sean."

"What do you want me to do Ava, beat it out of him? Although, I wouldn't mind trying," I laugh but she doesn't. "I'm just kidding."

"Go!" She points in Dillon's direction.

I let my head drop back as I reluctantly go find the young annoyance. I walk in on him standing around with his coat under his arm. I walk up behind him and grab hold of the back of his neck. "Come with me."

"Hey, what the hell?" Dillon cried out as I drag him into my office.

"Sit down!" I point to the chairs in front of my desk as I shut the door behind him. "Now talk."

"What do you want me to talk about?" He asked.

"Dillon, I am not going to play games with you. Now tell me why you are here or I will kick you out and deal with the wrath of my wife later."

He instantly sits up and takes a breath, "My father is real sick. I had to move back to North Carolina to take care of him and his business." Dillon suddenly jumps up with excitement. "I came up with this really great product Sean. I think you will love it, and with your new son it will be wonderful if you could … well, if you could endorse it for me. I have a sample in the car. I can leave it with you and Ava and you guys can try it out. I know you will love it, too."

"You know I don't endorse products Dillon. No matter how great it might be, I don't want to get into that business."

Dillon sits back down, defeated. "Sean please, I am begging you to consider it, just consider it. You are my only hope right now, otherwise I have to lose everything to a man I hate." Fisting his hands, he fights for his words before looking back up at me, "My whole world depends on this product succeeding Sean. Please."

"You obviously want me to help you with something Dillon, but I'm not even going to consider helping you until I know everything."

He hesitates, again struggling with his words. "It is really a long story Sean." He said. I huff, letting him know I am not budging until he talks. With a long sigh, he sinks down into his chair. "Do you remember that girl? The one I told you about ... Dani?"

Dillon causes me to sit forward when his eyes rise to meet mine. He looks scared and worried for the first time since I have known him. "She is the girlfriend you never saw again, the one whose father took her away in the middle of the night?" I asked, recalling his broken-hearted story.

"Yes, her ... I found her again, or rather, *she* found me. And now I need your help ... *we* need your help."